ESCAPE FROM ANCIENT EGYPT

A.K. TAYLOR

Soaring Eagle Books
Publishing Division of Soaring Eagle Publications LLC
1670 Chester Road
White Plains, GA 30678
www.soaringeaglebooks.org

This is a work of fiction. Names, characters, places and incidents either are the product of the author's imagination or are used fictitiously, and any resemblance to any actual persons, living or dead, events, or locales is entirely coincidental.
This book was printed in the United States of America.

ISBN 13- 978-1-943326-05-1
ISBN 10- 1-943326-05-3
LCCN- 2016902746

Edited by Timothy Staveteig
Cover Design by Mallory Rock
Illustrated by A.K. Taylor

For other works and to contact the author visit:
www.backwoodsauthor.com

Escape from Ancient Egypt

Egypt Ca 1300 BC

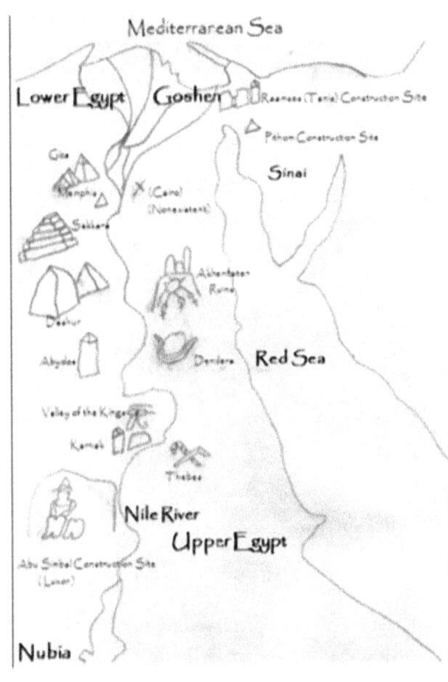

- CHAPTER 1 -

LIGHT FLASHED AS NEIKO stumbled from a portal. Her office was just as she'd left it, with a wide oak desk and a rolling chair, and a tall lamp in the corner, but now a layer of dust coated it. Papers and bills lay strewn around in complete disarray due to a hectic three-sided life.

Three years. Three years of hard adventuring had passed, and what did she have to show for it? Dark circles under her eyes, frayed nerves, and zombie like appearance and gait. A twenty-one year old shouldn't be subject to such stress; it just wasn't right, but not every normal twenty-one-year-old was a Chosen One of both a hidden land and another universe.

She peeked out of her blind. Warriors were still stationed outside her house, keeping watch. The Seven Chieftains and Seven Tribes council had to keep her under guard at all times for her own safety against their enemies the Crackedskulls, the Cursed Tribe, and their monarchs.

1

"None of my friends are doing anything, so I guess can update my logbooks—there's nothing else to do right now." Neiko sighed as she slumped in her office chair behind her desk. She had a tendency to talk to herself while alone. "I seriously need a break—I would like to go to a movie or something besides being stuck here. At least the Tribes built me this house and removed dodging my parents from the equation." She grumbled as she plopped two composition books on the desk and ran her hands through her hair. "Now I don't have to explain lapses in time or why I was about past 2 a.m. or worry about them getting hurt. I wished I could visit the Five Lands and not worry about getting kidnapped there, too."

"I guess I'll start with Hawote business first. There's not much to update on here," Neiko said as she opened the book to a blank page. Hawote was the hidden land that coexisted with the United States, Canada, and Mexico.

October 19ᵗʰ, 2001

It's been three years since Francesco was kicked out of the Tribes, and Eagle Claw has taken over as Grand High Mohican, but there are still moles in our ranks. Who would have guessed there were more? I think Francesco was just the chief-mole. Raven is daily turning up the heat and Outsiders can get hurt. He's putting more battle pressure on the Seven Tribes. It won't be long before he does more home invasions and/or public attacks.

P.S. The chieftains, my friends, and my enemies are starting to ask a lot of questions about my unexplained disappearances and unaccounted and unexplained lapses of time. I am told not to say anything. There is too much at risk. My world would be destroyed or worse—consumed by an other-worldly evil that I don't even fully understand...

Neiko pressed the pencil's eraser against her lips. "I guess I'm done with that one. Now to catch up on the Five Lands," she said, closing the other logbook, tossing it aside, and opening up her top secret logbook on the Five Lands.

ESCAPE FROM ANCIENT EGYPT

October 19ᵗʰ, 2001 Earth Time/The year of the Eagle Second Quarter of the Year: Waning Crescent of the Red Moon Their Time

The Attack Pack and I were successful in stopping Menes and his two dumb brothers from stealing the Tiger-eye of Luck from Mudara in the Great Plain in Qari. Ever since he has taken the throne as First Pharaoh, he has been trying to equip himself with powers and talismans stolen from others when he has unspeakable power at his fingertips. He has essentially become a petty thief. It's for everyone's benefit that he's such a dunce to not know what he has in his family. I know where the stuff is, but he doesn't know. The ancient city of his forefathers has almost everything he needs, and I found that on my first trip there which was 300,000 years ago their time. Raven has his Eye of Cygnus, and he'd never be able to get that. From what more I've heard about Osiris'(his father) past, I wouldn't believe he would let such an idiot come into the world and rule. My how the mighty clan has fallen! Osiris and the entire land calls Menes a disgrace and a laughingstock. When Menes leaves a threat, everybody laughs. If this is the future of the mighty clan that brought fear to the Five Lands years ago, everybody could retire early, but we must always remember the Dark Pharaoh…

On a personal note on Osiris: so many others and I would have believed Menes would have been the one to exile Ramses when I exposed him as an impostor and what he really was—which was both good and bad by the way. Anyway, back to the point. After finding out he wasn't the blubbering mess we thought he would be, SOMETHING, I don't know what, stirred in his soul that day—I know since I was there that day courtesy of Menes. Something dark. Something sinister. Something consuming. Was it vengeance? Was it something else? What stirred in him that day reminds me of that movie The Grudge—I hope it's not that serious. So what happens now? Only time will tell. I just hope the sleeping demon that everyone says Osiris was has not been awakened!

Now on the subject of Ramses, the Dark Pharaoh. My how times have changed. Maybe exposing his true identity wasn't such a good idea after all. He makes me pay for that daily in his pursuit of me. He's not showing all that he is, but it's enough to send the entire Five Lands into a clamor of fear. I fear, too. I have a threat over my head. He's going to make me permanently vanish someday. How, when, where, and all those questions no one knows—myself included. I know it's also a promise—he doesn't bluff. He and his minions are creating havoc all the time, especially Quicksilver, the Silver Assassin. I remember when he was human. I was there when Ramses turned him into those demon things called Shadow Warriors. I have yet to figure out what they are exactly, and rumor has it he has an entire army of them. Great Spirit be with us!

P.S. On the subject of transporting back and forth from Earth to the Five Lands. The constant switching between two difference space and time continuums seems to have an effect on the passage of time. On their time a watch is tactically useless, so I must use their devices and time keeping crystals for time there. Watches work fine here on Earth. I don't really understand how magic works. Forget about astrophysics—I am not sure if astrophysics rules work the same there as it does here. My friend Sito, the brainiac, would know, but he's been missing for eleven years—presumed dead. There are so many times his ideas and inventions could have aided us in our fights with the Crackedskulls—he may have been a help in the Five Lands. I wished I knew what happened to my pals there. Going on a tangent, so signing off for today—

Neiko's secret Indian phone rang—the one that hardly ever rang, the one that *she didn't want to ring right now.* She bolted downstairs. She hesitated as she reached it, groaning and mumbling to herself, and slowly extracted the phone from the end-table drawer beside the couch.

So much for a quiet evening, Neiko grumbled in her mind. "Hello?" she asked the caller with a puff of breath.

"Hi, Neiko, how do you like your new house?" asked Phoenix, Neiko's best friend in the Desert Storm Falcon tribe—her tribe.

Neiko's face contorted in confusion. *No emergency?* she thought, but said, "Oh, I love it! I'm so glad the Tribes built it for me.

It's the dream house I always wanted—loft upstairs, log cabin—everything. I was so ready to be on my own. Xartna and Sigma really know my style," Neiko replied, referring to the house plans. "There's no emergency? Why didn't you call on the regular phone?" Neiko asked.

Phoenix paused and, in a sheepish tone, said, "I didn't realize I used the wrong phone. I'm sorry about that, Neiko. But that's good—I'm glad you love your new home. Well, will you come over to my house? Where were you? I called for hours, but you weren't there. Why does it sound like you just run a marathon?"

Neiko had to think fast. "I had to run errands, you know how that is. I'm outa breath because I had to run downstairs from the office since I thought there was an emergency. I was writing in my logbooks—officer stuff. I really need to move the secret phone *upstairs* or get another one. Yeah, I'd love to come over. I need to get out of this house before I go stir-crazy," Neiko said, changing the subject before Phoenix asked any unanswerable questions.

Phoenix chortled. "See ya at seven, and I'll have dinner ready. I've invited Hawk, Eagle, and Monchiska to come over too. I wish Sito and the others could also be here," she said with sadness seeping into her voice.

Neiko bit her lip. "I know. I wish I knew what happened to them eleven years ago—I was just thinking about them myself. You still love him after all this time?" she asked, remembering the disappearance of Sito, his twin brother Tito, and their two friends Mactalon and Panthero. Neiko also remembered how much Sito's disappearance devastated her best friend, and Neiko had to help her friend through it countless times. Neiko hoped she wasn't having another relapse. Neiko didn't have the energy left to give at this point.

"Yes. You know we were childhood lovers," said Phoenix with a longing sigh.

"We'll talk more about it when I get there, okay?" said Neiko as she tried to muster up the strength for her grieving friend.

"Sure," Phoenix said, choking back the tears.

"I'll be there soon, just hang in there," Neiko said and hung up, showered, and changed clothes. She stuffed her buckskin clothes and war paint into a gym bag to take along just in case. She just never knew when the Crackedskulls may pull something and she needed to put on her warrior clothes. She checked with the warriors outside and they escorted her to her friend's house.

When Neiko arrived at Phoenix's house, everyone else pulled in at the same time. They all sat down and ate homemade enchiladas. It wasn't necessarily a normal Indian meal like deer meat, but it was always good anyway.

"I heard you've been going through one of your sad spells, Phoenix," said Hawk, and he shoved a huge bite of the enchilada into his mouth.

"Yes, I've been thinking about Sito again. He's been dead for eleven years," Phoenix said, starting to choke up.

"We never confirmed that the four of them are dead—they just vanished into thin air," said Eagle, trying to keep a positive frame of mind and arguing the matter. "We just presumed them dead."

"There has to be a logical explanation because people don't just disappear into thin air without a trace—especially four good warriors like them," said Monchiska, trying to comfort her. "It just doesn't make sense, and still doesn't for that matter."

"I guess so. Let's play rummy, shall we?" said Phoenix as she shook off the pain of his memory and wiped her eyes.

I want to get to the bottom of this and solve this mystery once and for all, mused Neiko to herself as she pitied Phoenix and hid her own sadness. She could only imagine what Phoenix could be feeling; she tried to imagine how she would feel if a similar thing happened to Monchiska. She wanted to know what happened and to make the perpetrator pay if it was the last thing she ever did before someone made her disappear.

Before Eagle passed out the first card, Little Bear, Phoenix's father, ran in.

"Everyone, prepare for battle. The Crackedskulls are attacking the Mohicans and Sparras. Eagle Claw has been captured!" he said.

Everyone jumped up. Neiko grabbed her gym bag from the kitchen counter and ran to the bathroom. Everyone else was went to their cars and pulled their clothes out of trunks and back seats and went into other rooms. Everyone ran out the door, piled into Little Bear and Phoenix's cars prepared for battle. The two vehicles peeled rubber on their way to the small territory in the northeast side of Hawote.

- CHAPTER 2 -

THE OTHER FIVE TRIBES came to the battle site and bailed out of the cars. The Crackedskulls were running amok, destroying homes, cars, buildings, property, and chasing the Mohicans and Sparras and terrorizing them. Great Spirit knows what could happen next, and the chieftains weren't going to sit around and find out before sounding the alarm. The remaining five tribes let out a shrill war call to let them know of their presence and charged under Neiko's direction. The small force of plundering Crackedskulls tried to retreat, but the Indians smashed into them. The Crackedskulls fought savagely, but the angry Indians' hunger for retribution was greater. The Indians wounded quite a few and killed a couple with clubs, slings, bows, spears, and tomahawks—they used native weapons to keep things quiet and not draw attention from Outsider authorities. The Crackedskulls answered back, and Indians were injured.

"Neiko, go and find Eagle Claw while we hold off these goons!" said Pike as he hit a Crackedskull across his eyes with the handle of his tomahawk.

"Righto, Pikey boy," Neiko said with a salute and knocking out a two Crackedskulls as she broke through and headed to Eagle Claw's house which was in the center of the territory.

The house was on fire, and Eagle Claw and his family were screaming as the flames got dangerously close to them; they were tied up and lying in the floor.

"Neiko, call for help. You can't do this alone!" Eagle Claw screamed from within as he wriggled.

Neiko looked and saw that they were fairly close to the entrance, and she saw a way to get to them. There wasn't much time. If she left to get help, they would be dead in a few minutes.

A few burns and some soot on my skin is a small price to pay for helping out a comrade. I'll just take another shower, she thought as she balled her fists and swung her arms like she was preparing for a long jump as she psyched herself up for what she was about to do.

She put her dagger in its sheath, took a deep breath to prepare for the risky operation, and ran into the burning house. She jumped over and ran around the flames. She crouched low to stay below the smoke and hot, toxic gases overhead. She made it to them and freed them from their bonds, leading them to safety as they dodged falling pieces of the smoldering roof. All of them heard the roof beginning to crackle and sag. They jumped out of the door, and the roof caved in just behind them, sending embers and sparks flying. They scrambled off the covered front porch before it decided to crash down upon them, too.

"Well, at least you're safe—but, I'm not so sure about your house," said Neiko, helping them to their feet and brushing off the ashes and soot from her clothes, hair, and skin. The black grime seemed to smear and mix with her sweat and war paint.

"Never mind the house. I'm glad you came because that could've been us in there!" Eagle Claw said, trembling at his close call.

"I am certainly glad you didn't listen to me and were stubborn just like always," he added with a good-natured and grateful smile.

Neiko looked around as more Crackedskulls came out of the woods, closing in on them. "Oh great. This is nice," she grumbled as she saw one hundred armed Crackedskulls with Karo, the General and supreme commander of the ground force in the lead. "Don't look now—we're not outa the woods yet. I think this situation just got a whole lot worse," Neiko said, gripping her quarterstaff tightly with both hands.

Eagle Claw looked around as the Crackedskulls closed in.

Eagle Claw's wife began to panic and gather her young kids around her like a mother hen as the older ones prepared to fight .

Deatheagle, the high commander of the Winged Warriors, and his two subordinate commanders surrounded them in the back.

"Well, well. I expected to find you here, Neiko. You are so brave and heroic that you are predictable. Well, the trap worked. Get them," Karo said with fiendish and conquering grin.

"What do we do with them, sir?" asked one Crackedskull.

"Take Neiko to Prince Bloodhawk. But, as for these other rats, take them away and kill them like we intended to do in the first place," Karo ordered.

"I don't think so, stinkweed!" said Pike with an insulting jeer that was just like he also said "Surprise!".

He had two hundred Indians behind him with their bows drawn and clubs raised. They fired on the Crackedskulls further from the apprehended hostages and wounded thirty-five. The Indians came from behind them, and the ground-force Crackedskulls were surrounded. The winged warriors flew away, and some of the infantry retreated. They then closed in and knocked out all the Crackedskulls that remained except for Karo.

"All right, pig dung, you go tell Raven if he tries another cheap trick like this again, then we will visit it back on him one thousand fold. Get outa here before we change our mind," Pike menaced as he thrust his spear at the general, and Karo ran off.

The Indians raised their weapons in triumph as they shouted and trilled their voices in victory calls. To everyone's surprise this battle was over just as quickly as it started. Raven must be getting sloppy.

Everyone, let's return home. We will celebrate this victory tomorrow night!" said Xartna, and everyone chanted as they left. The Mohicans and Sparras left with the other tribes so that they could find a place to stay the night and begin the preparations for rebuilding.

y

Neiko returned home late that night and went to her front door. She took her dirty tennis shoes off. The wood of her new front deck felt good to her tired feet. "Ohhh, that shower is calling my name and will feel sooo good," she said, closing her eyes and craning her head to stretch her neck and thinking about that hot, steamy water hitting against her tired muscles. She was glad she specifically asked for a massaging showerhead for her shower when the Tribes built her house.

She dug around in her pocket for the key. She had to get into the house first before she could get into that shower. She finally found the key, but then she dropped it on the mat.

"Aww, darn it!" Neiko grumbled as she bent over to pick it up with a grunt.

"Nice evening, isn't it?" came a familiar voice from behind her.

Neiko looked around, and Francesco was standing on her porch, smirking.

"Why are you here and what are you so happy about? We kicked your butts so bad tonight," Neiko said with cynical tone and a sideways grin. "Go away. You're not wanted. If you're still here after I get outa that shower, then your carcass is toast," she said with an ominous tone. She was tired and cranky and totally not in the mood for his antics or whatever messed-up scheme he was cooking up or whatever his purpose was for being here.

"I wouldn't be so satisfied about that victory tonight. And you are still painted for war—how nice. This will be the last battle you will win against us because you won't be here any longer," Francesco said, still smirking. The smirk became more dark and sinister by the second. "Second of all you're shower will have to wait—permanently. You won't be enjoying another hot shower ever again where you're going. You'll have plenty of the 'hot' part."

Neiko looked at him like he was mad. "What is that supposed to mean? What are you gonna do—kill me?" she asked with a sarcastic snort. "They probably have showers in heaven, but where you're going they don't. You'll stink like rotten eggs, burning sulfur, and soot in hell," she shot back. "In about two seconds I'll send you on your one way ticket if you don't beat it."

Francesco snorted and grinned like he had become Satan himself. "No. Remember when I said I would get you back for my humiliation and your sorrows would be one hundred fold? Here is that moment—your time has now come, Admiral. Don't tell me you honestly think you're that self righteous."

Neiko burst out laughing. "Just you being here makes me sorrowful," she slandered. "Why are you here anyway? I could beat you up with one hand tied behind my back! I'm not self righteous at all for your information. I think Karo and Deatheagle have more honor than a traitorous scum like you any day. Since you won't get lost, let's have at it—mano y mano," she said, dropping her key back into her pocket and putting up her fists like she was in the mixed martial arts octagon.

Francesco looked at her like she was nothing more than a Neanderthal that solved everything by hitting it with a club. "I'm not here to fight you! I'll let you figure this out on your own. And there is no way back," Francesco said as he pulled out a green crystal from his pocket. "It will be the same for you as it was for them…"

Neiko looked at it with surprise and raised her right eyebrow quizzically that asked "Hey, neat—what's that?". "Oh, are you gonna frame me like last time? Ha! That won't fly this go 'round. And what do you mean there's no way back…and who is the 'them' you're talking about? What kind of new toy is that anyway?"

Francesco said nothing as he rubbed the crystal. It began to glow. He mumbled chants, and it glowed brighter and brighter. Then he thrust his hands up and waved the crystal toward her. A green light surrounded her, and she disappeared.

- CHAPTER 3 -

NEIKO'S VISION TURNED FROM the green light to the world spinning around her in dizzying speed. Neiko wasn't moving, but she felt like she was in freefall—like someone had cut the cable from an elevator, and she was plummeting with it. Descending in what—space and time? The evergreen and colorful deciduous vegetation of the Hawote woodlands changed to a desert with a river with some greenery and palms nearby. The cool autumn air of Hawote in October transformed into stifling, searing, dry heat. Pyramids, sphinxes, and strange statues spun around her after her house, porch, and front yard disappeared within the vortex. It was nighttime in Hawote, but the sun rose and set as time flew by—from west to east—backwards. Beneath her bare feet the wood from her front porch turned to nothing then into hot, soft sand.

Neiko's world stopped spinning, and the sun was high in the sky. Neiko watched the sun to be sure it didn't move again. Wherever she ended up, she guessed the time must be about high noon there judging by the sun's position in the sky after a few moments of observation. The heat was intense, and she discovered she must be somewhere far from home. "Where?" was the ultimate question. A gust of wind blew the feathers in her long, black hair. Her hair wrapped around her face, and she brushed it back. Sweat beaded out on her body, and she tugged at her shirt and headband. "Phew! It's hot out here! Where am I—Death Valley?" she asked. Death Valley was the only desert place she thought of off the top of her head. She had never been there, but she'd read and watched TV programs about the place. She looked around, and a city was only a few feet away. She could see the buildings down below from the high dune where she stood. She took a deep breath and fingered the fringed sheath of her knife to reassure her confidence—without thinking and by instinct. Then after a few more seconds, she trudged down to the city in the soft sand from the dune to go find some answers.

Neiko entered the city still dressed in her buckskin, decorated warrior clothes and painted for war. As she took in the sights and from the confusion, she had forgotten she was armed. Her machete was sheathed to her back, and so was her knife on her side. Incense, perfumes, and music filled the air. She didn't recognize any of the smells, but the music seemed to be like Egyptian reenactments in movies. The buildings were white alabaster covered in brilliant wall paintings. Some men rode on camels like horses and others led them by a leash. Chariots cantered by. Neiko looked around in amazement. This ruled out Death Valley, Arizona. Neiko lifted her eyes to the sun to get a bearing on north. North was as good of a direction as any to begin a search for answers. After her eyes fell from the sun and to the north, she could see the Pyramids of Giza towering in the distance. She recognized them instantly. She had seen enough pictures and documentaries on the monuments—they were unmistakable. Even though they were miles away, they towered above the city and in view. This definitely wasn't Death Valley.

In that case I can get on the first flight home, she thought. She believed that she had landed in Cairo. This city came to mind because it's the only one close to the Pyramids of Giza. Then she realized she didn't have any money as she put her hands in the pockets of her buckskin shorts and only felt the house key. She had left her wallet in the car back at home when she left from Phoenix's house after the battle.

"Well, I can probably make up some story that I was abducted or something—which is sort of true. Really funny, Francesco. I guess you meant no way back since I'm broke. I'll hitchhike back to Hawote if I have to. I'll scrounge around to see if I can find some change for a pay phone on the road," she remarked to herself, and maybe the phone book would have some information on where to find an airport or something. But, then again, would the phonebook be written in English or Arabic? It was a chance she had to take. The worst that could happen was not getting anywhere.

Neiko began walking to find help, change, a pay phone, the U.S. Embassy, an airport, or whatever she could find first. After a few more minutes of exploring, she recognized the clothing of the people: white linen kilts, some wore robes and fine jewelry, some wore headcloths while others did not. No one seemed to be dressed like the Arab residents of 21st century Egypt. "Why is everyone dressed like ancient Egyptians?" she asked herself. She wondered if this was some sort of a cult or a weird secret society that lived like the Amish in Cairo.

A small group of armed soldiers marched in front of her, but they didn't pay any attention to her. They carried swords, shields, spears, and were dressed in ancient Egyptian armor. She had seen it in books and movies. They weren't carrying guns or dressed in desert camouflage BDUs like Egyptian soldiers of the 21st century.

She headed farther in to the marketplace. It was obvious since people had shops and bazaars selling goods. People were yelling and haggling. People thrust things at Neiko trying to entice her to buy. Neiko put up her hands and shook her head. She couldn't understand a word anyone was saying. Funny, no one seemed to be selling T-shirts, souvenirs, or that type stuff for tourists. Quite frankly, no one seemed to be selling any maps.

Neiko walked up to a man who was a merchant at a bazaar. He was selling all manner of fine jewelry. Heavy collars, bracelets, necklaces, arm pieces, earrings were on display. All gaudy like the ancient Egyptians liked. "Excuse me, can you tell me where I am? I seem to be lost. Do you know where I can find a map or where the airport is? A phone?" she asked as she made her hand like a phone and put it to her ear; her thumb the earpiece and her pinkie the mouthpiece.

The man looked at her startled because of her strange appearance and because he couldn't understand her. He was dressed in linen like everyone else and sported some of that same Egyptian bling since he was a successful jeweler.

"That's a little out of style, don't you think? I mean, guys don't wear eyeliner…and, that skirt and that sheet on your head are not how people dress nowadays. People dress like ancient Egyptians only on Halloween. Last I checked it was still three weeks away," Neiko said to the man as she shook her head.

The man chattered in a language she didn't understand—God knows what he was saying to her. He thrust at her a fine scarab necklace. Neiko looked at him puzzled with her right eyebrow raised. The language didn't sound like Arabic since she watched a lot of action movies. Neiko put up her hands and shook her head and signed "map" and "phone" and spoke the words in every language that she knew of but got nowhere.

"Never mind," she said, throwing her hands up in defeat and walking off with a frustrated sigh. "Okay, that is no language I know. I can usually tell, but it's not anything I've heard before except in a few movies."

Neiko stopped a scantily clad woman. She was topless with hardly anything to her loincloth. "Pardon me, do you speak English?

Greyhawk? Cherokee? Blackfoot? Or how about Spanish?" The woman looked at Neiko like she was an alien from another planet. "You need to get some clothes on, girl, before you get charged with indecent exposure," she said as she had unknowingly come across an Egyptian dancer. "Strippers wear more clothes than that when walking down the street in Vegas—or so I've heard or saw in the movies!" she mumbled, shaking her head. Neiko watched a lot of TV when she wasn't busy busting Crackedskull heads or going on quests in the Five Lands.

"Okay, I'm getting nowhere fast," Neiko grumbled as she looked at sphinxes and animal-headed gods. The Pyramids grew as she headed north. Neiko walked through the streets of the city looking at everything, and many people looked at her because of her foreign appearance. Some people stared. Many young men gawked at her beauty. Neiko found it annoying and tried to ignore them. *These people act like they've never seen an Indian before,* she thought as she twisted her mouth and shook her head. After some time it dawned on her that there was no trace of modern day technology. She hadn't even seen a car in the past hour which unnerved her. Neiko bit her lip as a weight began to grow in the pit of her stomach at this realization.

"It seems like ancient Egypt, but how in the world did I get here? Or, is this just some place he made up to make it look like…I— no, this has to be; I'm sure of it. But, I also need to find out where and when I am. I guess Cairo is definitely out. I think it was built later…if this is ancient Egypt, then I know there is a pharaoh here somewhere, and I know how they treat outsiders. I don't know how they would feel about Indians—most people don't like us anyway. And, who is the pharaoh? Now I know what he meant about me not returning. Well, I figured out what country I'm in at least—if that's even the case—" she mused, and then her thoughts were scattered because a group of men stopped in front of her blocking her path. She hadn't noticed them since she was in her own little world.

At the head was a rich man, clothed in fine clothes, gold and jewels. He motioned for his men to fan out to seal off her possible escape routes. Seeing her armed, some of other men drew their weapons. He looked at her closely—very closely. He rubbed his hands together and grinned like he had just found gold. There was another glint in his eye that she didn't like—the kind of look when someone is obviously checking you out. Neiko understood *that* very well.

Neiko looked at him with a frown and a cocked eyebrow. Her hand went to her knife, but she didn't draw it. Her insides told her to run, but she was so startled and confused she was immobilized like a deer blinded by headlights before they get run over. There were also too many of them to take down by herself, and she was surrounded in a tight circle.

But before Neiko could react, the man pointed at her and started barking commands to his followers. They were on her in seconds. They grabbed her and bound her wrists in front of her as they disarmed her. She tried to resist them, but it didn't do any good. "Hey, what gives?" Neiko asked as they dragged her along behind the man.

Neiko was taken to the man's house and put in a cell with three other men. The dungeon reeked of urine and BO. The floor was nothing more than trampled sand. Cells lined the hallway, and it was fairly dark. Very little light came in through the tiny windows in the cells in the late afternoon sometime before dusk. Then they shut the door and locked it and walked away laughing and chattering.

Neiko yelled at the men, saying, "C'mon, gimmie a break! I didn't do anything to you! I didn't steal your horse—or whatever you're accusing me of! Let me outa here!" she shouted from in between the bars and pushing on the door in aggravation.

The men didn't pay her any attention as they continued to walk away, laughing and talking.

"He didn't lose a horse. He just acquired another slave," said one of the men in the cell in English. He was covered in smudges, dirt, and had long, stringy, and ratty black hair. The man looked remotely like a Native American. His skin was not the golden bronze like the rest of the Egyptians—a red hue showed through his tan.

"Aye, I bet he will fancy this one because she's gorgeous which won't be good," said another.

"Hey, she's an Indian. Do you think she looks familiar, Mactalon?" asked the third.

Neiko looked at the men like her ears were playing tricks on her. Her mouth gaped open and she raised her eyebrows. "How do you know about Indians and how to speak English? And—how come you have a name just like one of my long-lost friends?" Neiko asked, perplexed. All three of these men had seen their better days, but in some ways they seemed almost familiar—like older versions of the boys that had been missing for eleven years.

"That's because Mactacon's my name. I am an Indian along with my pals here—Tito and Panthero. Nice to meet you, dear lady—it's nice to see an Indian again. But why are you here in Egypt?" asked Mactalon as he nodded her way. Neiko's buckskin clothes and appearance was unmistakable to him.

The three off them were in servants' clothes: plain linen kilts, and no shirts. Their appearance was homely because of their filthiness. Their hair was long and stringy, and strangely enough they didn't have beards, a tell tale sign that they were Indians. They looked as they hadn't bathed in weeks. They were covered in dust and had shackles on their ankles.

"Well, Francesco, the ex Grand High Mohican, sent me here. It's nice to see you guys aren't dead. I'm Neiko—do you remember me?" she asked with her eyes filled with hope.

The three looked at her closely and remembered the young warrior child. "Neiko? What a fine young woman you have turned out to be—and beautiful too! So why did the GHM send you here?" asked Tito.

"Because I exposed him for whom he really was—a dirty rotten traitor. Also, he was actually a Crackedskull who somehow wormed his way up to the top after he was adopted into the Mohican-Sparra. He used that to spy for Raven all these years. My being here is his revenge. I bet Raven and Bloodhawk will be mad to know that he did this. So where's Sito and what's your story?" Neiko asked with a shrug.

"Well, I have no idea where my brother is. We uncovered a plot by the GHM to send classified logs to Raven, and he disposed of us—the exact same task you were going to do but we stopped you, remember?" asked Tito as he shifted to a more comfortable position on the dusty floor.

Neiko nodded and couldn't imagine what might have happened if she was sent away instead. She shuddered at the thought.

"The three of us came together, but Sito got separated from us upon arrival—how—I don't know. We tried looking all over Egypt for him but had no luck in finding him. We came here and have been enslaved by Kenes—that's the rich jerk you met today," replied Tito.

"Where are we, and do you know who the pharaoh is?" asked Neiko as she hooked her thumbs in her belt loops and leaned against the wall.

"We are in Memphis right now—the old capital city of Egypt—it's still a booming city though. I heard that Seti I passed on recently and his son Ramesses took the throne about three months ago. Boy, Egypt is perilous in these days for foreigners and slaves," Panthero replied shaking his head.

Neiko looked at them with disgust with a "you've got to be kidding" look. "He wouldn't be THE Ramesses—uh—Ramesses II by any chance, would it?"

"Yup. The one and only Ramesses the Great," chimed Tito.

Neiko slapped her hand on her head and groaned. "Of course--Francesco's personal role model. He had a thing for this guy and knew a lot about him. It is on the borderline between an obsession and a fetish, if you ask me. He sent you here during Seti's reign, right?"

"Yep. We've been here for eleven years—and been serving Kenes for ten and a half. We spent six months trying to find my brother. We work in Kenes' gardens from sunrise to sunset—normally, but I hate to see what your service will be," said Tito. "That pretty face is going to get you into a heap of trouble here."

Neiko shrugged indifferently. "Things could be worse. I mean, we could be making bricks or statues for that tyrant Ramesses—"

Tito put up his hands and shushed Neiko. "Don't go around saying his name like he's your next door neighbor—that isn't done here! You only speak his name in reverence out of his presence!" Tito warned. "Furthermore, you don't talk bad about him behind his back—he finds out quickly somehow, and it's his personal pet peeve. I don't know how I know that, but trust me!"

Neiko shrugged and scratched her head with "so what" written all over her face.

"Well, everyone loves him except for people like us," said Mactalon.

"Is Sito still alive?" asked Neiko.

"Yes. Sometimes he's happy, but oftentimes he's extremely sad. We feel each other through our twin telepathy, and he feels my pain," said Tito.

"What're the only places you haven't looked?" asked Neiko.

"The only place we haven't gone is Thebes. Thebes is where Pharaoh is until he gets his new treasure cities built, and they will be finished in about another five years or so. We came to Memphis to avoid any confrontations from both Seti and Ramesses in Thebes. That was the last place we were going until we were captured and enslaved," said Mactalon.

"When we get outa here, that's where we're going. Don't try to stop me because I ain't scared of no pharaoh, especially when we mean him no harm," Neiko said, folding her arms.

"Okay, you are the same as we remember you. How old are you now, and have we missed anything?" asked Mactalon beaming with curiosity.

"Well, I'm twenty-one now. You missed when I was promoted to admiral, my graduation from high school, and the recent battle that took place before I got sent here that was a washout for the Crackedskulls—we spanked them good," Neiko replied with a sideways grin.

"Wow! We missed all of the important milestones in your life. And look at you, an admiral," said Panthero shaking her hand. Indian ranks were different than other known military ranks.

"Yeah, and things seem really sticky now since then. You were young kids when you were sent here too, right?" asked Neiko.

"Yeah, Tito and Sito were twelve, and Panthero and I were thirteen, while you were eleven. We five were the future special warriors, and we started out young too. At least you were able to fight one last battle before you left," said Mactalon with a wishful sigh.

"Well, I was glad to fight one last battle, too. I wanted to be there to watch the fall of Raven and Bloodhawk, and be the admiral to bring them down. Seems to me like Francesco is a little more unstable and dangerous," said Neiko as she bit her lip.

"I agree. He seems a little in left field to be looking up to Ramesses like a god or whatever," joked Mactalon with a snort.

"I know! You oughta have seen his house! He had pictures of the guy everywhere and used his name as the password for his secret stuff in his computer. It looked like Ramesses lived there and not Francesco!" Neiko exclaimed.

"Neiko, again—a word of advice—do not say the name of Pharaoh in public or where anyone else can hear you out of reverence because it's bad. I would hate to see what Pharaoh would do to you," warned Tito. "Only say it around us where only we can hear you. That's what we do."

"Okay, thanks for the advice—these people act like he's Jesus or something," she said with an apathetic shrug and an "I don't care" look on her face. The others snickered. "I know he hates most outsiders, but how does he feel about Indians?" asked Neiko.

"Close enough. It's like Amon-Ra incarnate," said Tito. He and his twin brother, Sito, and father were experts on ancient Egypt. "I don't know, and I don't really want to find out because I don't think he knows about our kind, and I plan to keep it that way," Tito said with dread and shaking his head.

"I would assume he would send the four of us to Goshen and not think twice about it," replied Mactalon.

"Where?" asked Neiko, fanning her hands out with an "I'm lost" look on her face.

"Oh, that's the place he's building his treasure cities, and that's where most of the labor gangs are," answered Mactalon. He only knew since it was the kind of place Tito mentioned to avoid in the beginning.

"Oh yeah! I remember that name now—" Neiko said nodding, but she was interrupted because a man rapped the bars on their door with the handle of his whip.

"Go to sleep," he snapped at them in Egyptian, but turned and left.

Neiko looked at him with her mouth hung open like she had just said "Huh?" silently.

"Time for bed," said Panthero as he stood up to go to a pallet in the floor in the back left of the room.

"Can you understand them?" Neiko asked, scratching her head.

"Yeah, if you live in a place long enough, you kind of pick it up. But Sito and I were better prepared because we studied this language as a hobby, remember?" said Tito as he fluffed his pillow and plopped down.

"Oh yeah, and Francesco knows the language and can write in hieroglyphics," Neiko said standing there and looking for a place to lie down.

"Shut up!" snapped the Egyptian. Apparently he hadn't left the hallway and still heard them talking.

Neiko turned around. "Okay, okay, don't get your panties in a wad!" she snapped angrily with her hands on her hips.

The others winced because they knew this could cause trouble.

The man didn't understand what she said, but he could sense the hostility of her remark. He started to unlock the door with a look of annoyance on his face. He was going to deal with this impudent slave and tell Kenes about this little upstart. But Tito stood up on her behalf by stepping in between them and putting up his hands in surrender.

"She didn't mean it, and we were just going to bed," he told the man in his language. "Right, Neiko?" he asked her in English.

She nodded as she slid behind Tito further but peeked from behind his back.

The guard looked at her and then at Tito and then walked away. Everyone released their held breaths.

"If you are going to make it in Egypt, then you have to control that temper of yours," Mactalon scolded as he thrust his finger into her shoulder. "It's dangerous for a slave to have a short fuse—definitely a pretty one. Besides, anyone who is not Egyptian is inferior—remember that—and they won't hesitate to do what they want to you," warned Mactalon.

Neiko nodded silently as she twisted her mouth.

They all lay down and went to sleep.

– CHAPTER 4 –

T HE NEXT MORNING NEIKO awoke feeling like she had been drugged. She pulled herself into sitting position and rubbed the sleep from her eyes. It took her a few moments to recall where she was or what happened. A coffee would be nice. *Oh wait, coffee hasn't been discovered in ancient Egypt*, she thought. She noticed that she was alone in the cell. She instantly wondered where her friends had gone. She picked herself off the pallet and paced around the small room. The sun shone brightly through the small barred window, and it was getting hot in the cell. It was anyone's guess what time it was.

"Ohhh, man, I feel like I have jet-lag or something," Neiko groaned as she rubbed her eyes some more. "If I went through time, is it called time lag? Does this Kenes guy have something to eat around here? I'm starved—"

Neiko's thoughts scattered when four guards came into the cell. One of them was carrying a plate of food—a silver plate at that. The guard tried to hand it to her.

Neiko cocked her head and turned up her eyes at the guard in distrust. *I've heard of stuff being handed to me on a silver platter, but this is ridiculous,* thought Neiko. There wasn't any way that could be for her, could it?

The guard kept saying a word to her and trying to give her the plate of food. Then he signed "eat" by placing his fingers at his mouth and repeating the word.

Neiko took the plate and backed away and began devouring the food. Surprisingly it wasn't stale or gross. The food was very tasty. *Is this what slaves get?* Neiko wondered. She pictured something disgusting like stale bread and gruel for slaves. After she was finished eating, the guards took her from the cell.

When Neiko was brought into the house, servants and slaves were bustling about, but there were no signs of her friends. Then she remembered that they worked in the fields and gardens. As the guards took her farther inside the house, she saw Kenes and two other wealthy men sitting down eating a fine breakfast. From a closer look Kenes and his two acquaintances seemed to be in their late twenties or early thirties, close to her and her friends' age. The guard who delivered her food went to Kenes and said something to him as he placed the matching silver plate on the table next to him. Neiko observed they were eating the same food she had just eaten minutes ago. Coincidence? *Nah,* Neiko thought shrugging off the notion she had been fed off of Kenes' table.

Kenes nodded and waved his hand. Then he and his friends seemed to stare at Neiko. Neiko felt a bit miffed and awkward by the attention she was getting.

Only Neiko had no inkling what was happening. She guessed the two men must be his friends. It seemed awfully strange to her that there was no woman there at the table with them. Neiko shrugged at that thought, too.

Suddenly a woman did appear with a broom in hand. She thrust it at Neiko and made sweeping motions. Could she be Kenes' wife? She was not a pretty woman, and she seemed like "the scary babysitter named Helga" type. That didn't seem like Kenes' type, but then what was his type anyway? Neiko could only guess as her mind reeled in trying to make sense of this morning's events.

Neiko frowned and snatched the broom from the woman's hands. "I know what that is and what it's supposed to do," Neiko muttered under her breath. "I can make this fun! Let's see," she thought aloud as she spun the broom like someone on the flag corp as she swept. Then she went as far as pretending the broom was a guitar, and she was putting on a rock concert as she sung the tune to "Smoke on the Water" or other tunes that came to mind.

The other servants watched her as they worked. They couldn't help but to gander at this madness.

"What is this girl so happy about?" asked one young servant girl to a man who was polishing the floor.

"Obviously she doesn't know how mean and cruel Kenes really is—he is as cruel as Khufu. She won't be singing that happy song for long after he gets through with her," said the man as he continued to buff the floor. He looked around and checked around for Kenes and hoped he didn't overhear, or he and the young girl would be punished for gossiping.

The young girl scampered off before the woman with the stick came by.

This woman was the overseer of the house, and she carried a rod with her at the ready to whack a slothful or disobedient servant. Seeing Neiko making a mockery of her work detail, she was on the overseer's radar. She rushed at Neiko with the rod raised to strike her.

Neiko saw her from the corner of her eye and held the broom up like a quarterstaff to block her.

However, a man came from the left like the roadrunner and stopped the woman's assault by grabbing her wrist and stopping her in mid-swing. "No! Lord Kenes gave precise instructions about that one. She is not to be harmed, or *we'll* be punished instead. Apparently you missed the meeting," said the man who was the chief overseer of the guards and taskmasters.

The woman scowled. "If you say so." The woman sauntered away muttering and clearly in a bad mood.

Neiko stuck her tongue out at the woman. "Yeah, that's right! Keep walkin'! He just saved me the trouble of kicking your butt!" she shouted at the woman as she poked out her chest. After that, she continued sweeping and playing with the broom.

Kenes seemed to be entertained by her antics as he watched her from the table, doorways, or any other place he could get a peek. His two friends joined him. Although Neiko's display was fun, it wasn't the only reason why he was watching her. Little did Neiko know that he had been watching her all morning. Neiko got into a fast-paced song, swept the floor, and concluded the act by tossing her broom and catching it. Kenes clapped along with his friends who also witnessed her show. "Nicely done," said Kenes.

Neiko made a face since she didn't do it for their amusement, and she didn't like being watched. Kenes also had that weird look in his eye again that reminded her of a coyote which had found its most memorable prey. Neiko shivered at the sneaky, predatory grin and what could possibly be going through his mind.

One of his guests looked at her strange apparel. "I have never seen a woman like this, and I have traveled as far as Syria. Where did you acquire a rare beauty such as this?"

"Oh, simple. I found her in these very streets. She is the fourth of these strange painted people I have been able to capture right here in Memphis. But, she is the only female. You're right—she is beautiful—that was the first thing I noticed when I found her. Although I have to say, when I found her, she was wearing paint on her face and carrying weapons like she had been in a battle," replied Kenes.

The other man looked at him with raised, inquisitive eyebrows. "A female warrior? Such a thing is unheard of. These people are barbaric, no doubt. I wonder if they are even housebroken. How much will you be willing to sell her for? I would pay a handsome price."

A shrewd light came into Kenes' eyes. "I'm sorry, Hotep, she is not for sale. I have my own plans for *that* rare gem. I'll offer you one of the painted men if you wish," he said with a flick of his hand and a callous frown.

Hotep shook his head at the offer and looked at Neiko. "Aw, come now, Kenes. You were willing to sell me that other slave—that Assyrian, remember? You also said you would never sell him."

"I know, but she is special—I can sense it, but call it intuition if you will. I may be able to make money off her and her friends, and she will please me in other ways," he said with a sneaky grin. "I won't be keeping her in the jail for long. I will dress those other three in their original clothing and tell them to fix themselves like I found them. You wouldn't believe what they looked like as you can see from the way she is dressed," said Kenes. "I saved their clothing because it is so rare and possibly valuable. I did have ideas of maybe making them my own attractions or additions to the zoo."

The three men snickered. There was a nice zoo in the northeast part of Memphis.

Another man, whose name was Het, was also curious. "How did you know she has three friends?"

"One of my guards told me of them talking like they were making up for lost time. He reported to me about the incident. I told him and the rest of my guards and taskmasters I will deal with that one personally. She's no good to me broken, scarred, and sullied. I must say, she has spirit. She got angry at the guard, and it seems she has a temper," said Kenes with a crooked grin. "All wild beasts can be tamed. She won't be sweeping floors and polishing dishes for long and will be dressed in fine linen and gold as my lady—the lady of Memphis," he said. "You know how I *always* get what I want. I always have the best as well."

"Does she have a name?" asked Hotep.

"It's Neiko, I think," Kenes replied.

Upon hearing her name, she stopped polishing the plates, looked up, and saw the three of them looking at her, smiling. She also figured they were talking about her. "Okay, stay calm," she reminded herself because the heat of her temper started welling up. She clenched her fists around the polishing cloth, shook, and turned away from her watchers. She went back to her chores in an effort to ignore them. Neiko didn't know how much she could stand of them staring at her and doing household chores forever when she had a war to win.

"You see? Her anger is rising, but she's trying to control it," said Kenes.

"Neiko—it fits perfectly. It's a pretty name, but has strength and spirit," said Het.

"Unfortunately, she cannot communicate with us like her friends can. I've had those three men for ten and a half years, but she's been here not even a day, and it seems she has just come here recently," said Kenes.

"I have an idea. You can make lots of money showing her off, but those other three are expendable. Why not use them as pit fighters? You can test the war skills of these foreigners against other peoples, and if they are good enough, you can make much off them as well," offered Hotep.

Kenes paused for a few moments in thought. "I like the sound of that. Neiko will stay with me and after the fights, I will charge for people to see her. She will be dressed in her native clothes, and her friends will fight in their native clothes."

Het smiled. "I would like for Hotep and me to help you along the way and give you ideas. We will also get those three savages ready and let them experience a few practice fights. We will keep this in Memphis till fame spreads, and one day go to Thebes. Then the real money begins."

Kenes rubbed his hands together. "Yes, that will be terrific. I think you have found us a gold mine! I will gladly split the profit with you, and when we get to Thebes, we will be rich! If those other three don't survive, then I'll keep Neiko forever!"

Neiko looked up at the mentioning of her name, and she sensed that they were planning something. Unfortunately she didn't know what it was because of the language barrier.

Neiko looked around as more Crackedskulls came out of the woods, closing in on them. "Oh great. This is nice," she grumbled as she saw one hundred armed Crackedskulls with Karo, the General and supreme commander of the ground force in the lead. "Don't look now—we're not outa the woods yet. I think this situation just got a whole lot worse," Neiko said gripping her quarterstaff tightly with both hands.

Eagle Claw looked around as the Crackedskulls closed in.

Eagle Claw's wife began to panic and gather her young kids around her like a mother hen as the older ones prepared to fight .

Later that night, all four Indians were lined up, and they were dressed in their Indian clothes. The three men were able to fix their hair and put on paint and their headbands and feathers.

"What in the crap are they up to?" asked Mactalon.

The three boss Egyptians looked at them in amazement while smirking at each other. "This will be a cinch," said Het.

"I agree," said Hotep, looking Neiko in the face—eye to eye—with his outlined eyes, but she turned away. He was still so jealous that Kenes wouldn't let him have her.

"All right, you three will start your training. Het, you will be responsible for that and get a few of my men to assist you," said Kenes as his dictated with his hand.

Neiko's friends were the subjected to excruciating military exercise. If they slacked off, then they were whipped or kicked and yelled at. Neiko stood there in disbelief unable to help them because Kenes and his men kept her at bay and a close eye on her.

Great Spirit knows where this was heading, Neiko thought as she stood there, helpless.

- CHAPTER 5 -

EARLY THE NEXT MORNING, Neiko came outside to see what had happened to her friends. They were gone when she awoke, and she hadn't seen them all morning after the guards fetched her from the cell. She wasn't given any chores to do that day. Her situation was becoming weirder by the day in her opinion, and it didn't make any sense at all.

They were running around the garden and showed signs of great fatigue, but if they slowed their pace, they were whipped. When they came her way, they stopped and flopped on the ground, panting.

"What's going on?" asked Neiko.

Tito swallowed and panted. "They—are—exercising us to death—again."

"What? Why? I know those three are up to something," Neiko replied. She remained clueless about what Kenes had cooked up for her though.

"No idea, but this seems like some sort of training. But for what, the army? We have been at it all morning long before dawn. We never trained this hard in warrior training," complained Mactalon as he sucked oxygen into his burning lungs.

"I know! It's not good to strain people in training," said Neiko, shaking her head.

Het came up with three canteens of water and threw them on the ground with taskmasters behind him. "Drink up. Rest time will be brief," he said curtly.

The three men turned up the canteens and chugged the water as it cooled their parched throats.

"Why are you doing this?" asked Tito as he breathed heavily.

"You will find out soon enough, savage," Het snapped and walked away like a runway model strutting his stuff.

The three Indians shot him daggers. They hated being called savages.

"Okay, no one will tell us diddly," grumbled Mactalon as he chugged down his water.

About ten minutes later, the three were back at training.

Neiko dug in the sand with her toe. "What am I supposed to do? I can't talk to my friends, and Kenes doesn't want me to work, so what good am I?" she mused as she sat under a palm tree and watched her friends in their hard training. She probably didn't want to know what was in store for her.

Later that night, everyone went out into an arena-like structure. It was like a much smaller and Egyptian version of the Coliseum where pit fights were held. The three of them were given weapons. "You will practice your fighting skills with your weapons in a mock fight. In a real fight, it is to the death. Then we will go into the city for real action," said Kenes.

"We don't fight and kill people for sport! We only fight and kill against people who try to hurt and destroy our land and our enemies—the Crackedskulls!" protested Panthero. "If you're looking for bloodthirsty savages, then I think you need to catch some Crackedskulls instead!"

"The men you will be fighting are your enemies! What land is this anyway?" asked Kenes with a snarl.

"It's called Hawote. You'll only make those men our enemies; we won't do it. I'd rather work in a mudhole than kill people without a cause!" snapped Tito as he threw down his spear.

"Me neither!" followed Mactalon, and he threw down his shield and sword.

"Right behind you, guys," said Panthero as he pitched his daggers.

"Pick them up, and you will do as you are told," growled Kenes as he puffed out his chest and jabbed his finger at them "If you refuse to obey, I will have you scourged with ten lashes. You've been warned."

The three of them spat at his sandaled feet.

"You are a heartless dog!" Tito said with hatred.

Neiko looked around, confused. She felt like she was watching a foreign movie that forgot the English translation captions. *Will someone please tell me what is going on?*

"Enough, tie them to the fence and whip them!" Kenes said vehemently. "It is time to *remind* you who is in charge here. This is what happens when I must repeat myself!"

They were seized and tied in a row as Kenes continued his rant. Seconds later, Het went and started to strike Mactalon with all of his strength. Kenes' other men whipped the other two.

Neiko ran up and grabbed Het trying to stop him. "Stop it!" she yelled, but he pulled free from her grasp. Hotep pulled her away before she could do further harm since she was about to side-punch Het into the stomach or groin. Hotep tried to restrain her, but she wriggled and bucked to get away from him to help her friends.

Kenes tried to stop her from interfering when she almost broken free from Hotep's hold. Kenes laughed at her as he held her wrists. "Look at this wild spirit, would you? I've never seen a woman this lively in all my days!" he chuckled with a strange look in his eyes that made Neiko's blood run cold like she was looking into the eyes of a stalker.

"Let her go, Egyptian dog breath!" Mactalon yelled indignantly between gritted teeth and grimacing at the pain as his eyes flashed in rage. He instantly guessed what was waiting around the bend for Neiko, and it turned his stomach and kindled his rage.

"Give them ten more lashes for insulting me!" Kenes shouted authoritatively as he continued to restrain Neiko.

The tormentors laughed as they struck the three because they couldn't bear much more and started groaning. When the assault had finished, they spat on the afflicted Indians and kicked them because they couldn't stand up due to the intense pain.

"Now get up and do your training. The next time you fail to comply with my orders will end in thirty lashes!" Kenes snapped cruelly after releasing Neiko to take center stage.

The wounded three tried to stand up, but they couldn't. However, the Egyptians kicked them mercilessly until they stood up. Neiko still tried to rush to her injured friends, but two of Kenes' men held her fast. She had even thought about attacking Kenes while his back was turned. While everyone watched, the three picked up their weapons and practiced in pain to sharpen their rusty warrior skills that night.

- CHAPTER 6 -

LATER THAT NIGHT, THE four Indians talked in their cell about the occurrences.

"This is hardly the worst thing Kenes has ever done," remarked Mactalon. "We've seen some real horrors in the ten and a half years we've been here. You really have to watch yourself, Neiko. I don't think you're going to be in here with us much longer."

Neiko furrowed her eyebrows and opened her mouth like she silently said "what?". "Okay, what's going on? Why is Kenes acting all weird and stuff?"

"We think Kenes has romantic plans for you. If you say no, he'll make you serve him whether you want to or not—he makes everyone do what he wishes whether they want to or not with force and cruel punishment—like tonight. I don't know how far his plans for you are gonna go," warned Mactalon. "It can be marriage and all it entails or just a "personal slave" if you get my drift."

Neiko looked like she would like to barf. "Wouldn't his wife have something to say about that? Wouldn't she smack him with that stick she always carries around?"

The three guys laughed.

"That's not Kenes' wife. That his overseer of the house. Kenes doesn't have a wife—yet," said Tito and he put a lot of emphasis on the word *yet*.

"Maybe he'd have one if he wasn't such a butthole," said Neiko, crossing her arms. "I'd hate to break it to him, but I'm not on the menu."

The four of them laughed.

"You won't have a choice against the lord and richest man in Memphis, Neiko," Tito said. "Like we just said; he'll make you."

"I'm glad one never forgets how to fight," said Mactalon, trying to turn the conversation to a brighter note. "We are a little rusty, but at least it's like riding a bike—it comes back to you."

"Yeah, I know, but we have to use our great skill for show, and we have to kill people without a cause. And if we don't kill the person we're fighting, then he'll kill us," fussed Panthero.

"Well, it seems that if you survive long enough, then I heard something about Thebes—I think," replied Neiko. She thought she picked out the name among all of the other unknown words.

Tito looked at her, horrified. "Pit fighting in Thebes? Those will be really tough matches, and I bet our fame would spread everywhere. I bet that would get Pharaoh's attention. If he feels threatened by us then, he could try to snuff us out. I mean, look what happened to the Hebrews—they get enslaved for just taking up too much space here. That happened just recently—like four to six months ago. To his fellow Egyptians he's a good and benevolent king; he just doesn't play around when he sees or sniffs out a threat."

"Hey wait a minute—I thought..." said Neiko but lost train of thought. "Where's Moses?"

Picking up on Neiko's thought, Mactalon said, "That's what we thought too, but he isn't even here—frankly I don't even think he's been born yet. The Exodus may not take place until about a hundred years or more."

"He isn't. Ramesses wouldn't have co-ruled with his father if he was," interjected Tito.

"Oh…well…I guess never mind Pharaoh. Our main concern is getting out of here, finding Sito, and trying to find our way back to Hawote, right? We won't be here long enough for Pharaoh to find out about us if we play our cards right and stay quiet," said Neiko. "However, the getting back to Hawote part may be a bit impossible unless Sito can invent a time machine out of…whatever-century-this-is' technology. Instead of a Deloreon, do we get a chariot to go 88 miles an hour?" Neiko snorted. "I don't guess there is a space-time vortex near the Pyramids of Giza either, huh?" she asked, throwing her hands up in frustration, and then snapped her fingers and said, "Oh, darn, I could have swiped the time crystal Francesco was using before I—whatever the heck happened."

"Neiko's right. We will have to disguise ourselves well once we escape because those creeps will run us down, or we could get picked up by some other rich jerk," said Mactalon and then he scratched his head. "The getting home part does present a bit of a problem indeed."

"True, but are there any ideas on how to break out of here? We've finished our training, and there's a match tomorrow. Besides, if we try to break out of this cell, there are too many guards—we won't get very far. If we get caught, then we will definitely get the whip or maybe worse," mused Tito. "I don't know how cranky Kenes will be if he had to come get us in the middle of the night."

"Well, then what? Just say we are able to get out of Memphis and reach Thebes, but we'll still have to find a place to stay. I mean, four Indians in the streets of Thebes would get Pharaoh's attention in a heartbeat, and that's the last thing we need," Neiko said.

"Good point—don't worry so much about Pharaoh, Neiko. You act like he's as scary as Satan or somthin'—like I said, he's really a good king unless he perceives a threat, and then he deals with it head on. I know a good man who lives in Thebes named Senu. He's just as rich as Kenes and is Kenes' rival in the slave trade. Most slaves want to live with and work for him because he is neither cruel nor abusive. He is like an Egyptian version of Schindler," replied Tito.

"Do you know where he lives?" asked Neiko.

"As a matter of fact, I do. He lives in the central part of the city and plenty far from Pharaoh and his palace, which is favorable. He lives close to the river and has prime riverfront real estate. Not only that, he is one of the richest men in Egypt—as rich as Kenes. Kenes is the richest man in Memphis, and Senu is the richest man in Thebes-- second to the pharaoh—of course. These two *are* bitter rivals—I can verify that, so he will protect us from Kenes if we can persuade him to," said Tito.

"The question is, how are we gonna get outa *here?*" pressed Neiko. They still hadn't addressed that part of the plan yet.

"Hmm, well—I bet we'll have to wait till after the matches tomorrow night or during. He has this jail crawling with guards due to all the escape attempts. That's the last chance we've got, and we'll have to improvise since I can't think of anything at the moment. We will be separated tomorrow so you'll have to follow our lead. But, the escape will be done sometime during or after the fights. Good enough?" asked Mactalon.

"Yeah, at least we have a prayer and a *somewhat* plan," said Neiko dejectedly as she rested her chin on her hands and sighed.

"I haven't seen or heard from Neiko in days!" said Phoenix to her father as they stood on the porch at their house. Phoenix had every nervous tick imaginable biting her.

"Hmm, this is strange. I've noticed that too," said Little Bear. "Worrying about it won't solve anything."

"The door was locked, and I didn't find the key to her house on the mat—you know—the one she keeps with her all the time. Her car was parked at the house, and I even found her shoes by the door that she was wearing when she came over. Dad, I think something's wrong," Phoenix said, starting to cry.

"Honey, don't cry. Does anyone else know about this?" asked Little Bear as he hugged her.

Phoenix shook her head. "I hope she's okay. I mean, Bloodhawk could've swiped her in the middle of the night, right when she got home," she sobbed.

"No, he couldn't. It would take Karo an hour or so to make it back and tell them about all the details of the defeat, and Neiko would have got home twenty minutes after the battle," said Little Bear.

"But you know how impetuous Bloodhawk is! He wouldn't hesitate for a moment to abduct Neiko. Besides, it could have been part of the plan," argued Phoenix.

"Phoenix, don't talk that way!" scolded her father.

"Okay, Dad, I'll talk to Monchiska and see if he's seen her," Phoenix said, and then ran to her room. She grabbed the phone and dialed the numbers to Monchiska's house.

"Hello?" asked Monchiska.

"Monchiska? Hi, it's Phoenix. I was wondering if you have seen or heard from Neiko," she said.

"No, I haven't seen or heard from her in days. Why?" Monchiska asked.

"I called for that exact same reason. I found her shoes outside her door, and the door was locked. I called her house for the past few days, and there has been no answer. Bloodhawk may be responsible," added Phoenix.

"It can't be him, and I have a feeling it wasn't. If he took her, then he would have come at least an hour or so later. Besides, Dad told me that there has been no talk about anything like that in the Crackedskulls from the spies' reports," interjected Monchiska.

"That's what my Dad said. It's like she vanished into thin air. She could have disappeared like Sito did eleven years ago," Phoenix said, choking up.

"Now wait. Don't jump to conclusions. Let's meet at Neiko's house and see if we can find any clues. I'll meet you there in a few minutes," Monchiska said, and they hung up with each other.

Then Phoenix grabbed her jacket and left to meet Monchiska at Neiko's house.

- CHAPTER 7 -

FRANCESCO PRANCED INTO the throne room singing and dancing a merry jig. He had been as happy as a lark for days.

"What are you so chipper about? I find it hard to frolic about after a defeat! Especially one this bad with so many losses!" snapped Raven as his amber eyes flashed in irritation. Raven was nine feet tall with snowy white wings and eagle like feet and eyes. "What is with you? You have been annoyingly giddy the past two days and driving me insane!" he said, clenching his huge fists by the shaven sides of his head.

Francesco smiled. "Oh, there is now hope of victory because I disposed of Admiral Neiko Kidd for good."

Raven's mouth fell open. "You *what?*"

Bloodhawk narrowed his inherited amber eyes. "What do you mean you 'disposed' of her?" he asked angrily. His massive eleven-foot form stood erectly in challenge to the small, scrawny man and fanned out his huge onyx-black wings and dug his talons into the stone floor.

"All I did was send her to Egypt about three thousand years in the past during the reign of Ramesses the Great—that's all," Francesco shrugged indifferently.

"What? How?" asked Raven in utter disbelief.

"With this," Francesco said as he took out the crystal and held it up and bounced it in his hand. "I made this myself with an ordinary quartz crystal and the Eye of Mohica. I can go anywhere I desire—past, present, or future—or I can send someone else. What makes it really great is when I return, the people I meet will have no memory of me being there. It's been tested and all worked out."

"Is it possible to return if you go?" asked Bloodhawk.

"Of course, you know me—I always have a way out," said Francesco.

Raven nodded and crossed his arms over his huge, well-built chest. "Good—because you will go to Egypt, find Neiko, and bring her to us. Do you get that?" snarled Raven with his amber eyes flashing.

"You mean I have to go to Egypt and look everywhere for her? That will be hard!" Francesco squealed.

"Hard? If you don't go and bring her back, then I will make you die hard!" snarled Bloodhawk as he shook his huge fists.

"Where did you send her?" asked Raven. "Then—Neiko isn't going to stay still. God knows where she could be after two days—" said Raven aloud as his thoughts were fleeting. "How much trouble can she get into in forty-eight hours? Trouble always seems to find her—she doesn't look for it."

Francesco shrugged like he didn't care which he didn't. "Memphis, and don't worry about the pharaoh finding her because he isn't there—he's in Thebes," said Francesco soothingly in an attempt to avert the savage wrath of the monarchs.

"You better hope that Pharaoh doesn't lay a hand on her—for your sake—because if he lays eyes on her, then that would pose a problem getting her back. I have an idea what could happen," Raven suggested.

"Yeah, and if he does, I'll kill you. And, that goes for any other Egyptians as well. Do you read me?" asked Bloodhawk curtly.

"Yes," Francesco said, annoyed.

"Good. You will go to Memphis tonight, and that is where you will start. Don't come back here unless you find her and have her with you. If she is dead, or if you fail, don't ever return because I give Bloodhawk permission to tear you to pieces upon sight. Now get out of my sight, you worthless, sniveling idiot," Raven scowled as he waved his hand in annoyance.

Francesco walked out of the throne room with a crafty smile on his face. He had his own hidden agenda. *I'll show them,* he thought maliciously. He walked into the foyer, took out the crystal, and prepared for his trip ancient Egypt. Raven's foyer turned into the green swirling vortex.

Francesco appeared in the northeast side of Memphis which was close to the Pyramids of Giza. Why not start his journey near one of the Seven Wonders of the World? After landing and getting his bearings, he put the green crystal back into his pocket and headed into the city to begin his search for the Chosen One.

Monchiska and Phoenix sat on the porch after their search. "Well, I don't believe this. It looks as if she disappeared without a trace. So I suppose we should call Xartna and tell him about this," said Monchiska as he picked up his cell phone.

Xartna was a member of Neiko's tribe who was one of the chieftains of the Seven Tribes Allegiance.

"Hello?" asked Xartna.

"Hey, pal, it's Monchiska. I've got some dreadful news. Neiko has disappeared—it's just like how Sito and the others disappeared years ago, and that is not good," said Monchiska.

"Oh no! What will we do? I have to bring this to the Tribes' attention tonight. And do you have any idea who may be responsible?" asked Xartna.

"No. Wait—maybe Francesco knows, and you know he has it in for Neiko. And, do you remember that threat of making her sorry? I have a hunch he may have something to do with it. And remember, he didn't particularly like Sito and the others that well either. Who knows, they may have found some dirt on him," proposed Monchiska.

"Hmm, well, that does sound logical, but we need more evidence so we can conduct a search for her, and maybe even find our long-lost comrades," mused Xartna aloud.

"Yeah, but the thing is, there is no evidence. We searched Neiko's house inside, out, and top to bottom, but we found squat," said Monchiska dejectedly.

"Well, I don't know what else to do. All we can do at the moment is tell the Indians and wait and see if Neiko will return on her own," sighed Xartna.

"Well, thanks. See ya tonight. Bye," said Monchiska and then hung up.

"Oh no, I fear she met the same fate as my sweetie did," Phoenix said, crying.

Monchiska gave her a hug. "Don't cry. We'll get to the bottom of this, and if Francesco's the one involved, then I will finish what Neiko started," he vowed.

- Chapter 8 -

IT WAS THE NIGHT for the pit fights to begin, and the Indians' imprisonment to end—or so they hoped. Many rich families brought in their finest combatants to do battle in the fights Kenes was hosting. The Indians were dressed in their clothes, and they all possessed weapons, including Neiko. Neiko was shown before the contests in her warrior regalia, along with her weapons. Guards and Kenes himself watched her closely to make sure she didn't try anything. Many people paid to see her, and they looked at her amazed. But she looked at them sternly, folded her arms, and stood in a proud Indian stance.

"Attention, everyone. Let the fights begin!" said Kenes loudly, and everyone herded to the arena. Several fights passed on, and each Indian dreaded when he would be next.

"Okay, we're all outside and armed. When the first one of us fights and wins—hopefully, then yell out a hawk's call for a signal. We need to strike like lightning. Neiko will follow our lead just like we went over. Everyone understand?" asked Panthero.

"Roger," Tito and Mactalon said in unison.

"You're next, savage," snapped Het as he shoved Mactalon toward the arena.

Mactalon walked into the arena to meet his opponent with his shield and sword. A tall Philistine met him on the field with a spear. He laughed at Mactalon's appearance because he was taller than the poorly armed Indian was. The signal was given, and the fight began. The two fought skillfully as people cheered. Mactalon's three friends yelled to him to wish him luck. The Philistine kicked him and sent him to the ground. He raised his spear, ready to kill Mactalon, but he defended himself with the shield. Without thinking, he sliced the Philistine in the leg and got up.

"I will kill you, painted warrior!" snarled the Philistine in pain.

"C'mon, kill me!" Mactalon challenged.

The wounded Philistine charged and tried to stab again, but Mactalon fended off the attack. Mactalon lashed out and cut the spear in half, scoring a cut down his opponent's chest. The Philistine howled in pain and tried to use the spear as a club to pound him. Mactalon defended himself, but the angry opponent cuffed him in the side of the head, sending him falling to the ground. He tried to stab again, but Mactalon painfully jerked to the side to dodge the spearhead. He thrust out his sword and stabbed the Philistine in the chest. He groaned, crumpled to the ground, and then lay still. Mactalon staggered to his feet, panting. The crowd was taken aback because this Philistine had been a longtime champion.

"Way to go, Mack!" Neiko yelled from a distance.

"Way to show 'em!" called Tito and Panthero in unison.

Mactalon raised his shield and bloodied sword in victory. He took a deep breath, threw back his head, and let loose the shrill call of a hawk, which was the signal. Tito and Panthero knocked out their guards and sprinted to meet Mactalon. Seeing them and following their lead, Neiko cuffed her two guards, drew her sword, and wounded two more who were trying to catch her. She found a rope she could use to slide down to make a shortcut to the field because Egyptians were coming from both sides, cutting her off. She put the sword in between her teeth and slid down onto the field to her friends. The four ran out of the arena, with a mob of Egyptians chasing them. They found four bareback horses, unhitched from a chariot, and tied up at a watering hole. They grabbed the reins, jumped on the backs of the horses, and rode off toward the south—toward Thebes—as they lifted their weapons in triumph and yelled in victory calls. Kenes sent men after them as he went to his house to gather a band to hunt them down.

The four traveled in the desert, along the river, heading south for days. They made a rest stop for supplies at Abydos. They also had to give Kenes' scouts the slip at this riverside town before they could cross the river by ferry to Dendera. The next day they crossed the river to the east to Dendera and continued following the river south for around a day. They could now see the city, Thebes, clearly in the distance.

"Thebes dead ahead!" shouted Tito, and they kicked their horses to a run and rode to the city.

They all marveled at the splendor of the place as well as keeping an eye out for Sito. Music filled the air and people bustled about. This place seemed even larger and more bustling than Memphis. Monuments, statues, jugglers, and markets were everywhere, along with peasants and snake charmers and workers.

"Wow! This place is kinda cool," said Neiko as she scanned the area.

"Yeah, I know, but keep your eyes open," warned Tito.

Several platoons of soldiers marched through, and several people peered at the strange-looking newcomers.

"How are we supposed to find Sito in all of this?" complained Mactalon. "I mean, he could look like everyone else, you know."

"Yeah, it seems like we're playing a live version of Where's Waldo," grumbled Neiko.

"Mactalon's right. Maybe we should try to find Senu first," said Panthero.

"How will we find his house? The further we move in, the more crowded it gets," said Neiko.

"Just look for the nicest house in Thebes," said Tito.

"Uh, correction—if we look for the nicest house, then we will end up at Pharaoh's house. So I think you mean the second nicest," said Mactalon.

"You know what I meant," Tito said, shoving his friend playfully. They explored the winding streets and alleys of the city, but there was no sign of Sito or Senu.

"I think we would have a better time trying to find an Apache in downtown Atlanta," grumbled Neiko.

"There they are! After them!" a voice yelled, and they turned and saw Kenes with a band of armed men on horses. Among the numbers were also the scouts they had ditched back at Abydos.

People screamed seeing the weapons and backed out of the street. The Indians bolted forward in a full-scale retreat. They couldn't risk a battle or be recaptured. The Egyptians divided up and started gaining. Kenes and a small group came from the front, and the Indians split up, with Neiko going left and the others going right. Kenes and his small group went after Neiko, while everyone else of the party went after the others. Neiko rode street to street aimlessly, trying to shake her pursuers. She saw a stand with huge melons on it, and leaned over and grabbed one. She turned and threw it at the group hoping to hit someone. She was able to hit one man in the eye. He didn't see a low-hanging rope, and it hooked him in the chest. He flipped off the back of the horse and landed on the ground. The remaining nine men still chased her. Just ahead was an overhead ledge where bricks were lying, and only a few logs supported them. Neiko sliced the rope binding the supports with her sword, and the bricks fell, toppling five more men. The man who had put the bricks up there called after her, shaking his fist angrily.

"Sorry!" Neiko called back. Neiko turned a hard left and fell into a mob of people. She rode through and fought to get to the opening in the street.

"Excuse me, pardon me, sorry—comin' through," Neiko said as she and her horse fought through. She made it to the middle of the street, but there was a mob on the other side. Kenes and his remaining four men had her trapped. Neiko brandished her sword, bared her teeth menacingly, and gave a shrill war call. "Come and get me if you dare!" she challenged.

"Get her!" commanded Kenes, but no one noticed a man who walked up with his wife and a large number of people behind him. He watched in amazement on what was going on and was somewhat entertained. Neiko charged on her horse and jumped onto one of the men. They both fell off as the horse fell, and she landed on top of him, knocking the breath out of him. She dealt him two side punches in the jaw, and a final double punch in the forehead, knocking him out. People looked at the battling group, horrified as Neiko picked up the fallen Egyptian's spear and stabbed an oncoming man's horse. The horse died, and they both fell over. The horse fell on the man's leg, and he couldn't get up. Neiko hit him in the head, making him unconscious.

One of Kenes' men dropped his staff and ran off.

"Do something!" Kenes shouted at his remaining man.

The man jumped off the horse, tackled her, and tried to restrain her. The pair wrestled on the ground, but Neiko was able to free her right arm. She socked him in the nose. He growled in pain, but he kept holding her. She grabbed his hand and bit it as hard as she could; he let go, yelling in agony. She kicked him between the legs, and he doubled over and danced in anguish. She picked up her spear and hit him in the chin with the butt; he landed face down in the sand,

motionless. Kenes was taken aback by Neiko's skill. She ran and jumped up on the horse tackling him and sending him crashing on the ground from the horse.

"How do you like being hit and beaten? You want to enslave me, do *you*? Huh?" Neiko snarled, punching Kenes mercilessly in the face in a left-right manner.

Kenes didn't understand her, but he could hear the hostility in her voice. Kenes pushed her off of him and tried to make a hasty retreat. He had to return home to get more reinforcements and come back for her. Her friends were going to die, and she was going to be his even if he had to have her in chains to keep her under control. As he tried to flee, Neiko stabbed him in the leg, and he fell down. She tied him by one leg to his own horse with the rope he had brought, as he lay on the ground. She tied the other end to the saddle tightly. Then she stood over him and put the point of her spear to his throat. People covered their mouths in fear, and the woman hid behind her husband because she wasn't sure if Neiko was going to kill Kenes. "Try to hurt us again, and I'll kill you," she snapped as she pricked his neck with the point. She took the point from him and slapped the horse's flank. It ran off, dragging Kenes behind it, who yelled curses and threats to her as he was dragged away. His threats didn't mean anything to her since she couldn't understand him. Neiko raised her spear in triumph and yelled, "Victory! Indians rule, and Egyptians drool!" Then she released a shrill call and watched Kenes disappear. "Yeah! Who's the better fighter?"

Soon a shadow loomed over Neiko, and she saw it in front of her. She spun around and stood face to face with a wealthy man. She poised her spear, ready to kill if he tried to capture her. A few soldiers began to draw their weapons and approach her with angry faces, but the man raised his hand stopping them. The man seemed to have an aura of complete control about him. She held the spear at his chest, but he didn't fear her. "Are you Senu?" she asked. She repeated the name and pointed at him in trying to make him understand her.

The man stared at Neiko in order to get a better look at her. As he peered at her face, his hand went to a huge jade scarab that hung around his neck that rested on his muscular chest. It finally sunk in what she was trying to ask him. "I am not," he replied shaking his head.

Neiko was dressed in her buckskin tank top with buckskin shorts and no shoes; her tennis shoes were still on her front porch where she left them. She was wearing her falcon headband, and her hair was fixed with hawk feathers. She had armlets on the tops of her arms with feathers, and an eagle and bear claw necklace. Her face was painted in red and black—she had a black bird's foot on the T-zone of her face, red stripes on her cheeks and chin, and lightning bolts under her eyes.

Neiko studied the man. He was wearing fine linen clothes with a jeweled collar. He wore gold bracelets that came from his wrists to his elbows. He also wore a blue—and white-striped headdress, but she didn't notice the golden cobra with jeweled eyes coming from his forehead or his beard. He wore rings on his fingers and a heavy gold necklace in addition to the large scarab amulet that he continued to hold and stroke with his fingers. He was well-built, young, and fairly tall. He had a strong jaw, and his dark, piercing eyes, which were outlined, never left her.

"Okay, do you know where I can find Senu?" she asked, not letting down her guard.

The man looked at her, baffled, and she took a step backward. "A woman who can fight? Where do you come from?" he asked.

"Huh?" Neiko asked, dumbfounded because she couldn't understand.

"Wait—I remember now. You are one of the painted people—like Sito—who my father found years ago and took in. But unlike him—I like you—a lot. And you look so familiar to me—like the one I have been searching for," the man said rubbing his chin as he stared into her face, and she took a few more steps back. He had released the massive charm. "Could it be you at last?"

The woman, who was dressed like him but wore a golden vulture crown gawked at her, concerned, and looked at him confused. Apparently, she had no idea what he was speaking of.

"Never mind. Since you know nothing of Senu, I'll find him on my own," Neiko said backing up with her spear still raised and her eyes still on the man, watching his every move.

The man started to approach her, but Neiko poised her spear in warning, stopping him in his tracks. "Back off," she said as she twisted her hands on the shaft trying to conceal her fear. Her heart was hammering in her chest.

The man's eyes sparkled, and he smiled at her. Neiko looked at him coolly. He reached his hand forward and said, "Take my hand and come with me. Come," he said, beckoning her with his fingers.

Neiko's eyes widened, and she shook her head. "Ok-kay, I can understand what that look means! I have friends to find and no time to flirt with some rich dude I don't even know. I don't take orders from nobody! Now if you will excuse me," she said, backing away again at a quicker pace.

The man lowered his hand and took a few steps forward. He was not so easily deterred and challenged her. Obviously, he was very stubborn.

Neiko frowned and narrowed her eyes. "I don't think you get the message. Maybe I should put it in terms you can understand," Neiko said, as she drew a line in the sand with her big toe. "If you cross this line," she said, pointing at him and then the line, "Then I'll kill you," Neiko said, thrusting her spear at him.

The man looked at the line and then at her, but he smiled broader. "You have spirit, but I fear nothing. You are coming with me—like it or not. Guards, get her and bring her to me," he said, pointing at her, and three soldiers came at her.

"Oh crap! Time to go!" Neiko said as she ran to her horse, jumped on, and rode away barely escaping the advancing soldiers before they could grab her. She went off in search of her friends and Senu's house.

- CHAPTER 9 -

NEIKO RODE THROUGH THE streets of Thebes that night, searching frantically for her friends. She had eluded several groups of soldiers who tried to catch her and hid in the crevices to avoid others who were searching for her. It didn't seem to take very long for the man to sic the entire Egyptian army on her. Neiko instantly guessed he must have quick access to the military.

She asked several civilians about Senu. She had to say "Senu" and sign or draw "house" and try to sign or depict "the way". She was able to get a few people to draw sketches in the sand for her to follow. It took a bit of work, but she was able to somewhat communicate. Finally, she came to the place she believed to be the house from what her friends and the villagers said. She knocked on the door and prayed that it wouldn't be the man she had met earlier that afternoon or she would be in a fix for sure. A rich man came to the door. "May I help you?" he asked as he looked at her.

"Senu?" Neiko asked and held her breath in anticipation.

The man nodded. "I am he," he replied. Senu was a young man, about the same age as Kenes, but a little taller. His kind eyes studied her. "Do come in," he said, pulling her inside. He led her into the dining hall where her friends were seated and eating.

"Neiko! Thank goodness you made it! We thought we had lost you or Kenes got you!" Tito exclaimed as he ran up and hugged her with the others on his heels.

"What happened?" asked Mactalon.

"Oh man. I spanked Kenes and his men good, and I gave Kenes a sting he won't forget and a good road rash. I doubt he'll try to make money off us again or think twice about making me his personal slave. And then this other rich guy tried to get me, and he looked at me funny like he got shot by Cupid or something—almost a love at first sight kind of thing," Neiko said, remembering the man and his actions distinctly.

"What guy? And what do you mean he looked at you funny or knew you?" asked Mactalon, alarmed.

"This guy was an Egyptian version of Bill Gates or something. He wore gold like it was a common item. And—I dunno, his eyes sparkled, and he smiled at me with that kind of smile—you know. It was weird—he looked at me like Bloodhawk does," said Neiko.

Tito gasped. "That's not good. He liked you, Neiko—I mean, like for a wife—not just a slave. I bet you would make a unique one."

"He already had a wife, I think," Neiko said, rubbing her head. "But anyway, I just think he liked my fighting skill. That's all."

"It doesn't matter. Egyptians can have as many wives as they want, especially ones that rich. The least little thing can set off a man's affection--you know that—I bet it has happened a lot in Georgia, too. I'd wager he was overwhelmed by your beauty even if it is hidden in all of that tough war paint," Tito said, poking her strong arm.

"You're right, you're right. You know what? He had soldiers working for him, and he had all these people with him who were bald in funky robes—it was like some parade," Neiko said.

"Hmm, those bald men were priests—and soldiers? The more you say, the more I don't like. Were they like bodyguards?" asked Tito.

"Yeah, but that guy could have been parading because he just got hitched," Neiko suggested.

"Well, he may just be an army man—like a general. But with priests too? Neiko, did you get a good look at him, and could you identify him if you saw him again?" asked Tito.

"Yeah," Neiko said and shrugged.

"Okay, did you happen to see if he had a cobra on his headdress?" asked Tito curling his forefinger and putting it on his forehead then paused. "Or a strange looking beard?" he asked again depicting the beard.

"Nope, I don't remember seeing them," Neiko shrugged. Unfortunately for her in her panic, she didn't see them during their encounter and those were fine details that her mind didn't think were important compared to escape.

Everyone sighed with relief.

"Good. If he did have a cobra and the beard, then that would have been Pharaoh. The last thing we need is you catching the favor and getting hitched with the pharaoh. So you are okay now because he can't get to you, and he'll give up soon," Tito added.

"I'm not so sure about that because he sent soldiers after me, and I dodged several groups on the way here and trying to find this place. They are patrolling the streets and may even do a door-to-door search," Neiko fretted.

"Neiko, don't worry. Senu will help us out. When he can't find you, you'll be old news," Tito concluded.

"What?" asked Senu since he heard his name mentioned.

Tito told him everything that Neiko had told him, why they were in Thebes, and about their escape from Kenes.

Tito and Senu talked for a few more minutes and then Tito walked up and offered some news to the others. "Senu says he will protect us as much as he can, and he will do his best to keep Neiko safe, but we must pose as servants and he'll supply servants' clothing. He said he will also try to help find my brother. Sito used to work for Seti in his court, but he hasn't seen him since. Senu knows quite a bit since he serves in Pharaoh's court as a courtier and as a lord. It's possible Ramesses could have sold him elsewhere, so it's evident Pharaoh knows of our kind. We arrived when Ramesses was young, and I'm not sure how he will take us."

"If push comes to shove, we may have to ask him where Sito is," said Neiko cringing.

"No, you will not address Pharaoh because I won't take any chances. He may make a request for you, and all he has to do is say one word. Then you will belong to him, and we will have to find a way to get *you* out of trouble. And most of the time, women do not make requests," cautioned Tito. "No offense."

Neiko nodded silently. "Good point. I don't really want to meet him either. But I would like to see the look on his face when I show up and ask him where Sito is," Neiko said, smiling.

Mactalon giggled. "I can imagine, but that is the last thing I want to do. If he is still there, I don't think he would have a problem handing him over, but if Neiko tagged along, he may ask for her in exchange. She'd be stuck there, and he'd have a problem about letting her leave. I told you that pretty face would get you in trouble, Neiko."

"Yeah. What will we do when we find him, and what if we can't find our way back to Hawote?" asked Panthero.

"I don't know, I guess move to another country--maybe to the Serengeti. What do you think?" asked Mactalon.

"Cool! I always wanted to go there, and I wonder what it's like in this time," mused Neiko.

"Maybe. We'll have to worry about cannibals and headhunters, but it's safer there than it is here," said Tito.

The friends talked that night about their plans for the future. Senu gave them their servants' raiment, and they went to sleep.

CHAPTER 10

THE NEXT MORNING, THE Indians had breakfast with Senu, his three wives, and his fifteen children. They talked about a lot of things.

"You won't have to address Pharaoh about your brother because he and I are good friends. I could go further than you could—that is—if we cannot find him elsewhere. I can tell you right now, Ramesses will be annoyed of your presence there. He doesn't like the company of savages—no offense by me—his words not mine, especially invoking him to a request," offered Senu.

"That's good. Thanks for all you're doing. What would he do if he found out you were helping us?" asked Tito. "I wonder if he has some sort of beef with my brother for him to say things like that," said Tito as he rubbed his chin in thought.

Senu shrugged at Tito's musings. "He would do nothing to me about helping you—if you brother is now overstaying his welcome or whatever the case is. He doesn't show much concern in the slave business unless the work forces are unsatisfactory in Goshen or in Luxor or his monuments are unfinished when he wants them finished. He has no concern about my disputes with Kenes or what we do as long as we don't start a war," replied Senu. Suddenly there was a knock on the door. "Clean this up, just in case it's a patrol. I will answer the door," he said, getting up. The Indians followed his instructions. He ran and opened the door to a patrol.

"Good day, Senu. Have you seen a strange-looking warrior girl around?" asked the captain.

"No, I haven't," Senu replied, shaking his head.

"We must search the house, just in case—it's orders—no mistrust," the captain said, and Senu led them in. Servants darted about doing their chores. The Indians cleaned the dining hall, and the soldiers closely checked the house. The soldiers left, and the Indians gave each other high-fives on duping the soldiers.

"That's that. Senu is such a genius, and they had no idea she was right in front of their faces! I bet that guy will give up pretty soon," said Tito.

"I guess they thought I was still wearing my other clothes," said Neiko, laughing as she fingered her garment.

Senu ran up to them. "I have some important news. I will be having a dinner party tomorrow night, and I have invited several of other men of the wealthy elite and their families to attend. They will come from all parts of the country, and that man may come to the party tomorrow. This mystery man could be anyone. Do you have any ideas on how to hide Neiko? I fear that he may still recognize her in servant clothes especially the way you say he looked at her so profoundly. Even as a servant, her beauty shines through."

"I got it! Why don't we dress her in fine clothes and make her look like a goddess? We have to make a cover story, and Neiko will pick out an Egyptian name," said Mactalon.

"Very good. I will get my wives and a few of my servants to assist her in dressing, but she must have an escort. One of you will do; the rest will be servants," Senu said.

"I know! I will be her brother. You can help me dress up in some of your clothes, and it'll be perfect; we are almost the same size," said Tito switching his forefinger between himself and Senu.

"I want to be the brother because it was my idea!" Mactalon protested.

"Please, don't fight. Tito will do the brother role, but there is one thing more. She cannot speak or understand our language like you three, and that will give it away," mused Senu.

Panthero pondered. "I know! She will pretend she's deaf and mute."

"Hmm, this may just work. Bring Neiko here and tell her the plan. And she must choose a name now," Senu said.

They brought Neiko over and told her the plan.

"Now you must have a name," said Tito.

"So do you! Most of the Egyptian women's names are long mouthfuls and things I can't spell or pronounce. Besides, the only one I can think of is Hatshepsut, but it doesn't fit, and I don't particularly like it," said Neiko.

"My name will be Thutmose. Make one up, and I will judge if it sounds Egyptian or not," offered Tito.

Neiko racked her brain, but nothing came to mind. "I can't think of anything."

"Neiko, do try," said Senu as he studied her frustrated face.

Neiko thought harder because she knew this was the last step of the plan and one of the most important parts. Then one name popped into her head. "Sat-Hathor," she said finally massaging her aching head.

Senu smiled. "A pretty name, and it fits. What do you think, Tito?"

"Good choice, Neiko. Sat-Hathor it is. I can't wait to see what you look like tomorrow night," Tito said.

Everyone prepared for the party, and they put in place the finishing touches on the plan.

– CHAPTER 11 –

NEIKO AND TITO PUT the last touches on their disguises and everything was ready. Tito and Senu worked with Neiko in proper etiquette so that she would fit in. She also got plenty of practice on her handicap charade. Everything was in place, and then the guests started arriving. Within two hours, all of the invited guests had arrived.

Tito walked over to Neiko to have a quick word. "Do you see that guy anywhere?" he whispered.

"No. I guess he had a party of his own," Neiko shrugged.

"Stay close. There are a lot of people looking at you," said Tito slipping his arm into hers.

"What am I doing wrong?" Neiko asked, trying not to move her mouth.

"Nothing. All of them are looking at your beauty, that's all. You have a lot of guys checking you out," whispered Tito.

A young man approached them and started talking to Neiko, but she looked at him like she couldn't hear. "I'm pleased to make your acquaintance," he said as he took her hand and kissed it. "You are—"

"This is my sister, Sat-Hathor, and my name is Thutmose. I'm afraid my sister is deaf and mute. And you are?" asked Tito.

"Sut. A truly beautiful rose; she may have a few thorns, but it does not change—" he started to say, but Tito cut him short.

"Listen. Our parents died years ago and left my dear sister in my care. I will choose whom she marries, and I'm sorry to say you will not do. Excuse us," said Tito as he took Neiko away from Sut. "I bet I'll have to drive off these guys with a stick! That is the only drawback of making you beautiful, but no one knows who you are," he mumbled to her.

"Yeah," Neiko muttered not moving her mouth. Then she saw a familiar form from the corner of her eye. Francesco had come in the door, and she poked Tito's arm and pointed him out. It was anyone's guess how he had snuck in unannounced and uninvited, but then again he was an excellent deceiver.

"What? Oh my gosh! What is that loser doing here? How did he *even* get in here or find this place?" Tito asked, and hot anger welled up in both of them. "Let's go tell the others," he said, leading her to the Indian party, and they told them.

After a quick word, the four split up started to subtly close in on Francesco. Neiko remained with Tito to keep up the sister/brother façade. They heard a trumpet sound a proclamation, and a man and his wife walked in with ten armed bodyguards. It was the man Neiko had seen. Neiko tugged on Tito's sleeve frantically. "That's him! Oh gosh, there he is! That's the guy that I saw who tried to get me!" she whispered, pointing at him. Tito looked to where she was pointing, and his mouth dropped open. He grabbed her hand and placed it down at her side. He hoped the man didn't see her pointing at him. "Don't point! Do you have any idea *who* that is? That's Pharaoh! It was he all along! Oh—you are in *big* trouble. You can't slip up now—I won't let you out of my sight. I hope Francesco doesn't give us away just to be mean. I'm gonna go tell Mactalon, Panthero, and Senu about this ASAP. Senu can't protect you from Pharaoh if he finds out you're here, and *he's* in danger too. I'll be right back. Don't move or bat an eyelash—stay right in this spot!" Tito said firmly and then ran to find his friends.

"Oh no! I prodded the pharaoh with a spear? Oh great—now what? My luck he'd think of it as a turn-on," Neiko grumbled.

Someone came from behind and slipped an arm into hers. Neiko gasped with surprise and turned; it was Sut. "Come now, Sat-Hathor," he said, trying to lead her off. She shook her head and pointed to the floor, signaling she couldn't move from that spot. "I do not care what your brother says. Let's go eat together," he said, pulling her from her spot to vacant places at the table.

Tito ran up to Mactalon and Panthero with the news, stopping them from corralling Francesco. "Guys, I have terrible news. The man that Neiko was talking about was indeed Pharaoh. He just arrived a few minutes ago."

Both of them gasped.

"Oh no! She's in for it now! What are we gonna do?" asked Mactalon anxiously.

"We have to stick with the plan, and I have to find Senu and talk to him about this. One thing's certain—Senu won't be able to keep her safe if Pharaoh finds out she's here," replied Tito.

"That's just peachy. Do you think he's gonna torture her to death because she waved a spear in his face?" asked Panthero.

"I don't know. I believe he could take her to his house for servitude or—" Tito gulped.

"Or what?" asked Mactalon.

"Or he may take her for his wife," Tito said in dread. "I think she would be in very high favor. If that happens, that would complicate things to the nth degree—"

"But he's already got one!" Mactalon interrupted in protest.

"He's the king, and can do as he pleases here. And people had more than one wife in this time period, you know. We're not in Europe, so he can have whoever he wants. If we object, maybe he won't turn a deaf ear to us and let her go," Tito said.

"Yeah right! Not only is he the king, they think of him as a god! Do you really think he would let Neiko go if he's madly in love with her?" exclaimed Panthero. "Let's be realistic here!"

"Yeah—true—and I know all of that nonsense. What makes it worse is that he is one of the most popular pharaohs in history in a lot of ways."

"I don't care, and it don't matter what we know because the past is the present right now. Things will change, especially if she gets married to a god-king. That will be a disaster to Hawote, but I don't know about history itself," Panthero mused.

"You are absolutely right, and we have to keep that from happening. History in Hawote will definitely be messed up, and Neiko will not be the liberator of Hawote. And, if he likes her enough, then she will be written about on the walls and remembered as the warrior queen or something like that instead of what we know her to be," said Tito. "To add, she might get plastered on the great temple of Abu-Simbal along with or instead of Nefertari."

"That is unbearable, but we have to check more into this. Francesco has the answers, and we will make him tell us," said Mactalon.

"Not only that, he has our way home!" concluded Panthero.

"Huh? How do you know? How can you be sure that Raven just sent him here alone?" asked Tito.

"That was his voice we heard before we ended up here, remember? Remember what Neiko said the other night about that weird crystal he had on him? Speaking of Raven, I guess he sent him here to find Neiko and bring her back, and Raven couldn't get here. You'd think he has to have a way to take Neiko back to Bloodhawk, right?" mused Panthero. "Call it a hunch."

"He's right, Tito. If Raven and Bloodhawk showed up, that would freak out the Egyptians—Horus and Ra have come," Mactalon joked. "Now we just have to find a way to get to Francesco tonight and not draw attention to ourselves. But how?" asked Mactalon.

Tito grinned at Mactalon's joke and nodded in agreement. "I'm not sure about how to engage Francesco, but we have to wait till Pharaoh leaves that's for certain. Let's hope he leaves before

Francesco does," Tito replied. "It's a good idea to keep an eye on both Francesco and Pharaoh after I talk with Senu. Then, I will stick to Neiko like glue."

"Good plan. I don't think it will be hard to find the king. Look," said Panthero as he pointed in that direction. Men who were talking with him surrounded him, and many women were flirting with him hoping to get his attention as the queen looked at them annoyed. The three of them giggled at the sight.

"I bet every girl in Egypt is over there flirting, and the queen is about to have a fit. Haven't you noticed that Neiko wouldn't be caught dead over there? I remember when we went to a party in Georgia in elementary school, and all those girls were flirting with the cutest guy in the room. Neiko was on the other side of the room while every other girl was around that boy. I remember he wanted to have a dance with her and sought her out, but she turned him down! Speaking of Neiko, where is she?" said Mactalon.

"I left her over there. I hope and pray that scenario doesn't happen. I don't know what Pharaoh would do if she told him no—I don't know how he takes rejection. I bet he would think she's from another planet in doing that. I hope it doesn't catch his favor that much more because if you remember, when a girl plays hard to get, a boy usually likes her better, and he keeps trying to win her. You know how her luck is when she tries to be tough with guys—especially ladies' men—which he is. She usually is ready to punch them when men won't let her be," mused Tito.

Mactalon giggled, remembering. "Uh-huh, I can just imagine her in that state with the king. Also he is the most popular guy in the room, and one of the cutest."

"Neiko wouldn't think so. She would say he's the meanest, ugliest, stuck-up jerk in Egypt! Oh boy, I can picture it now!" said Panthero laughing. "He may be a god-king, but he is still a man, and I believe Neiko would have a hard time trying to douse him with her tough, critical ways. You can figure out how tenacious he is from reading about him, and what kind of a guy he is. Ladies' man is darn right. He is Neiko's worst nightmare from what you told me."

"I know, that's right. She would definitely go berserk if he went after her and tried any of those old, cheap moves or threw that Pharaoh protocol at her. She'd probably sock him in the face, and then she'd be in a mess. We'll chat later—I have to find Senu. I know one thing, from what Neiko says about the way he looked at her, I think she'd have that problem if he found out she was here," said Tito, and he went off in trying to find Senu.

– Chapter 12 –

TITO WENT THROUGH THE crowd trying to find Senu. He pushed by the dancers, musicians, jugglers and groups of people talking and the game table. Senu had been close by the feasting table most of the evening. He wasn't hard to miss because he was always surrounded by people since he was an excellent host and handled a group well. He was always well known for throwing the best parties and having the best of everything including entertainment. Egypt's elite always felt at home at Senu's including Pharaoh. Senu's house was one of the few homes he felt comfortable in besides his own. Not even protocol kept Pharaoh away from Senu's house when he wanted to come.

Tito located Senu among a crowd of the wealthy still by the feasting table and talking with Ramesses. Tito swallowed hard and went forward anyway. "Senu, I need to speak with you right now," Tito said while turning slightly away from the king in order to avoid his eye.

Senu looked at him with raised eyebrows and at full attention. "About what?"

Tito sighed in agitation. "About my sister—it's *urgent*," he said, motioning for him to come with him alone.

"All right, Thutmose," Senu said with a nod to Tito. "Excuse me, my king," Senu said with a slight bow to the pharaoh.

Ramesses nodded with a good-natured smile. "Do hurry back, Senu."

Senu nodded as he went with Tito to a secluded corner away from all the other guests. "What is it? Did she find the man? Is he here?" asked Senu frantically as his eyes darted among the crowd.

"Yes, and you were just talking to him," said Tito.

Senu's eyes widened and his hands went to his head in a panic. He began to pace the floor. "Amon-Re, Anubis! I cannot help her if she gets into trouble—you have to prevent anything that may cause a problem—is she all right?" he rambled in panic and shock. "I am now in peril! If something happens, I could be ruined or worse!"

Tito grabbed him to stop him from making a scene. "Stop that before somebody sees you! Yes, she's fine. The others already know. What else shall I do?" asked Tito.

"You mustn't let her anywhere near Pharaoh—just in case. He may recognize her by the looks of things," whispered Senu urgently.

"Why is he here?" asked Tito with a shrug.

"He is one of my invited guests to the party, but I thought he was too busy to come. He is a frequent visitor to my home when I have parties because I am the second richest man in Thebes to himself and because we are friends. I am just as surprised as you are that he is here. He has been talking about Neiko all evening—that is what he was talking about when you came. He remembers every detail of that day distinctly as well as every detail of her and the way she was painted, everything. He has stayed up for days waiting for her arrival or any news at all. He says he will not rest until he finds her. Seeing her fighting skill, her inner and outer strength, and fearlessness mesmerized him—although I feel he is not saying everything. That wasn't all he saw that day. It seems like he knows her somehow. Women like her are extremely rare. He wants to take her in and decide what to do with her. I'm glad he doesn't know of her beauty that goes with her strength and fighting ability. This is a grave situation, and you must warn Neiko. If he were to find her here and uncover her identity, then I believe he will want her for his wife—maybe even his Great Wife," he said.

Tito put his hand over his mouth to hide his gasp and sighed in agitation because the "Great Wife" was a really big deal. Tito then rubbed his temples to relieve the tension. "Right," he said as he looked in the direction where he told Neiko to stay, but she wasn't there. "I *told* her not to move from that spot! I have to find her because she could be in a fix! Men have been after her all evening!" Tito said frantically as he pulled at his head cloth as he searched the crowd for any sign of Neiko.

"Who?" asked a voice from his left. "Who is lost?"

Tito turned to his left to the speaker and was face to face with Pharaoh himself. "My sister—I seem to have misplaced her," he said nervously as he avoided eye contact with the king and fidgeted. Tito had to ignore his impulse to bolt.

"I do not know you. Are you new to Thebes?" Ramesses asked, cocking his head and looking at him with a grilling stare.

Tito began to sweat. "Er—yes, my sister and I do not get out much ever since our parents died. Sat-Hathor cannot speak or hear, so she gets into trouble from time to time," Tito fibbed trying to create a believable sob story so Pharaoh wouldn't ask too many questions.

"I am sorry to hear that." Ramesses scanned Tito's features from one angle then another. "Have we met?" Ramesses asked, looking at him with recognition. "It seems like we could have met somewhere—in some ways you remind me of a servant of my house: Sito," he said with a frown as he rubbed his beard in intense thought. He spoke Sito's name with a twinge of hate.

"No. You must be mistaken. I don't even know whom you speak of," Tito lied. Ramesses could never know that Sito was his twin brother or they would be busted. Great Spirit knew what would happen next. "Now, if you would please excuse my abrupt leave, I have to go find my sister—please excuse me," Tito said thinking fast and trying to get away. He remembered to bow to the king during his exit.

Ramesses put his fists on his hips in a dominant stance. "I want to meet your sister. When you find her, bring her to me," said Ramesses. "She seems to be the one woman I *haven't* seen," he said with a small grin.

"I'm very sorry, but that isn't possible—please forgive us. She cannot speak or hear, and she is terrified of strangers. We live an isolated life, and the only person she knows besides me is Senu. She is also petrified of pharaohs—she also has very crude manners unfit for your attention," Tito said trying to keep his composure and come up with something to deter the king's curiosity.

Ramesses folded his arms and looked at him with an aggravated stare. "Do as I command. Let me see her. Why do you hide her from me, Thutmose? I will not harm her. I will only take a few moments of her time. Now go," he snapped, waving his hand.

Tito sighed with relief and walked away and wiping the sweat of fear from his brow. "Oh boy. I have to do it so I don't arouse his suspicions—he already knows something's up," he sighed and looked around for Neiko. He then saw Sut escorting her around, and Neiko was trying to get away from him. Tito stormed up and pushed Sut away from her. "Didn't I tell you to keep your hands off of my sister?" asked Tito angrily.

"I don't have to listen to you—you are not my king," Sut snapped as he thrust his finger at Tito. "It is not good form to keep her sheltered all her life," Sut retorted.

"I don't care, and that's none of your business! She is the most prized possession I have because my parents are dead, and she is in no shape to go and meet strangers! Don't you tell me how I should and shouldn't care for my sister. Find another woman and leave her in peace. We will be on our way. Come, Sat-Hathor," said Tito as he put his arm around her.

Sut grabbed her arm and pulled her away from Tito. "You will go in peace, Thutmose! She will remain with me the rest of the evening—"

Tito socked Sut in the nose and jerked Neiko from him. "No! She won't be with you or any other man here! Lay another hand on my sister again, and I'll cut it off!" Tito said in hushed whispered that carried through the crowd as he straightened his back and poked out his chest.

Sut pinched his nose to stop the bleeding as he backed away. "This is far from over, Thutmose! You will pay for this," he snapped and stormed away.

"Anytime!" Tito retorted and started to escort Neiko to a place where they could talk, but the queen stopped them.

The queen had an inquisitive look on her face. "You are very protective of your sister. I admire that. You look like someone I know. Your name is Thutmose, is it?" the queen asked.

Tito nodded silently. "My queen, this is my sister, Sat-Hathor."

"Queen Nefertari," she said bowing her head.

Tito bowed in signal to Neiko, but she curtsied. Tito slapped his forehead with his palm when he saw Neiko curtsy. "Pleased to make your acquaintance, and so is she. I speak on her behalf."

Neiko's cheeks flushed. *Oh, right I was supposed to bow not curtsy. We're not in Europe*, Neiko, she said in her mind, scolding herself.

Nefertari was a bit confused and shifted her eyes at the pair with a curious smile. "Why doesn't she talk?" asked Nefertari.

"She is unable to hear or speak—forgive her, my queen," Tito said.

"I understand. You have my permission to call me by my name," Nefertari said.

"Why are you not with your husband?" asked Tito.

"I got bored listening to him talking about his treasure cities and kingdom. That is all he speaks of—well—until that warrior showed up. Now all he speaks of is her. She was so interesting, but I was a little frightened of her. I was surprised she didn't run him through with that spear, but he knew she wouldn't—somehow—unless he tried to take her by force. He has spoken so highly of her, and I like to hear him tell the story of that battle she fought against Kenes. I overheard you speaking of your family to Sut, and I pity you. I thought that was so unkind in the way he was trying to take her from you. He is so desperate to find a wife, and Sat-Hathor was what he was looking for," said Nefertari.

"I know, that is another reason why I don't take her places that often, and I saw that you had the same problem," Tito said.

"Oh yes," Nefertari said rolling her eyes. "He pays no attention to them, but it does make him feel good about himself. But how does she feel about it?"

"Oh, she gets annoyed by it, and she can't stand to be bombarded by strangers. She is so shy—she is afraid sometimes," said Tito with a sideways smile.

"That is so refreshing and impressive. She was the only woman who wasn't throwing herself on my husband to get his attention. She seems to cleave to you and no one else. Most want to have the attention of all the men in the room, but Sat-Hathor just wants to be beside her brother. I admire that," said Nefertari.

"How do you feel about that warrior girl?" asked Tito. "I hope you don't mind me asking—I don't mean to be nosy."

Nefertari smiled. "Oh no, it's all right. In what way do you mean?" Nefertari asked as she pursed her lips and shrugged.

"In every way. And what would you say if your husband took her as a wife?" asked Tito. "Aren't you and wouldn't you be jealous?"

"I admire that warrior girl for who she was. I wish I could fight like that and have no fear of anyone or anything. I could plainly see she feared nothing. I would love her to be part of the family, and she didn't want to come willingly, so that shows she is not easily won, and that is special. Also, it's strange…she reminds me of someone that a person I know speaks much of. Most would come running if Ramesses asked them for their time with him. That girl is very unique, just like your sister," Nefertari said, smiling at Neiko. "As for your other question, it would be safe to say that I would not be jealous. No one woman can expect to have all the attention of our God-king."

"Really, how interesting," Tito said trying to fight the urge to pry further into her business.

"In a way, you remind me of someone I know. His name is Sito. Do you know him?" asked Nefertari.

Tito shook his head. "No. I've heard *of* him, but I don't know him," Tito fibbed.

"Oh, you just seem to remind me so much of him like if you were twins or something," said Nefertari with a chuckle.

Tito chortled with a nervous smile but said nothing.

Neiko looked at her with a "what-did-you-just-say" look and remained silent and then cut her eyes to her escort.

Tito smiled. "I appreciate the earlier compliment for my sister, and it's not often you comment on another woman, is it?" asked Tito.

"No, and I bet you are proud of her—you should be," said Nefertari.

"Thank you. I talked with your husband earlier, and he wants to meet my sister. I shutter at her possible display of poor manners. She is shy and afraid of strangers, even your husband, the king, but he insisted, so I must be going. Thank you for your time, Queen Nefertari," said Tito, bowing.

"There you are. I have been looking for you," said Ramesses, appearing out of the crowd like a ghost from a wall and walking up to his wife and kissing her on the cheek.

Neiko looked up from the floor to be face to face with the man she was hiding from. She tried to lead Tito away frantically, but he wouldn't budge. "This is Sat-Hathor, my king," said Tito signaling

Neiko to stay still. He gave her a stern, "don't-rabbit-or-we're-dead" look.

"You and Nefertari became acquainted, Thutmose?" Ramesses asked with a pleasant smile.

"Yes, and she has spoken highly of my sister," Tito answered with a timid smile.

"Good. I was wondering what was keeping you—I don't have patience with some things," he said, furrowing his brow. "I saw you deal with Sut harshly about his dealings with your sister. You care much for the well-being of your sister—how nice," Ramesses said, looking at Neiko in the face.

Neiko turned away and looked at the floor as she fidgeted nervously.

"My sister has been a handful this evening," Tito said in an attempt to prolong the conversation and to avert Ramesses' attention back to him.

Ramesses didn't respond to Tito's comment. Neiko had his full attention. "She is quite shy," Ramesses said, taking her hand and kissing it.

Neiko pulled it away like an asp had bitten it and looked at him in the eye to read his intentions with her fierce emerald-green eyes.

Ramesses looked into her eyes with his dark brown eyes. Their eyes locked because he noticed her eyes seemed *very* familiar.

Tito saw this, and his mind started racing especially since he could see some electricity from Pharaoh's eyes. He jabbed Neiko's arm to get her attention and to get her look at him to break the connection. He pointed to his eyes, to Ramesses, and shook his head to sign: you're not supposed to look at Pharaoh in the eye. He turned back to Ramesses and asked. "Is there something wrong?"

Ramesses looked at Tito with an irritated frown at the interruption regardless if it was tradition that no one gave royalty eye contact; he *wanted* to gaze into her eyes. Ramesses' brow furrowed in deep thought as his eyes fell to her face. "No, she seems familiar—like we have met somewhere. Do you think so, Nefertari?"

Nefertari looked at Neiko. She turned the corners of her mouth down and pursed her lower lip and shrugged. "No. I have never seen her before till just moments ago."

Ramesses crinkled his nose and shook his head at Nefertari's negligence. He looked at her from head to toe with his eyes studying her. Then he gripped her chin and tilted her face to his.

Neiko swallowed hard; her heart was thumping in her ears. Neiko shut her eyes and her mind screamed, *Please go away. What is going on? Please don't recognize me.*

Tito's heart started pounding; his breath shortened, and he gritted his teeth.

Ramesses released her chin, but his eyes never left her like he was in a trance. "I can't place you, but those eyes are so familiar—I know of one with eyes of emerald that I seek and yearn for. I know you—somehow—somewhere. Are you she?" he said softly in lingering thought. He then broke the entranced stare and shook off the spell by shaking his head. "Your sister is truly a beautiful desert flower."

Tito breathed with relief at the close call. "Thank you. We must be going. My sister and I haven't had much time together this evening. Excuse us," said Tito.

"Very well, you may leave," Ramesses said, waving his hand and smiling since his request was satisfied.

Tito and Neiko quickly walked away nearly running.

"Thanks a lot, Tito! That was too close!" Neiko squeaked. "Why did you just stand there like that?" she demanded like he had gone nuts.

"I'm sorry, Neiko. I was hoping to warn you, but he got to us first. He demanded to meet you, and I tried to make up something to keep him away, but he wouldn't buy it. He's a stubborn son-of-a-gun just like in the history books. At least he didn't recognize you. He knows your eyes, and he knows you somehow. Nefertari was so kind, and she thinks highly of you also. Nefertari also said I looked familiar. I wonder if she knows where Sito is—I think she does; she mentioned she knows him," said Tito.

"I know, maybe she does, and that would be good. I'm glad he didn't find anything else familiar, or I'd be in trouble," said Neiko with a deep exhale.

"I talked with Senu, and he said it seems he has a quite flame for you," Tito said.

Neiko looked at him like she had just seen a zombie. "I gotta stomp out this little flame before it becomes a doggoned forest fire!"

"Too true. There is more at stake. If you marry Pharaoh, then all of history will alter—definitely if it plays out like I hear from all the gossip. I won't bother to explain because it's not gonna happen, and you wouldn't understand. All of history is at stake here, and so is our future...so is the entire land of Hawote including Raven and Bloodhawk's. If we don't get out of here, then the guys and I will be goners, and you'll be someone else's arm ornament and eye candy for sure—possibly Pharaoh's if we're exposed. You, Neiko Kidd, will not have ever liberated Hawote, and Bloodhawk will never have fallen in love with you, and your parents will not have ever known you—I think. I have to find out from Francesco on how this will work exactly. I assume you will have to die here in Egypt for the 'cease to exist' part to happen. You will be up the creek if you are taken as a wife by anyone—especially Ram—I mean Pharaoh," Tito replied. "Now you've got me doing that!" Tito said jabbing her playfully.

Neiko giggled, but then her face was fierce. "Oh my gosh. Francesco is gonna pay for this!" Neiko hissed in vengeance between clenched teeth and fists.

"I don't think he intended for your predicament with Pharaoh to happen. I think he wanted you to be enslaved or dead. And, I bet Bloodhawk made plenty of threats about this whole gambit altogether. If Neiko Kidd never was the Liberator, then the Crackedskulls will probably dominate, and I believe that is what Francesco wants. Your suffering is when you are working to death and separated from

Hawote, knowing no one will know you, and history will reverse to the Crackedskulls' favor," said Tito.

Neiko clenched her fists, gritted her teeth, and shook with rage. "Where is that weasel? I'm gonna wring his scrawny neck!" she growled, holding her hands like she was actually choking Francesco.

"Neiko, calm down. Pharaoh is watching you," Tito warned, nodding in Ramesses' direction. "I will handle Francesco. When I do, you will remain with Mactalon and Panthero or Senu."

Neiko nodded, and she turned and saw Pharaoh staring at her and smiling as he was talking with a few men and women were swooning all over him. He was also clutching that large amulet as he watched her. He ignored the women flirting with him; his full attention was on her and not them.

Neiko clutched Tito's arm tightly as she looked at him with a "get me out of this" look.

"It'll be all right," said Tito comfortingly.

"I hope so," Neiko said.

Tito put his hand on her shoulder. "Neiko, trust me. I'm gonna go find Francesco and interrogate that weasel till he turns blue. Go and find Senu or Mactalon and Panthero! You'll be safe."

"Okay," Neiko said as she let go of his arm. Their friends were in close proximity to their position.

Tito disappeared into the crowd.

- CHAPTER 13 -

TITO SURVEYED THE crowd and finally found Francesco in a corner guzzling down wine. "Well—look what trash the desert coughed up," Tito snapped in English. "How in the world did you find your way to this party?"

Francesco looked and saw Tito. It took a few moments to figure out who he was. "Tito? I remember when you were a twelve-year-old! My how time has flown—no pun intended. How in the world did *you* get to this party? Coming to this party was easy. All I did was follow the trail of gossip from Memphis to Thebes about three painted men and a woman. Naturally, you made quite the ruckus. Then, I saw the crowd of people flocking to this house, so I let myself in to enjoy the new, hottest gossip. Gossip spreads in crowds like this. It's not as easy as going to the nearest grocery bazaar and picking up an issue of the *Egyptian Inquirer*."

Tito scowled. "Enough, wise guy. I want some answers. What is your plan? I want to know when history will change—if that's part of your plan!" Tito said poking him in the shoulder with his finger.

Francesco chuckled. "I will tell you since you won't be telling anyone or able to stop me. Hawote will remember you no more once you pass on here in Egypt and all of the history surrounding you will change. Once Neiko dies here, Bloodhawk will never have known her, nor will her parents or friends—it will be like she never existed or was ever born. What a shame," he said with a cold, evil grin.

Tito shook his head and rolled his eyes. "I bet Raven and Bloodhawk would have something to say about that. Where did you rip that off from—*Back to the Future*? I thought you were loyal to them."

Francesco cackled at him cruelly. "Loyal? That was forty years in the past. I have been waiting to do them in all this time! They don't treat me with any respect. Ever since I found out that I could do time-travel with the Eye's magic, I have constructed a back-up plan. I made a crystal for that purpose, and I have done extensive studies on this time period. It's one of my favorite places, so I chose it to dispose of Neiko the Kid. Raven sent me here to get her back. Ha! I will show him! I will remain here in Egypt to ensure that she suffers many pains, and once she is dead, I will return to Hawote and go on with my plan. The entire land of Hawote will eat crow by the time I finish!"

Tito looked at him horrified like he became Hannibal Lector. "What plan? You mean there's more?"

Francesco slapped his head with his palm. "The downfall of Raven and Bloodhawk, of course. The whole history part is only half of it! Once they have their victory celebration, I will poison their food. They will die, and I will become the Pharaoh of Hawote. Any who resist will die—that's Crackedskull and Indian alike. I originally planned to wait till Neiko was wed to Bloodhawk and dead from giving birth to his child from the curse. I planned to do this instead since it was taking *way* too long. I may have been adopted as a Crackedskull, but I am not a Crackedskull!"

Tito's mouth fell open. "You plan to assassinate Raven and Bloodhawk? If you had succeeded back then, what would have happened to Neiko? If you are not a Crackedskull or an Indian, then what are you? I don't even think Raven could come up with something so heinous or so off kilter!"

Francesco snorted. "Yes, you stupid Indian! I would make her my palace slave to make her suffer somehow. The rest of my past...well, that's my little secret. I will be the beginning of a new Hawote—I will unite the opposing forces to one nation and begin the reign of a new emperor—the Pharaoh of Hawote!" Francesco said like he was preaching to his own imaginary congregation.

Tito looked at him as if he was the Valedictorian of a private school of lunatics. "Keep preaching to the choir, Francesco. Oh my gosh—do you actually believe you could do that alone—all by your little scrawny, weak self? Ha! The Crackedskulls are diligent followers to their rulers, and they despise you! The Pharaoh of Hawote indeed! Karo may be a big muscle head, but he'd snap you like a twig. Now I get why you look up to Ramesses the Great because you want to mimic him in the land of Hawote! Let me tell you something—it won't work. Ramesses may be an egotistical tyrant, but he is not a lunatic. Good luck with trying to outdo him in a place not even he could rule!"

Francesco snorted cynically. "Mimic? I want to be greater than he is! I want to be better than any that has ever lived! I would be careful with that word 'lunatic' if I were you. All the great minds and geniuses have been called such by those *half* their mental capacity. Since I am here, I will go and learn a few things from Ramesses by becoming his servant."

Tito burst out laughing. "You—serve Pharaoh? What could he possibly do with a back-stabbing, conniving jerk like you? If I know anything about Pharaoh, he ain't a fool, nor is he that dumb."

"You wait and see—I will get into his court," Francesco said cockily.

"Yeah, I bet you will—why don't you try getting into the court of Genghis Khan or Ivan the Terrible or Vlad the Impaler instead? They seem more like your kind of company anyway. You might score with Ramesses the Great if you can suck up well enough and inflate his ego without getting caught. I can already see you kissing Pharaoh's royal fanny! Good luck! You just go and tug his kilt until he gives you a job, and I hope you get chores like shining his sandals or feeding him grapes twenty-four-seven!" Tito punned scornfully.

Francesco narrowed his eyes at him angrily. "Do you think I'm joking? You haven't changed at all. I will take any job he gives me just as long I can win his respect, so he can teach me all there is to being a pharaoh. Being privileged enough to be his cup bearer is more than the respect I *ever* got in Raven's court!"

"Oh yeah, I forgot you worship the ground Ramesses walks on from what I heard. He will not teach you anything! He is not that stupid because he will feel like you are going to overthrow him!" Tito said as he looked at Francesco as though he were in his underwear.

"You're right—I do admire him, and I will not directly ask him to give me a class. That wouldn't happen. I suppose Neiko told you I think highly of him since she broke into my house and snooped around in my stuff to expose me. I will study and observe as I serve in his house. Now if you will excuse me, I have to speak with him now!" Francesco snapped and mingled in the crowd.

Tito left the vacant corner and found Neiko. They couldn't leave the place for two reasons: getting the crystal from Francesco, and now because of Pharaoh's eye being on them. An abrupt leave by any of them, especially Neiko, would arouse his suspicions.

"Well, did you find out anything?" Neiko asked, fanning out her hands, and he told her everything he had learned. "You're serious? Oh my gosh! He's crazy! Well, I know how he made the crystal and now how much he is against everyone—but now he wants to be the Pharaoh of Hawote?" Neiko asked shaking her head in disbelief.

"You know how he made the crystal? How?" Tito asked in complete shock.

"It's a complicated story, and there is more to it than him just making the crystal. I know where the Eye of Mohica came from, but I will get into that later—maybe. Sito must know about this too," said Neiko. "For now, let's keep this between us."

Tito nodded silently in agreement. "Okay, I'm gonna go talk with Mactalon and Panthero about this screwed up plan Francesco has. Be back later," Tito said and went to find his two friends.

Neiko watched him leave, and someone bumped into her from behind. It was Francesco; he seemed like he was in a hurry like the white rabbit.

Had Francesco inadvertently run into her on his speedy passage to somewhere? Had he not recognized her? Neiko needed to find out where he was headed. She followed him at a discrete distance. Francesco made his way to speak with the king. Seeing Ramesses, she halted her pursuit or else the king may find her again—without her friend to help her this time. *I wish I could eavesdrop, but I can't understand this language, and I would get in trouble because that twerp would expose me*, she thought as she watched him. She was ready to pounce on him once he was finished with the king.

Francesco approached the pharaoh and bowed. "Good evening, my king."

Ramesses looked at him with complete suspicion. "Who are you? I do not know you," his said with a keen edge of distrust.

Francesco smiled. "I know. I am Francesco from Hawote, vizier to His Majesty, King Raven of Hawote. I have come to Egypt looking for a new home, and I wish to grant you my services," Francesco said cordially. He was skilled with court protocol and addressing royalty.

Ramesses eyed him with suspicion, narrowed eyes, and frowned like he smelled a dead rat. "Oh? I have heard of this land—I have no need of you, so be off," his said, flicking his hand. "I am sure there is another ruler in another land that would be interested…"

"Oh please, I want to be your vizier, please? I want to counsel you…" Francesco pleaded, interrupting him.

Ramesses' eyes darted around in disgust. "I have one already. And one is certainly enough. Stop groveling—you repulse me with your sniveling—how *dare* you interrupt me! I will accept no foreigners into my court. Out of my way," he said as he shoved past Francesco, nearly knocking him down. "I am not fond of this Hawote," he muttered under his breath.

"Where are you going?" Francesco asked, trying to catch up with Ramesses.

"I want to see someone, and it is none of your concern! Leave my presence!" snapped Ramesses as he stood erectly and clenched his fists like he was an alpha male wolf defending his territory.

Francesco stopped his approach and took a step back with his hands up in surrender. "Whom?" asked Francesco, following as though he were still part of the team.

"Sat-Hathor. Ask no more." Ramesses growled, taking one antagonizing step toward Francesco.

Francesco cocked an eyebrow. "Sat-Hathor?"

"Yes—I did not stutter! She may not hear or speak, and she may tremble in my presence, but I have unfinished business with her. Enough! Leave me alone! If I must tell you this again, I will have you arrested!" Ramesses said, turned in a huff, and stormed off.

"I will have a lot of work to do to win his appreciation. Sat-Hathor? Of all his million wives he had during his life, I never read of one with that name. And, she is deaf and dumb, and fears pharaohs? I have to find out about this Sat-Hathor for myself. I have heard rumors about Pharaoh seeking a warrior girl, and she just vanished? If Tito is here, I wonder if Neiko is also—I wonder if she is the warrior girl he's looking for," Francesco mused aloud as he tried to find out where Ramesses had gone. "If she is, then Neiko is my ticket in!"

Neiko saw that Francesco was looking around—probably for Ramesses. She had lost sight of Ramesses because he left the scene so abruptly. His body language told her that Francesco had ticked him off. Francesco also had the look of a definitive eureka moment—just like someone had flipped the switch to the invisible light bulb over his head. It was anyone's guess *what* he was thinking about. She took great pleasure watching Francesco's plan blow up in his face and his 'favorite pharaoh' snubbing him. "There's snipe wad, but where's—never mind, maybe he took his queen and left—I have a few choice words to tell that—" Neiko said as she thought of a thousand names to call Francesco.

Neiko flexed her arms and her muscles rippled beneath her gold armlets and showed nicely in her sleeveless linen dress as she started to close in on the Crackedskull. She was prepared to fight. Suddenly someone grabbed her arm from behind. She spun around to confront and wallop the culprit thinking it was Sut or one of the ten—twenty—or she-lost-count men trying to get her. When spun around, there stood Ramesses, the last person she hoped to be there. She was certainly glad she didn't unload a punch on the pharaoh— that would have been *very* bad. She tried to swallow the knot in her throat and tried to stop her body from shaking. She hoped he hadn't overheard her talking to herself.

Ramesses didn't release his grip on her arm immediately. He ran his thumb over her taut muscle since they were still rippling in his grasp and visible to his attentive gaze. "You certainly are strong—you must work very hard at home, don't you? Why are you nervous? I won't harm you," Ramesses said kindly as he slipped his arm into hers and escorted her to where he had been most of the evening. She kept her eyes on Francesco watching him. He noticed her watching him and studied her behavior very closely.

I just gotta get to that pipsqueak, but first I have to get outa this, she thought. Neiko tapped his shoulder getting his attention. She signaled with her two fingers "walk" and pointed to Francesco.

Ramesses looked in Francesco's direction and then back at her with a cocked, confused eyebrow and a disdainful frown. "You must speak with him—but you don't speak. Why do you want to go *there?* No, you are coming over here with me," he said, walking with her arm in arm and firmly tugging her into the opposite direction. She stopped him by planting her feet and signaled she had to go alone and it was important. He looked at her with raised eyebrows, but he didn't release his grip. After a few more moments of silent coercion, he finally released her and walked away.

Neiko sighed with great relief as she walked in Francesco's direction. She didn't think it would have been as simple as that. She also hoped and prayed he wasn't watching. She stopped to look around, but she had lost sight of Ramesses. Shrugging, she continued her bee-line to the Crackedskull.

Francesco had no luck in finding out who Sat-Hathor was, so he went to his corner to binge on more wine. He was about to take a drink when someone shoved him from behind which caused him to drop his golden goblet and spill it all over his tunic. He spun around, and he saw a beautiful woman in front of him. After a few moments of studying her, he narrowed his eyes when he recognized Neiko. "You," he snarled in venom, baring his teeth in hatred.

"Yeah, it's me. Miss me? Tito told me about your plans—really original—the run-of-the-mill, stereotypical schlock for psychotic dorks like you. But hey, it's the new millennium in Hawote, right?" Neiko said shrugging and fanning her hand like she was putting something on display.

"Ooh, you are always a permanent cramp in my plans! I can't ever get rid of you! You just wait until I tell the pharaoh you're the warrior girl and where you are—right here under his nose. I'd just *love* to see what he does to you, and I think you will have bigger fish to fry than little old me. I won't be in Egypt long. I will leave you here to die where it's seventy minutes or seventy years from now—it doesn't really matter to me. You may just be the ticket I need to win Pharaoh's favor and enter into his court!" Francesco said.

Neiko's smirk faded into a scowl. "Oh yeah? Tell Pharaoh, and I'll kill you. Besides, I don't think he likes you very much. He just gave you the sandal instead of the boot—get it? In case you're wondering, yeah I saw it. You may just need to stick your head in the sand for the next fifty years after *that* failure. You can beg till you turn green, and he won't listen to you."

"You can threaten me all you like—I am used to it by now since it happens to me all the time. I'm sure Ramesses will *love* to hear where the warrior is hiding, and I'll be the man to tell him," Francesco said, starting to walk toward the king.

Neiko clenched her fists and shook them at him. "You don't think I'd do it?" Neiko yelled at him and everyone stopped what they were doing and looked—the musicians also stopped, and Ramesses looked at her with a gaping mouth because the "mute" had spoken just like a miracle had taken place. "I'll show you, you scalawag!" Neiko screamed as she tackled him sending him crashing onto the hard marble floor. In her fury, she lost all sense of reason, and battle fire shone in her piercing green eyes. Neiko landed on top of him and pinned him. She grabbed him by the throat with a vise-like grip and started to squeeze. Neiko banged his head on the hard floor as she tried to strangle him. Francesco coughed and wheezed as he fought to get air and tried to remove her hands from his throat.

"I'm gonna wring your scrawny neck for everything you've ever done to me and everyone else, you despicable traitor," she snarled, squeezing harder and digging her thumbs into his trachea.

Ramesses came out of his shock and he pointed to her. "Seize her!" he commanded his soldiers.

Hearing Ramesses' voice with him pointing at her and seeing the guards advancing, Neiko realized what she had done, but it was too late. She didn't need words to figure out they were coming for her and her cover was blown. They grabbed her, pulling her off of Francesco and bound her wrists in front of her. Two men held her fast, while another kept a hold of the strand of rope that served as a leash.

The guard pulled her arms so she was unable to move.

Francesco sat up and fought to breathe and coughed as people closed in to investigate.

Ramesses briskly walked to her and looked her in the face as she struggled to break free from her captors. "Is it you—is it finally you? You *must* be the warrior from days ago, but are you the one I yearn for? Let us find out. Bring me some black and red paint!" he commanded. "Half of the mystery will be solved now!"

"Tito, Mactalon, Panthero, help! Senu, please, somebody help me!" Neiko cried out trying to free her hands from the rope.

"Neiko! Oh no! Hang on, I'm coming!" Tito ran up to rescue his captured friend, but the remaining guards blocked his path, thrust their spears at him, and prodded him with the points.

Ramesses looked at Neiko in shock with an open mouth, and then looked at Tito and narrowed his eyes venomously. "Thutmose? So, Sat-Hathor's real name is Neiko, is it? How dare you lie to me!" harangued Ramesses with narrowed eyes. "Let's see who Neiko is, shall we?"

Tito sighed. "My real name is Tito, not Thutmose. I am not an Egyptian, and these are my friends, Mactalon and Panthero. I have a twin brother—"

Ramesses' eyes narrowed in venom "How dare you mock me! I know who you are and *exactly* what is going on here! You are Sito's twin brother, and those two are his friends that he speaks of," Ramesses barked indignantly as he pointed at Mactalon and Panthero. Then he shook his fists in wrath at the mockery they made of him from the sham.

"I..." Tito began, but fell silent since he couldn't think of anything else to say without putting him or his friends in danger.

"Here is the paint, my king," said a servant.

Ramesses dipped his finger in the black paint, and approached Neiko, ready to paint her face, but she writhed and bucked, dodging his finger. "Hold still! Secure her!" he commanded. Another guard gripped her face and her head, forcing her to remain still, and he smeared the paint on her face just as it was on the day he first saw her.

"No!" screamed Mactalon as he tried to attack the guards kamikaze-style to intercede for Neiko, but a guard stopped him and pushed him away.

Pharaoh then painted the red on her face, and the face matched exactly.

"Behold, the warrior!" said Ramesses, displaying the apprehended warrior girl. "Now I will take you and find out more about you and if you are 'the one'," he said with his dark eyes burning with longing.

Neiko looked around at everyone's shocked faces and heard their gasps; they were pointing at her and whispering. She looked at the floor, knowing she was helpless, but other than that she didn't have much of a clue about what was happening. Ramesses' chest swelled with pride.

Nefertari looked at her in shock, and she cupped her hand over her mouth as she saw the true identity of Sat-Hathor.

"Let us leave—come, Nefertari. Bring her," Ramesses said, snapping his fingers and waving his arm.

Nefertari obediently came along with Neiko being dragged behind them.

Senu stepped in front of Ramesses cutting him off. "I can't let you do this."

Ramesses looked at him like he had gone mad. "Step aside. You owe me an explanation, but later…"

"I cannot," Senu interjected putting up his hands. "Please, I beg you as a friend. She meant you no harm. It was an accident and a simple chance of fate! She only meant to defend herself, and she was frightened."

Ramesses rolled his eyes and shook his head. "I know that! I am perfectly capable of determining the actions of a warrior because I am one myself. I command you as Pharaoh—step aside!" Ramesses commanded aggressively, but Senu did not move, and Tito and the others stood behind him. "What is this? What is going on here? I want answers, and I want them now!"

Senu took a deep breath. "These four are travelers, and they took up residence here years ago. They have suffered from Kenes' hands, and this warrior girl is a friend of theirs."

"Lies! Nothing but lies! I know who they are—invasive savages! Barbarians! You have broken my trust, Senu, and for what, slaves? I have had enough!" Ramesses shouted, shaking his fists. "I will interrogate you later about this once I cool down. I hope for your sake you have a good explanation for this, and we can rebuild our friendship."

Tito stepped forward another step showing no fear even though Ramesses was making quite a scene. "We aren't invaders. We'll be on our way if you let our friend and my brother go."

"You are in a position unsuitable to make demands—especially to *me*," said Ramesses with a scowl.

"What do you mean you search for 'the one'? Neiko can't be the one you're looking for," Tito argued.

Mactalon had to bite his lip to keep a straight face about Tito's last statement. "I don't think that mind trick works on the strong-minded, Bro," he said.

Tito shook his head at his comedian friend. Now wasn't the time to be funny.

Ramesses shifted his eyes at Mactalon, but then looked back at Tito a cocked eyebrow and his head slightly tilted to the left with a suspicious glare. "That is none of your concern—I'll be the judge of that. How do you even know about that—that is *my* secret! You may go your way, and I will send you your brother—I would like to be rid of him sooner rather than later, but she is coming with me. Out of my way, savage!" he snapped as he tried to bulldoze by Tito.

Tito stood his ground and blocked the pharaoh's passage. "I've heard you talk about 'the one' quite a few times tonight," Tito retorted.

Ramesses recoiled like a defensive cobra and looked at him with a that-was-gutsy-and-foolish look in his face.

Neiko watched the standoff and knew her fate was in the balance. Her heart raced, and she began to perspire.

Senu stepped in between the contenders and ushered some space between them. "Ramesses, I implore you—you may take her, but not at this hour, please? She is not properly prepared for your presence. To rebuild our trust, I will prepare her for your arrival, and you choose the day. She is not ready to depart the care of her friends. Can you find it in your heart to understand?" asked Senu, pleading as he folded his hands like he was praying.

A great annoyance crossed Ramesses' face. "Very well, since you are so persistent on the matter and *only* because you are my friend," he said, waving his hand in disgust. "I will return in one week at sundown. I will gladly pay you for your trouble and loyalty in great riches and livestock. But, she better be here—if you try to double-cross me; I will strip you of everything you own and let you rot with the vermin in the mud pits of Goshen after you are charged with treason before the public. Is that understood? One week—and dress her nicely, but in her native attire. What she wore on the day of our meeting will not do. Preparing her for me is a start to rebuilding my trust in you, Senu. If you weren't my close friend, I would have you executed for this. Release her," he said and snapped his fingers.

The guards let go and cut the rope binding her hands. Neiko rubbed her wrists, joined her friends, and looked at Ramesses with raised eyebrows. She didn't know what just happened, but she could figure out that she was off the hook—for now.

Ramesses and his guards marched out of the house. He swaggered in his great arrogance as he left like the prized game cock of the barnyard. Neiko wrinkled her nose and curled her lip at him in scorn. The other Indians shook their heads, but they were relieved that he left.

They were safe for the time being. They had one week to sort this thing out and avert it.

<h1 style="text-align:center">– CHAPTER 14 –</h1>

<hr>

AFTER THE PARTY THAT NIGHT, Senu and the four male Indians sat down to counsel about the events of the evening in a secluded room while the servants cleaned the dining hall. The Indians told him the truth of who they really were and the importance of finding Francesco and not allowing Neiko to be taken by Pharaoh.

Senu's face was filled with confusion and disbelief. "Three thousand years in the future? That man sent you here to do away with you? I cannot comprehend this, but you haven't said anything that has been untrue. If you tell Ramesses the truth, he will laugh and say it is all nonsense."

"I don't care what he thinks. If we are able to return to Hawote, then we don't have to worry about it, but if not, we have to let him take Neiko," complained Mactalon.

"Did you see the way he looked at me?" Tito said pointing at himself with both fingers. "He knows Sito and can't stand him by the way things look—God knows what has been going on between Pharaoh and my brother the past eleven years. I get the impression he doesn't like our kind—which doesn't surprise me. I think we're going to have big time problems in dealing with him. He's gonna send us my brother but not Neiko," Tito said. "Senu, what does he mean when he wonders if Neiko is 'the one'?"

Senu shrugged. "I haven't the faintest idea. You will have to find this Francesco person and return to Hawote. You have exactly one week. What will you do if you are unable to accomplish all of this in time?" asked Senu.

"We have no choice but to let him come and get Neiko—for your and our own safety. If we pacify him, then we can find Francesco without any confrontations with Pharaoh. But, then we have to find a way to get Neiko away from him—and by the looks of things, it won't be easy," replied Tito as he ran his hands through his long dark hair.

"Yeah, you heard what he said to Senu, and we can't let anything happen to him because of all the kindness he has shown us and the good things he is doing for everyone—which he didn't have to do in the first place. All of these servants will then have a master that will mistreat them, and it will be our fault," whined Mactalon.

"We do have an inside friend. Queen Nefertari seems to like our kind for some reason. I'm sure she could help us out in some ways if we need it—maybe. She seemed to recognize me. I wonder if she has any idea about what is going on," mused Tito aloud.

Everyone shrugged or scratched their heads at the notion.

"That's good. She seems so good-natured, unlike her puffed up, ill-tempered husband. I'm also wondering if Sito may still be at the palace, but I wouldn't think he is doing very much," said Panthero. "But, we can't be sure Pharaoh didn't kick Sito out or if Pharaoh would ever send him to us."

"He's there alright. He said he would, and I think he'd deliver on his promise," corrected Tito.

Senu sighed helplessly since there wasn't too much more he could do without putting himself or the Indians in more danger. "I'm glad that you care much for me, and I will allow you to stay as long as you need to. If you need my help, don't hesitate to ask. I will try to find your brother, but make the palace the last place you search—I may even need to avoid the place myself for a time. The Pharaoh needs to cool off. We have no other court appearances this week; I can't use that as an excuse. Are there any more of you in Egypt?"

"Nope. Just us five Indians, and Francesco, the Crackedskull," replied Panthero.

"Good. Ramesses already feels threatened by you—why I don't know. If he found there were thousands of you, he would go berserk and would maybe drive you out or even try to exterminate you. I must be off to bed. Good night," said Senu, yawning and arising to leave. He left the hall.

"Okay, good night," Tito called after him. He called Neiko in and told her everything they had discussed.

"That's good that he is opening his house to y'all, but I really don't want to go to the palace alone. I can't handle the thought of going there at all," complained Neiko. "What is all this talk about 'the one'? The one what? Is he gonna send me on a quest or something?"

Tito shrugged. "I don't know—I don't think it has anything to do with questing. My brother may be there still, but we won't know for sure till we start looking—and we have to find that creep Francesco as well," said Tito.

"Do you really think you can do all of that in one week? You ain't superman! If time does run out, I want you guys to come with me because I can't communicate with Ramesses. I don't want to face him alone. I know for a fact that he is going to try to tie the knot judging from what you guys say, but the question is when. It would be good if he waited years. I know I will have a fight on my hands, and if it comes to that, then I'll try to run away," said Neiko.

"Neiko, I don't think he will want us anywhere near you on that day. From that day forth, you will be his property, and we feel he doesn't like the rest of us very much while he adores you," said Tito.

"Great, that's nice," Neiko grumbled with a disgusted frown and an eye roll.

"Tell you what, if you are forced to go, then we will find a way to get in somehow. If we have to, then we will use some of Francesco's old tricks. But I believe Nefertari can help us. If Sito is there, then try to get him to talk to her and see if she can persuade Ramesses to accept us as servants or something. I'm sure he'll listen to her, and she knows how to push his buttons," said Tito.

Neiko gave a questioning look to Tito that said "how do you know?"

"Call it a hunch," he replied.

Neiko shook her head. "Okay, I'll give it my best shot," Neiko promised. "I know one thing, you guys aren't the only ones who are trying to get into Pharaoh's court."

Now, Mactalon rolled his eyes. "Neiko's right. We have to worry about Francesco getting in there, too. He will make Neiko's life miserable and put in a bad word on us just to be a jerk. I'll bet Ramesses would try to be rid of us and Sito as well, and Neiko would have no hope at all of escape."

Neiko shuddered. "Not only that, Francesco would leave me there alone, and the five of us will be trapped here which I think was the whole idea in the first place. I will have to live there and be a faithful wife until he dies, and that'll be torture. Is he one of those that lived and ruled for a couple years or a decade? If so, I can leave right after that."

Tito shook his head. "Neiko, you haven't studied, have you? Ramesses lives to be in his mid to late nineties—or even a hundred. He rules Egypt for another sixty-seven plus years—this doesn't even account for the co-rule with his father who has just passed! You will be there a very long time, and you will have to be a faithful wife for that long—maybe longer if you add years to his life. You will be old, and you may die first. Nefertari won't be around that long either—she lives to her late twenties or early thirties at the most—which is another ten years or so. You will have your hands full after she's gone."

Neiko moaned in disgust and covered her eyes with her hands. "I didn't learn about that in history class! Oh no! What am I gonna do?" she whimpered. "I can't stand him for two seconds—I can't handle him for seventy years or more! Ugggh!" she groaned. "How old is he anyway?"

"Twenty-three. I asked Senu about him before the party, and he is our age—only two years older than you. He and Nefertari have only been married a year, so he is just starting out."

"Great—wonderful," said Neiko sarcastically. "This ship is on course, but you and I aren't supposed to be here, and this is not supposed to be happening!"

"I know. That's why we must find Francesco before all of history and the future is shot! Senu said we need to help in finding something suitable for her to wear, just in case," reminded Tito.

They went to bed with dreams of escape and nightmares if not.

The next morning they talked with Senu about making the just-in-case preparations for Neiko.

"How did he want her to dress?" asked Panthero.

"He said in her native clothes, but they must be presentable. He said the clothes she is wearing now will not do, and she cannot wear face paint," replied Senu.

"Do you have any tanned animal skins like deer or leopard or anything on hand? We will have to make them because we know how they are supposed to look."

"I do have some tanned leopard and antelope skins, a tiger that I killed a few weeks ago. I haven't done anything with it. Will that be acceptable?" Senu asked.

"Yes. Bring them here, and we'll get started. Can you find Francesco for us?" Tito asked.

"Yes. I will get right on it," said Senu. "He should be easy to find—he sort of stands out."

The four men snickered. A pasty white man among dusky Egyptians made "standing out" an understatement.

The Indians worked on Neiko's clothes the entire day. Senu and some of his servants assisted them in making her attire. Neiko's raiment consisted of an antelope skin top with a beaded eagle on the breast and fringe at the neckline. The beads were not the tiny Indian beads, but some assortment that Senu had on hand. They made her skirt of tiger skin and a cape of leopard skin. She wore no shoes, but sported her falcon headband, hawk feathers, armlets, and necklace of bear and eagle claws.

"What do you think?" asked Mactalon.

"I love this outfit. I wish you guys could make something like this back home."

Senu looked at her amazed. "The outfit is extremely nice, and she looks beautiful. This will do nicely." Then he paused as his face took a worried expression, "But, I had no luck in finding Francesco."

"I bet the scum wipe skipped town or he is already trying to get Pharaoh's appreciation," Mactalon grumbled. "I can't say he's hiding in his favorite spot with his rodent kin because sewers haven't been invented yet."

The five men laughed at the joke.

The Indians spent the rest of that day together. They also tried to make plans for every outcome imaginable when they got the crystal.

- CHAPTER 15 -

ON THE FIRST DAY of the week they discovered Sito was at the palace, yet they could not risk going in or Neiko would be called prematurely. They then made preparations to leave town if possible.

However, on the second day they discovered that Pharaoh's army had closed off all exits of the city and checked everyone coming in and going out. It was apparent that Pharaoh did not trust the Indians at all. That evening, news spread that a royal decree was made that if the Indians were caught leaving the city they were to be arrested on sight and charged with treason. Neiko, in contrast, was to be brought to Pharaoh immediately following their capture. What happened to the rest of them was anyone's guess; it was either hard labor or death for each.

To make matters worse, on the third day, Kenes came back into town with a mob. He found out that the Indians were at Senu's house. He immediately went to Senu's house. He threatened to sue Senu and press charges against him for theft of property if Senu didn't return all four slaves back to him; he mostly wanted Neiko, but he asked for the others for spite and to get his revenge on them.

The two rivals began arguing, until Senu broke the news to Kenes that Pharaoh had a claim on Neiko and was coming for her in four days. Things were now out of Senu's control, and he certainly wasn't going to give her friends to Kenes so that he could kill or mistreat them for ruining his chances at having a rare, trophy wife.

On the fourth day, several of Senu's friends from the court brought news that Kenes was trying to buy Neiko from Pharaoh. Kenes presented him lavish gifts and made extravagant offers to entice him to sell Neiko and remove his claim. Senu's friends talked about how Kenes' even went as far to offer Pharaoh gold mined from the ancient mines of the kings of the Old Kingdom as a last desperate attempt to succeed. Others said the offers he made would make a tax collector blush and maybe even make Khufu jealous. The surprising thing was that Pharaoh refused all of Kenes' offers and sent him on his way back to Memphis.

Kenes didn't take this very well and was distraught from his terrible loss. Not even he was gutsy enough to challenge Pharaoh head-on. This occurrence was the talk of the city, and it just struck home how serious this situation was for the Indians. For many of the court, what had taken place surprised even them; Neiko had to be truly special for Pharaoh to refuse to accept such offers and gifts for the sake of a woman. Neiko was told about the event, but it only added to her anxiety. She was really in this over her head.

The remaining days passed surprisingly fast, but they had not found Francesco. They didn't leave the house after the third day for fear of being assaulted by either Kenes' or Pharaoh's men. The dreaded date came. The Indians were perplexed that Francesco just seemed to disappear in society and that their luck had unraveled in such a short time.

Neiko put on her new clothes. She paced the floors in great anxiety and watched the sun as it moved in the sky. Evening came, the sun began to set in the horizon, and she became very nervous. "I can't do this," Neiko groaned as she fidgeted.

Then there was a knock at the door, and everyone jumped.

Senu opened the door, and a messenger was there. "May I help you?"

"Pharaoh has come for the warrior, and he awaits," the messenger replied.

Senu saw Ramesses walking to the house with an armed escort a few feet behind the messenger. Following him were other servants bringing in gifts for Senu. "All right, I will notify her," he said, but the Indians were already there and crowded behind him.

Neiko saw Ramesses advancing as she peeked from a crack between Senu and Tito, and she hid behind Tito.

"I can't do this, Tito! Don't let him get me, please! I'm scared!" Neiko fretted, grasping his arm so tightly that it cut off the circulation.

"Ouch! Neiko, calm down. Get a hold of yourself! We will try to come in, I promise. I need blood in my hand or it will rot and fall off," Tito teased.

Neiko slapped his shoulder playfully. "Tito, that's not funny—" she started to say, but Ramesses was in the door, and she darted behind Tito again.

Tito looked at Ramesses and laughed nervously. "She doesn't want to come alone. May the rest of us accompany her? We will not cause any trouble, I promise. Er, she also can't communicate with you."

Ramesses scowled at him. "No, I am not going to deal with you, your brother, and your friends and let you hamper my plans or stand in my way. Tell her it is time. She is no longer your concern. I am aware she cannot speak our language. In that case there may be a delay in me sending you your brother."

Tito gritted his teeth, trying to stifle his anger at Ramesses' harsh and uncaring remarks. He took Neiko by the shoulders and looked her in the eyes. "Neiko, it's time, and he won't allow us to come with you. You will have to handle this on your own in the meantime. Don't fear him—just think of him as Bloodhawk who is down to our size. It is in everyone's best interest if you leave with him. Now go," Tito said painfully, trying to stop his tears.

As they were talking, Senu and Ramesses said a few words to each other. The servants gave Senu his reward for his obedience, which were chests full of gold and jewels. Senu tried to be grateful but a twitching in his jaw and a crease in his brow showed he was not genuinely happy about the lavish reward. After that, Pharaoh motioned for Neiko to come to him.

Neiko nodded sadly to her friend, threw her arms around Tito, and held on. She was trying to delay leaving as long as she could. "I'm gonna miss you," she said, letting go and hugging the others as Ramesses fidgeted impatiently.

Neiko sighed and walked to him. He took her hand and started to leave. Neiko looked back at her friends, and she saw Tito bowing his head in dread. Mactalon and Panthero stood there completely helpless. Neiko pursed her lips, turned around, and looked forward as they walked to Pharaoh's chariot. Neiko climbed on first, and Pharaoh came on behind her. Seconds later he cracked the whip, and he and the escort left for the palace.

As they continued their journey to the palace, Neiko neither spoke to Ramesses nor looked at him. Her fear had turned to anger and disdain. *Treat him like Bloodhawk*, popped into her mind in Tito's voice. *Oh yeah, I can do that!* she thought in her own voice.

The palace was secluded from the common area of the city, and it was majestic. Neiko took in the grandeur to get her mind off of her situation. On the way in there were small sphinxes—mostly of Ramesses or his father—on either side of the walkway. She looked at the carvings, paintings, and hieroglyphs that were ever present. It was also decorated with statues of the gods, along with many statues of Ramesses.

They went inside and the place was spectacular. "Wow!" she said, looking around at the brilliantly painted walls and rich decorations. Dogs, cats, and peafowl lay all around, and servants bustled everywhere. She took in every detail, and she didn't notice him watching her as she checked his home out. She looked at all the people, hoping to find Sito. She saw a man reading a papyrus. He was dressed in Egyptian clothes, but Neiko recognized him.

"Sito?" Neiko asked.

Hearing his name, Sito looked up from his papyrus and looked at her. "Neiko? Is it really you?"

Neiko ran to him and threw her arms around him. "Oh, I'm so glad to see you. You're alive! We have a lot of catching up to do. I have more good news, Tito, Panthero, and Mactalon are here too, and they are staying with Senu."

Sito quivered with excitement. "Oh, that is great news! Where have they been, and how long have you been in Egypt?"

"They spent half a year trying to find you, and they have served Kenes for ten and a half years. I've been in Egypt for only two weeks, and I'm already in and been in trouble," Neiko said, pointing her thumb at Ramesses nonchalantly.

Sito laughed. "Well, you have been the talk of the palace—I've been wondering just who was causing all the ruckus. I should have known it had to be you. You seem to have become a fine fighter, and beautiful too. How's Phoenix?"

"She's okay. Everybody thinks you guys are dead, and they will think I am too before long. Phoenix mourns you every day even though she tries to put on a smiling face," said Neiko.

Sito sighed. "Oh my," he said, rubbing his head. "Has she found someone else?" he said with a twinge of hope that she hadn't.

"No, but I have more news. Francesco's here in Egypt; he has our way home," Neiko said and then told him everything she had told the others about all of their adventures in Egypt. "So what's your story?"

Sito sighed. "Actually, I don't have much to tell. Seti found me in the streets, and he took pity on me—which surprised me, and I am truly grateful. He was amazed at my ability to handle people and to speak his language. He took me in and made me his personal scribe and advisor. Ramesses has never liked me; I really can't go into that toxic history—I was told not to. When Seti passed on, he told Ramesses it was his dying wish for me to remain here—that's the only reason why I'm still around. Nefertari also made it plain that she wanted me to stay. Ramesses agreed, but he will not let me do anything for him. I have also heard he doesn't like the others that well either. Ramesses despises me, and if he finds a liable cause, he will get rid of me."

Neiko bit her lip and shrugged with "Ok-kay" written on her features. "Nefertari seems to be on our side, and maybe you can talk to her and see if she can talk him into letting the others come in too," suggested Neiko. "We all need to be together to fly this coop."

Sito nodded in agreement. "Hmm, she has always thought highly of me for some reason, and I think I may just do that. It would be nice to see them again. They are safe at Senu's house, but we need them here for when we are able to return to Hawote provided we get the crystal," said Sito.

"Francesco plans to come here too and try to worm his way into the court. He won't give up," said Neiko. "He's the one who has that ticket home."

"Oooh, this can't be good. From what you told me, he will leave you here with Pharaoh while the rest of us are dead or in slavery. It sounds that Ramesses doesn't like him either. We have to all be together to return home like you said," said Sito.

"Yeah, but I don't know how this will work out," said Neiko.

"It will. Let's pray tonight," suggested Sito.

Ramesses came to investigate and was a bit suspicious since he didn't know what was going on. "Do you two know each other? Tell me the truth and don't lie to me," he said with a suspicious glare, but there was another glint of warning toward Sito. There was evidence of something going on between them.

"Yes, I do know her. We were best friends in Hawote. It has been a long time," said Sito.

"Very well. I think I have a use for you after all. You will teach Neiko our language, and translate for us till she learns. You better not give her any ideas or say nasty things about me about behind my back," Ramesses warned. "There are 'certain things' I do not want told to her—I will tell her myself in due time. I also want her to be speaking well in basic speech in a fortnight. I want to be able to speak to her without you having to translate private things."

Sito rolled his eyes and tried to conjure up retorts in a respectful way even though Ramesses was being condescending. He had to be careful now because Ramesses was now Pharaoh and not the spoiled prince with whom Sito had spent eleven years in contention.

"Can you really expect me to make Neiko learn any faster? Do you honestly believe I have control over that? I'm sorry, but you put unrealistic demands and deadlines on me!" Sito said. He didn't tell Ramesses that Neiko was a very bright and fast learner.

"If you *were* any sort of teacher at all," Ramesses said with an arrogant snort and his right brow furrowed in a snobbish glare. "If you do not meet my expectations, then I will find her a new teacher—"

"You can try…" Sito said and paused. "Unfortunately, you will not find a soul from Nubia all the way to Syria who can speak any of the languages Neiko speaks. I can not only be more than adequate, I can be your only hope!"

They seemed to stare each other down eye to eye and square off at each other. Neiko looked at them and scratched her head. She even wondered what was being said.

Sito broke eye contact and then said, "I'll do as you wish, but don't expect the impossible just because you have a lack of patience and an impulse control problem." Sito knew the main reason for this impossible deadline was for an excuse to get rid of him and that he wanted to be with Neiko without him there and knowing what was

going on. Neiko's lack of communication was one of the few things keeping Ramesses from proceeding with the wedding much faster.

Ramesses crossed his arms and scowled at him but said nothing. He remained there.

Neiko shifted her eyes between the pair. "What was that all about?" asked Neiko.

"Nothing," Sito replied, shaking his head. "He wants you to be speaking pretty well in two weeks which I can't guarantee. He doesn't know you are smart and a fast learner on language."

Sito and Neiko kept talking, but Ramesses watched them closely. Sito took Neiko on a tour of the palace while Ramesses followed close behind.

Later that evening Neiko was taken to her room, and she went to sleep.

– **CHAPTER 16** –

TITO AND THE OTHERS walked down the streets of Thebes on their way to Pharaoh's palace to make an appeal for their stay there. Out of nowhere Francesco appeared a few feet away. "Where do you think you're going?" asked Mactalon in English. They only spoke Egyptian to the Egyptians. "Where did you come from all of a sudden? We've been looking for you!"

Francesco looked at them coldly with his blue eyes glittering in a shrewd smile. He didn't respond to Mactalon's questions. "I'm on my way to the palace. Where's Neiko? Oh yeah, yesterday was the day, wasn't it?"

Tito smiled cannily. "Yep, her time ran out. We're on our way to the palace, too."

Francesco's face darkened with disgust. "Oh no! Why did I have to bump into you—today of any day of the week?"

"We can travel as a group, I suppose," said Panthero.

"Very well, but I'll fix you and your twin brother with your little friends. Neiko is already taken care of," threatened Francesco.

"Oh yeah? We'll fix you first!" Tito retorted as he thrust his finger at him and poked his shoulder.

The group then remained silent until they reached the palace, but Francesco shot daggers at his companions, and they shot some at him. They sighed and went in, ready for what was to come. Things didn't look good for any of them, Francesco included. They remembered Ramesses didn't like any of them. Ramesses was sitting on his throne speaking with several advisors and Imenhotep, the high priest.

In the middle of his conversation with Imenhotep, Ramesses saw the four of them coming, and he became extremely exasperated as he squirmed in his throne as though someone had put fire ants in his kilt. "What do you want?" he asked moodily.

"We have come to make an offer," said Tito.

"For what?" Ramesses asked.

"We..." Mactalon started to say, but Tito elbowed him the ribs.

"Let me do the talking," Tito cut in.

"Tito!" Sito exclaimed, interrupting the conversation and dashing out of a hallway with Neiko on his heels. The twins hugged each other tightly, and Mactalon, Panthero, and Neiko joined in to one large group hug.

"At last we are together again, brother!" said Sito.

"Yes, and we are the five-some again! It has been eleven years!" Tito cried.

While the Indians were enjoying their reunion, Francesco stood away, looking at them mockingly.

Ramesses studied the occurrence carefully.

Nefertari walked in and saw the five embracing each other; she looked at them shocked.

"Ramesses, let me introduce everyone," said Sito. "This is Mactalon and Panthero, who are my friends, and here is my twin brother Tito, and, of course, Neiko. This is Francesco, a Crackedskull."

"I have met them already. A Crackedskull you say? Ah yes—Crackedskulls—I recall you are enemies from what I have heard," Ramesses said with a knowledgeable nod.

"We are Indians as I mentioned to you before a long time ago. Neiko, Tito, and I are Desert Storm Falcons, Mactalon is a Scraah Wareagle, and Panthero is Chang Battlehawk. We are members of the Seven Tribes allegiance of Hawote," Sito stated.

"I have heard you speak of your Seven Tribes already. Who is your king? I know Raven is the king of the Crackedskulls, but what about the Indians?" asked Ramesses as he pointed at the other Indians.

"We don't have a king. We worship Great Spirit, or we also call him God. His rules are the laws of our nation, and we have relational rules between tribes. We have chiefs and chieftains that lead the defense and well-being of every other Indian, and the Seven Tribes are the main warrior forces. That's only a small part of the vast land," commented Sito.

"What nonsense! What kind of a place is that? How does anything work there?" asked Ramesses as he shook his head.

"Each tribe is responsible for their people, and we are all brothers and sisters in a way. All of us get along unlike we used to," continued Sito.

"This is ridiculous! Do you have war?" asked Ramesses

"All the time. We fight against Raven because he wants to sack all of Hawote into absolute rule and make all Indians his slaves. We will never have a mortal king because all kings are tyrants, and we hate tyrants!" Sito said firmly.

"Impossible! No such place could possibly exist!" Ramesses snapped, standing up. "You are making this up—you have always talked about a fantasy world."

"I'm sorry to say everything is true," said Francesco, cutting in. "Raven and the Crackedskulls will change that very soon and make it into a more organized place."

"Whatever you just said, I don't think so!" Neiko shouted.

"How dare you!" Francesco snapped.

"You need to pipe down, you pin-headed geek!" shouted Mactalon.

"You know, Francesco, you are an embarrassment to the Crackedskulls, you weenie!" Tito shouted.

"Oh, you will pay for that with your life, Indian scum!" retorted Francesco.

"Your mama!" Mactalon shouted.

"You know what? You are so far over your head in Raven's stuff that I can't figure out how you can still see what's happening!" said Neiko.

"I'll teach you real suffering, you little witch!" Francesco shouted.

Since all this was in English, Ramesses couldn't understand what was said, but he could see the hostility break loose. "Sito, translate!"

"Little witch! At least I ain't Raven's talon-kisser!" Neiko retorted. She was referring to Raven's huge eagle-like feet.

"You sack of belly button lint!" Panthero hurled.

"You Indian dogs! Savages!" Francesco shouted in his defense.

"In your face, camel cake!" said Mactalon.

"In your ear, cow derriere!" Neiko retorted.

"Francesco, you are a belligerent old fart and a steaming pile of horse dung!" Mactalon shouted. "You are so mean that you give even savages a bad name! We ain't savages—you are!"

Suddenly everyone started shouting and talking at once—four Indians against one Crackedskull. The name-calling and argument got worse, and Sito couldn't keep up. He became so angry he joined in the heated dispute. For a moment everyone had forgotten why they were even there.

Ramesses became lost, and he began to get annoyed with the quarreling foreigners. "Silence!" he shouted in aggravation and rage.

The six stopped in mid-sentence and looked at him in shock. "Are you here to bicker in my presence? If so, leave and take your argument elsewhere. Sito, you are free to leave if you wish. If so, I can find her another teacher."

"Does that mean Neiko is free to leave, too?" Sito asked.

"No. She stays here," Ramesses said, shaking his head.

Neiko stamped her foot angrily since she heard her name spoken and whatever was asked was turned down. She had learned the word "no" already.

"Then—I cannot leave," said Sito.

"Fine," Ramesses said, annoyed.

"The rest of us want to stay here with my brother and Neiko, and we will gladly work as compensation. All of us are a family," said Tito.

"What shall you do? I have no tasks available for the lot of you," Ramesses said, hoping to ditch them.

"They can help me," Nefertari said, stepping forward. "They can be my servants; I can never have enough."

"This will be a great opportunity for you to learn of this Hawote and the other information that you seek if you let them stay. You can be rid of them when you choose and use them to get closer to her—just like you planned," Imenhotep whispered in his ear.

"Very well. Well, Francesco, do you have a request?" asked Ramesses, fanning his hand.

"Yes. I want to stay, too, but I'd rather serve you in any way I can," Francesco said.

Ramesses rubbed his chin. "Hmm, I am in need of a scribe, and you'll seem to do nicely. Sito, you will continue to tutor Neiko in learning our language. The rest of you will begin your duties tomorrow, so make yourselves at home to some extent—but don't touch anything or cause trouble! Do what you need to do to be ready. That is all."

Francesco walked off and went to find a room while the Indians walked out to the garden to talk; Nefertari was right on their heels. Once they got outside, they talked about everything, including their victory in moving in and catching up.

"One thing I need to bring up—I don't think he'll let us remain here long—my guess is that he'll get rid of us shortly after the marriage ceremony, feast, and jubilee, so we have to get that crystal ASAP. Ramesses has a *very* short clock, and it's ticking. All six of us need to leave. That's right—we have to take Francesco with us. We can throw his butt in jail once we get back," said Sito. "With all this we have on him, he'll go away a long time."

"Aww, I was hoping to leave him here, or I could go tell Raven what he's been up to," Neiko said.

"Neiko, I know you have a lot of animosity toward him, but we don't need to leave any traces of us being here—not a good idea. Just think about what he could screw up if he stayed behind."

"Right—I know. I know. It would be good for a little payback," said Neiko, deflated.

"Yes, I agree with you, but we need to be objective here," Sito said.

"Sito, may I join you?" asked Nefertari.

"Yes, of course," Sito said.

Nefertari looked at Neiko and smiled. "Is this the Neiko you talked so much about?"

Sito nodded silently.

"It is such an honor to finally get to meet her, and I'm glad to meet your brother and your two friends," Nefertari said, beaming and clasping her hands together in excitement.

"Why yes, it is. You have never mentioned that to Ramesses, have you? The things I told you not to mention, still don't. Otherwise everything will get nasty real fast," cautioned Sito.

"All right, I won't, but it may be very possible he already knows," Nefertari said with a concerned look. "It seems like he knows something's afoot, and he is not so easily fooled on certain things. You should know by now that he can be very perceptive when he wants to be."

Neiko looked at her as she bit her lip. "I hope what she said was good."

"It is. I've been telling her about you. Don't worry, she hasn't mentioned a word to Ramesses, and she won't say anything," coaxed Sito.

"Phew! I'm glad she's a friend!" Neiko said. "Told her what exactly?"

Sito shrugged and avoided the question.

The group stayed in the garden till the evening. Everyone got caught up, and Nefertari got to know the rest of them.

Everyone went to bed early that night.

- CHAPTER 17 -

ONE WEEK PASSED AND everyone had grown accustomed to his or her new lives at the palace—well sort of. Neiko's other three friends worked diligently in whatever work detail was available in the palace and gardens. Francesco did well as royal scribe and won brownie points along the way. Neiko, in contrast, had no chores. She did absolutely nothing except learn her new language with Sito's mentoring.

The first day Neiko learned basic words like cat, dog, bird, sun, crocodile, hippo, fish, please, and phrases like I want, I need, I love you. The next day she learned more words and phrases and a bit more about how to ask for things and table etiquette and some court etiquette—things important for a new queen to know. As the week progressed, he expounded on her vocabulary and reviewed others. Neiko also wanted to learn how to write and read in hieroglyphics. Even though most women didn't learn this, Sito felt it was a good idea, and it would help Neiko learn the language much better.

On the third day of teaching, Pharaoh demanded an evening with her. He was going to see how well she was progressing and test whether Sito's teaching was up to his expectations. The main reason for his request, however, was to begin courtship even if it was small talk and simple conversation. Much to his distaste, Sito had to be present.

During one of her daily language lessons after the first week, she decided to ask Sito some questions. "Sito, I've been wondering—why am I here? I mean, I don't have any duties, and I just do—whatever. I tried to sweep the floor, and Ramesses—or Pharaoh—whatever you wanna call him—personally took the broom away from me! It makes no sense," Neiko said, shrugging. "He hasn't said a word about it!"

Sito bit his lip and shrugged, acting nonchalant. "I know. I've been wondering the same thing. I know that he hasn't said a word of your cause in being here—maybe he's waiting for the appropriate time. Let's just continue with your lesson, shall we? You are doing very well, and you will be speaking proficiently in about another month or so," said Sito.

"Thanks, at least I'm good for something around here," Neiko muttered, and they continued with the lesson.

y

Francesco approached the royal platform, and he knelt. "You called, my king?"

"Yes—about a personal matter, but it is very important to me. You seem to have the answers I want, and you are the only one who will answer me—Sito thinks he can keep secrets from me and eludes my questions; I have ways of finding out what I want to know," he said, jabbing his finger into the elaborately carved, gold armrest of this throne. "I want to know everything about this Hawote and of Neiko's importance in it—in doing so, I will grant you higher favor. Sito seems to stress she is so important—is she the Neiko who is the 'warrior child'? What do the rest of them do?" asked Ramesses as he stood up.

Francesco looked at him with raised eyebrows, puzzled at Pharaoh's knowledge. He must have learned a lot from Sito, and Pharaoh's questions and remarks piqued his interest. "Well, Sito specifically said everything about Hawote itself from what you told me yesterday—except about it coexisting with a place called Georgia—it is woodlands that are owned by Indians and Crackedskulls. Neiko—she has a lot of importance because she is the Liberator who leads the Indians' opposition against King Raven. Yes, she is the warrior child—also known as the 'Chosen One'. I'll tell you more about her background since I don't know what you do know. Anyway, she was only a child when she began fighting—she began warrior training when she was six, and at eight years old, she was on the battlefield. She became Captain of the Falcon forces when she was nine years of age. She freed what are the Seven Tribes when she was ten. She is the superior officer of the Falcons, and three years ago she became Admiral—the only one in history. Captain was the top rank for thousands of years. Sigma, the Scraah chief, let the entire land vote on it. They wanted to elect her as the first Admiral. Not only that, every Indian looks up to her—she is the heroine of all time, and she is distinguished. You personally witnessed her skill. And above all, Raven's son, Bloodhawk, desires her. He has tried countless times to seize her on the battlefield so he can take her hand in marriage, but she fights him and escapes his grasp all the time. He has never managed to capture her but once, and he did it personally when she mysteriously disappeared and then returned—it's still unexplained. She was alone, but she escaped somehow. She has beauty to go with her brains and strength so she can be quite dangerous especially if she is feeling threatened or trapped. Those other four are just followers and comrades of Neiko. Sito used to be the inventor, and his brother lent a hand. So that is all."

Ramesses' eyes sparkled as he pondered, trying to piece together and align this information along with the information he had secretly acquired from Sito years ago. He smiled shrewdly since he now knew what he wanted to know. "Interesting. The warrior child is now a woman. So, is she a princess?"

"No. Well, ninety-eight percent of Indian tribes have no kings, so there are no princesses. She does come from a lineage of great chiefs. King Raven wants Neiko to be his son's wife—that is—if he ever acquired her. If the Liberator was by his side and out of battle, then the war would end. She would never accept his proposal—she is as stubborn as she is beautiful. It is also rumored she is in love with someone in Hawote, but no one knows whom," Francesco added.

"Well, that is quite remarkable. There is nothing like it in the known world—anywhere," said Ramesses. "She not being a princess is of no consequence to me," he added, pressing his fingertips together in a rhythm as he reclined in his chair.

"Well, look at it this way—there has never been anything like it in Hawote either. So why is this important?" asked Francesco.

"I have my reasons—I wanted to know if she was 'the one', but I believed you have sealed the case. I also have news I want you alone to know. I have chosen another queen to sit beside me, and I will address her later," he said, smiling. "If certain things are met, she will be my Great Wife."

Francesco's mouth gaped. He knew Nefertari was supposed to be his Great Wife until she died in a few short years. "You are extremely happy about it, aren't you? What do you mean by 'the one'? Who is it—if you don't mind me asking. I am curious, and I may even help you find her and get her if you'd like," Francesco said.

Ramesses smiled. "That may not be necessary," he said and paused. "I won't answer your questions now because I want to surprise everyone—and I have a few loose ends to tie up and a few other unanswered questions I must find the answers to. But, I will say the ceremony of our uniting will be in three weeks," Ramesses said, dancing around before he sat back in his throne. His hand went to the large jade scarab amulet that sat heavily on his chest. "I can't tell you about 'the one'—that is very private information. Not even Nefertari knows about 'the one'. I will tell 'the one' once I find her and at the appropriate time—if she isn't here already."

Francesco looked at him, with a raised eyebrow and a crooked grin. "She must really be something. And do you know if she likes you back? Good luck in finding 'the one'."

"No, but it doesn't matter. She will be easy to get, and she can't say no. Once I choose someone inferior to me, they cannot stop it. I speak, and it comes to be," Ramesses said emphatically.

"What do you mean easy to get? Would her parents protest? What do you mean by inferior? I'm so curious!" Francesco said, rambling in his own curiosity.

"Don't worry—you will find out soon enough. And her parents are of no concern," Ramesses said. "I think they are not even worried in this situation whatsoever," he added elusively.

"You are so sure about it, aren't you?" mused Francesco.

"Of course. One word is all I need. I presume things weren't this way in Hawote, am I not right?" asked Ramesses.

"You are absolutely right. People court for years before they marry, and both have to love each other and agree. The man proposes to the woman, and if she says no, it's over. Of course there are men who will try to pursue a girl till they agree to be courted!" Francesco replied.

Ramesses shook his head. "This is madness! I cannot see how anything works in this place. It is a nightmare given by the god Set himself! They do take marriage seriously. And how many wives can you have?"

"One—at one time you could have more depending on where you were from," commented Francesco.

Ramesses' mouth fell open. "This place is ludicrous. I plan to have many. I will have my favorites, and Nefertari is one of my favorites."

"She is your only wife at the moment," Francesco corrected.

"Not for long. I like this other I have chosen very much, and I feel she will be another favorite from what I hear and see," Ramesses said.

"Do you know a lot about her? How do you know her?" asked Francesco, pressing him. Francesco pretty much had the whole thing figured out. He knew so much about Ramesses that he could read him like a book.

"I know much, and I see her once in a while in the passing," Ramesses said, and they heard voices coming their way.

"Sito, this guy at the party named Sut drove me crazy, and Tito punched him in the nose," said Neiko in Egyptian. "How was that?" she asked.

"Very good," Sito replied in the same language. "We will have little or no English or any Indian languages since you know enough now. You need the practice—Pharaoh has us on a tight deadline."

"Okay, but I think we took a wrong turn," Neiko said, looking at the two as they looked at them.

"I agree. Let's go to the garden and meet the guys. I think they said we were going swimming today in the river," said Sito.

"All right! Let's get moving!" Neiko said, as she ran toward the garden, with Sito right behind her. "Can we go wrestle some crocs, too?" she added.

"Maybe…I don't know why you and the guys want to do that—that's dangerous!" Sito scolded.

"They're just bigger alligators," Neiko interjected as their voices trailed off from the two listeners. Then a door closed.

"What was that all about? I can see Sito is teaching her well," Francesco replied.

"Yes," said Ramesses, smirking at her. "Mention nothing of this to any of them, but you can say something about me choosing another wife."

Francesco nodded. "All right, but does Nefertari know?"

"Yes, and she is as curious as you are since I have spoken so little about it to anyone," Ramesses said.

Francesco tried to read between the lines and made a conclusion to see if his presumptions were correct. "I must be going. I have that tablet to read, and some loose ends to tie up," he said, and Ramesses nodded, allowing him to leave. Francesco went after the pair of mischievous Indians.

– CHAPTER 18 –

LATER THAT NIGHT, THE five returned from their dip in the Nile and came in making a lot of noise. They were sharing about their feats with the crocodiles. Francesco was leaning on the wall, smiling shrewdly at them.

Seeing this, Mactalon had something snide to say. "What are you so happy about?"

"I know something you don't know!" Francesco sang and danced jeeringly.

"Oh, what's that—you finally realized you don't have a brain?" asked Neiko.

Francesco smiled at her smugly with a self satisfied and shrewd smile. "No, I know of someone who's in *love*."

Sito looked at him coldly. "Oh, do you mean you finally found a girl you like? How nice. Is she a lanky dork with a big ego to match yours?"

He chuckled at him. "No, I'm afraid you're wrong. Pharaoh has chosen someone to be his second wife, and I can tell he *adores* her."

"Who is this unlucky victim?" asked Neiko, tossing her arm with a look that she could care less.

"Yeah, who would want to agree to be united with a conceited jerk like him?" asked Tito disdainfully.

Francesco laughed at them. "You better be glad he didn't hear that, Tito. He would have you beaten and mauled. He didn't mention her name, but I think I know who she is. She cannot object because she is inferior to him."

Neiko cocked an eyebrow. "Inferior to him? Well, that's the whole doggoned country for that matter—I think he felt his mother was inferior to him. That ain't much to go on, know-it-all."

Francesco laughed at her until his side ached. "You are so blind to the situation that it's hilarious! Do you not see it?"

Neiko shrugged. "Oh puh-lease! See what? If she says yes, that's her choice, and I wish her a long, happy life. Second of all, there's no way the girl all the hullabaloo is about is me—he likes me a little bit—maybe, and I'll just be some lowly secondary wife at best. I'll be below Nefertari, not above her. Furthermore, I wouldn't be caught dead near that conceited tyrant if I was her. I really hope that girl knows what she's getting herself into," said Neiko. "Why should I care? This doesn't involve me anyway! Even if it was, he can count me out!"

Francesco laughed even harder. "Like I said before, the girl has no choice. She can protest all she wants, but it will not change a thing. I think *he* decides who goes where. Neiko, Egypt is very different from Hawote in many ways, including women having no rights in choosing their husband. If a god-king picks her, then do you think she stands a chance? I don't think so. You have so much to learn."

Neiko shrugged indifferently. "Yeah. She can ditch the sucker by skipping town! If you can't do it by any other means, then run away—it's not that hard. Besides, I don't think he would waste time looking for that one chick while there are plenty of others who would love to be picked. I'm not gonna be here long enough to care about all the laws and rules here…I'm just passin' though."

Francesco sniggered at her. "If you say so. But, you are wrong about a lot of things. That is true about many, but this particular one—if she ran away—he would tear the world apart trying to find her. I believe he would make sure that she can't leave. He is not a pushover by any means. I don't believe she would make it far because he would know how to cut her off. And, how could a girl outwit Ramesses the Great in his own domain and on the battlefield?"

Neiko stretched her arms. "Oh, it couldn't be that hard. He would be easy to dupe because he is so blinded by pride and probably lovesickness that he wouldn't know what hit him. He could be a challenge if he wanted to be. What makes you such an expert on him anyway? Are you now his personal shrink?"

Francesco sneered. "A woman outfoxing him on the battlefield? Ha! You're dreaming! Let me share with you something I studied. He is also an early warrior—at the age of eight—and one of the greatest military leaders who ever lived. I don't believe any girl could outsmart him single-handedly while he has soldiers backing him up, and he is a worthy opponent himself."

Sito put his hand on her shoulder. "He's right, Neiko. I know the exact same thing—Seti told me about it."

"Good for him!" Neiko said with a sarcastic expression on her face and having both thumbs up. "Who cares? I don't have to worry about that Great Wife stuff because that's some other chick—I won't be around long enough *to* care. Saves me the trouble of making him eat a stick. I'm the last person on earth he would want for a Great Wife, and he wouldn't miss me if I left. Well, guys, I'm going to bed," Neiko said, stretching and beginning to walk off.

Francesco smiled at her cleverly, but no one caught it.

"Wait, you mean you won't stick around for the belching contest?" asked Mactalon, stopping her.

"Well, maybe I'll stay up a little longer," Neiko said.

Francesco swaggered off to find Ramesses.

"We will go into the dining hall, and we only have water to drink, so this will make it a challenge," Sito said. Everyone went into the hall and sat down. Sito brought out a jar of water and five golden goblets.

"Who goes first?" asked Neiko as she poured the water.

"I will," Tito volunteered. Then he drank the water in one gulp, waited, and finally burped. Everyone went in turn, and the two finalists were Neiko and Mactalon.

"Okay, let's have a showdown. These two have had the loudest, and we now must have the longest," Tito said.

Mactalon drank the water, and his burp lasted for two seconds, but Neiko had one that lasted for ten, and she was the winner. "Neiko! You are a champion belcher."

"I know, but just think what it would be like if I drank cola," Neiko said, chuckling. They burst out laughing, but it was cut short because the doors slammed against the wall, and they jumped. Ramesses stood in the doorway with his arms folded over his bare chest; he was not happy.

"What is this?" Ramesses snapped angrily as he entered the room.

"It's a private party. Please go away," Neiko retorted in Egyptian. "No Egyptians or Pharaohs allowed."

Ramesses' narrowed eyes pouted in a hot-tempered manner. The vessels in his neck were showing, and the muscles in his jaw were twitching in his fury at her smart aleck retort that he was unwelcome. "Where have you been?" Ramesses asked, putting his hands on his hips and looking at her sternly. "I have been looking for you all day!"

Neiko looked at him like "who me?" and "why?" and cocked her eyebrow like he had gone nuts. "I went for a swim in the Nile with my friends. Is there a problem?" Neiko asked with a look that could peel the paint off a battleship and flicking her hand like a wet cat would flick its tail.

"You didn't bother to tell me where you were going, and you were gone for an entire day! You had me worried because you could have been eaten by crocodiles or mauled by hippos," Ramesses said, thrusting his finger at her like a scolding parent.

Neiko grunted like a stubborn teenager. "So? I can take care of myself. I'm not a wimp, and you're not my keeper or my babysitter! You are certainly not my father, so stop acting like it, would ya? Besides, you were busy!" Neiko said, slamming her fist on the table in rage. "And furthermore, we were wrestling *with* the crocodiles…"

Ramesses interrupted her. "You could have taken the time. You will tell me where you are going, and you will ask for my approval. Understand?" Ramesses dictated. Neiko's last statement took a moment to sink in. Such a thing was unheard of. "You what?" he asked like she had just said she had jumped off a cliff.

Neiko looked at him as though he were mad. "What? I'm twenty-one years old, and I'm not a baby! I've dealt with things a lot worse and scarier than crocodiles or hippos!" she snapped, looking at him hotly. "I don't take orders from anybody! Don't you tell me what to do!" she screamed as she shook her fists and stamped her feet. "We wrestle with…uh…er alligators at home!" She said 'alligators' in English; there were no alligators in Egypt so there was no word for them. Noticing his confused look Neiko said, "Alligators are animals that live in Hawote that are a lot like crocodiles."

Ramesses was miffed and snorted. "You will not take that tone with me! I care for your well-being, and I make rules to keep you safe. You *will* obey! Is that so hard to understand? You *won't* be wresting with crocodiles again, do I make myself clear?"

Neiko threw her hands up in aggravation. "Since when do you care? I don't have to do anything you say. I don't have to listen to you, and I can do what I darn well please! You may rule Egypt, but you don't rule me!"

"Soften your tone and watch your words—you are speaking to a god-king!" Francesco reminded harshly as he walked up and stood beside him. "Haven't you forgotten something? You are in Egypt and under his authority—he has absolute authority here. Must I remind you Hawote's laws and ways of doing things do not apply here?"

Neiko narrowed her eyes at him. "I don't care! He's not *my* king! I answer to *no* king! And—oh, look at Pharaoh's little lapdog, and ain't he ugly—just a weenie dog on a leash," she scowled indignantly. "Shut your mouth and stay out of it, lackey!" Neiko made sure she learned that word.

Francesco gritted his teeth in anger. "You just wait—Ramesses will fix you!"

"Yeah right. I won't be around long enough because I'll be at home doing my duties. I'm just passin' through." Neiko waved her hand in a carefree manner.

"You will not be going anywhere," decreed Ramesses as he thrust his finger at her again.

"Says who?" Neiko asked, folding her arms, with her eyes blazing.

"I say so, and I have spoken. If I must, then I will enforce my rules and make certain they are obeyed; you will obey *me* after I finish," Ramesses said, waving his hand haughtily, and he turned and left with Francesco on his heels.

Neiko shot them cold daggers and stuck her tongue out at him as she stomped her feet angrily and shook her fists. "And stay out!" she called after them.

Sito and Tito came to calm their angry friend. "Neiko, you need to be careful. I would hate for him to demonstrate his power in some way by either restricting your freedom even more than it already is, or we could pay the price of your defiance."

"I'm sorry. I got carried away, but he made me so mad. I hate guys with big egos, and he is acting like my babysitter—it's getting on my nerves," Neiko said, huffing in fury.

"I wonder why he is so anxious to show so much concern in your affairs. He's been doing that more than usual here lately," mused Sito. "I didn't think it would get *this* bad."

Neiko shrugged. "I don't know, but I'm gonna find out."

"I think we all will pretty soon," rejoined Sito in a soft whisper.

"Let's go to bed," said Tito, yawning.

- Chapter 19 -

"I NEED TO TALK TO YOU," Francesco said as Ramesses sat down and rubbed his eyes. He had followed him into the vacant throneroom.

"I wish neither to talk nor counsel. Leave me," Ramesses said as he rubbed his eyes in frustration as he sat on his throne. When the court was empty, he came here to think.

"It's about Neiko," piped up Francesco

Ramesses perked up. "What about her?" he asked with a flat tone.

Francesco smiled. "I know you are in love with Neiko; I also know she is 'the one'. I wanted to tell you that I figured it all out and about some things she said earlier this afternoon."

Ramesses looked at him mystified. "How did you figure all this out? How do you know that she is the one? You must say nothing about this! This is a secret I have harbored a long time. Not even Nefertari knows about this!" he reminded with secretive motions.

Francesco bowed. "Agreed. Figuring it out was simple. I am very good at analyzing situations and people. I can see how much you care. Neiko has no idea you are in love with her, and she certainly don't know about the other thing and what awaits her—including becoming your Great Wife—not just your wife."

"How would you know?" asked Ramesses with cynical expression and a snort.

"I know her very well, and I spoke with her earlier today," Francesco said, and he told him everything that was said that afternoon.

"Is that so—she thinks it is someone else entirely? And did she say that about her being the last I would choose for my Great Wife and that she will not have anything to do with me?" Ramesses asked.

"That's right, and she will be in for a big surprise. She will be in shock at first and *will* fight you—that I can guarantee a hundred percent. You have to show her who's boss. I believe you will be able to handle her if you are going to invest in it for the long haul. She will be totally yours if you can ever get her to cave in, and that's the hard part since she is wild, iron willed, and will not be caged. The key is finding a weakness and hitting it hard, and at the same time showing her that there is no escape."

"Hmmm, she is like a diamond, but all have a weakness, and when it is struck it shatters," Ramesses mused. "I already know about the other—I have been long prepared."

Francesco smiled. "Precisely. You find the weak spot, and she will shatter into your hands—that is the key in winning her. Although, I do know this—it will be easy for her to agree to marry you, but the rest will be very hard. To what extent do you want her to commit herself to you?"

"Fully—in mind, body, heart, and spirit. The wedding is only the beginning—as you already know," said Ramesses. "I want a real, worthwhile relationship with her; she is not merely a one night fling—never was. As you said, I am investing in it for the long haul."

Francesco winced. "You have your work cut out for you, but I know you can do it. However whatever preparations you have may go out the window. You can't prepare for Neiko."

"I will not stop until I win her completely. You seem so uncaring to what befalls her or her friends," said Ramesses offhandedly. "You are wrong about me not being able to prepare for her resistance properly—it is merely a game of strategy that I excel at. How do you think I win battle after battle? This is merely a battle without weapons that I *will* win. I won't back down; I won't be defeated. I will break through her defenses, and how ever long it takes is no consequence to me; she won't be going anywhere any time soon—I'll make certain of that. I will conquer her and take all, and she will be mine for all eternity."

Francesco shrugged then smiled devilishly. "They never liked me anyway. I think she is better off with you than in Hawote. I will gladly assist you in your endeavors."

Ramesses smiled. "Thank you. You are so much different from any of those others you speak of—any of them at all."

"I know. That is why I left," Francesco said with a good-natured smile. *I will also make sure Neiko never returns to Hawote and spends the rest of her miserable life with him. I could do without the romance though—it's so disgusting!* Francesco thought with his stomach feeling queasy and a sickened look on his face.

The next day, the Indians went out into the garden to sharpen their fighting skills. Neiko was the instructor, and she started out with weapon exercises. They did them with staves that they broke off of the trees in the garden. Sito held the stick and tried to remember how to use it. "It has been a long time since I held a weapon; I hope I can still fight."

"That's why we're doing this. We're can polish our skills. I want to keep our skills sharp just in case we need them," said Neiko.

"Yes, and we are going to make sure you get your technique back," added Tito.

"All right, we will start with staff and spear. You will need to pretend your staff is a spear since Pharaoh will not allow us to use them, and we can't do any type of slings or bows and arrows. Follow my lead," Neiko said, practicing swings, lunges, and spins until they had clean, quick movements.

"Now, we will practice tree climbing. We will climb every tree in the garden that is climbable, and there are a few that will be a challenge. Then we will climb that tree over there. We will have several laps on the wall for balance, and take a long staff with you so no one will fall. After that, we will have a few duels with short staffs. Try not to hit too hard, because this is not a battle. You can also do a few sword duels with your staves if you wish. I will lead and join you," Neiko said, and they began the itinerary.

Upon hearing the claps of staves, Ramesses and Francesco decided to investigate. They saw the Indians in their duels. Each of them was moving with lightning speed with Neiko giving tips, waving her staff, and demonstrating other movements.

"What are they doing?" asked Ramesses.

Francesco rolled his eyes. "Warrior training. I remember those days vividly."

Ramesses gave a curious look like he couldn't place Francesco in warrior training. "That was when you were spying for Raven, correct?"

Francesco nodded. "Yes, and I had to do everything an Indian chieftain had to do, and I know little of fighting. I do have the ability to fight, but I cannot teach, because I only know a delicate form and not hard-core Indian fighting—it is not good against spears, tomahawks, and such."

"Then what is it good for?" asked Ramesses.

"It is good in sword fighting, but I barely have time to practice because I'm busy man in Hawote. However, I enjoy my work—I exercise my brain while the Indians flex their muscles and plan strategic moves for battle. They have no form of culture, and they do not have a mind to concoct what I can. Crackedskulls are just as bad as Indians in that they want to solve everything in violence, and Bloodhawk is a very good example—he wants to solve everything by smashing it with his huge fist or digging his claws or talons in it. He constantly wants to kill someone for the least little thing, and I was always threatened by him. I didn't think much of it. His father was never that way. Raven says it will get worse as he gets older, but he also says Bloodhawk will be a great king, and the Indians will fear him. I would too if I had to face a bloodthirsty giant," replied Francesco.

"Is he really that large in stature? How can you kill him?" asked Ramesses with his eyes full of curiosity.

"Easy. Bloodhawk is all brawn and little brains, and he will fall to my amazing brainpower—that's how," said Francesco, poking out his narrow chest.

Ramesses chuckled at him. "You are so sure about that? If he caught you, he would crush you like a bug, and your brain could not save you."

"That's why I plan things fully, and I won't be returning there in the near future because I have a death curse over my head. The Indians want to run me through because of my service to Raven, and Bloodhawk and Raven both have a death threat over other matters. That's why I left, and I really don't want to return until later. You are the only person that has appreciated me for my work, and I greatly thank you," said Francesco.

"You have served me well, and you are doing extra for me— why is that?" asked Ramesses as he pursed his lips and looked at him with a discerning look.

Francesco smiled sheepishly. "That is because I heard of your fame from as far as Hawote and felt it was a great opportunity for my career. I will gladly do more."

"That is not necessary, but I thank you for offering," said Ramesses.

"All right, men, another twenty on the wall!" said Neiko, and they climbed the tree and jogged on the top of the wall.

"What are they doing now?" asked Ramesses, and then he saw Neiko on the top of the wall. "Egad! She will fall! Get her down!"

Francesco shrugged. "Balance exercise. She has been on things much more difficult."

"I do not care. Get down, all of you!" Ramesses thundered at them.

"Okay, training's over for today," Neiko said.

"Aww, what else can we do?" asked Tito.

Neiko looked at Francesco shrewdly. "How 'bout a little target practice? See target? Ammo—old fruit. Come back tonight when he's outside writing."

The five-some looked at Francesco and giggled with mischievous looks in their eyes. "What will we do till then? Nefertari said we were off for today," wondered Sito.

"I know! Let's play games. Like baseball, volleyball, kickball, maybe a little football, and perhaps soccer," said Tito.

"Okay, I can live with that," Neiko replied.

"I made a football, soccer ball, and a volleyball in my spare time. Let me go get them," said Sito.

They looked at him puzzled.

"You did?" asked Neiko stopping him.

"Yes, I've had a lot of free time on my hands, and I have made a lot of other things, including a baseball bat and four mitts, but we don't have enough people to play a game. We have no bases."

"We can just bat, and each person has three outs apiece. We have two outfielders and a catcher. When you have your three outs, then it's another person's turn. We won't keep score on any of the games," suggested Mactalon.

"Okay, I will get the equipment," said Sito, and he ran inside.

- CHAPTER 20 -

AFTER THE SUN SET, the Indians waited for their opportunity to pull off their prank on Francesco. They had plenty of rotten fruit. They spotted Francesco on the patio, writing, while they were hiding in the bushes.

"Move in," whispered Mactalon as they quietly snuck closer.

"Fire!" shouted Neiko, and they threw all the fruit they had at Francesco. He became covered in smelly, gooey juice and fermented insides. Mactalon came up with an overripe melon and spiked it on his head, and he became bathed in the juice and the fleshy inside. His papyrus was messed up, and he was covered in rancid fruit.

"Argh! My paper is ruined, and I'm filthy! You just wait!" Francesco snapped as he stood up.

The Indians laughed at Francesco as he stormed into the palace. They followed him laughing so hard that their sides hurt.

"What's the matter—need a bath?" asked Sito, as the Indians dragged the filthy Crackedskull outside and threw him into the lotus pool. The water was cold; his teeth started chattering, and his lips turned purple. Each Indian gave the other a high-five and went inside the palace.

Francesco got out, clutching himself, and wringing out his clothes. As he walked inside, Ramesses and Nefertari met him.

Upon seeing him, Nefertari cupped her hand over her mouth and giggled. "What happened to you?" she asked in between chuckles.

Ramesses pinched his nose at the horrible odor. "What is going on here? Did you know my lotus pools are *not* for swimming?" he asked, as he pulled off a leaf from Francesco's collar.

"Five Indians thought it was funny to throw rotten fruit on me and throw me into the lotus pool. The paper you wanted me to do was ruined, so it will be completed later than you wanted," he said with his teeth chattering.

Ramesses frowned. "Never mind. I have a few things to discuss with you. Do not worry about your clothes because you will have new ones. I will change a few things around here. Those five will be wearing their native attire no more. They will not be permitted to leave the palace or be let near any weapons of any kind, and they will not be using my trees for staves. You will convey this message tomorrow to them. And—oh, yes—there will be a dinner tomorrow night to tell them the news."

Francesco's eyes glittered. "Yes, but I know those five won't listen to me."

"If they don't, then tell me, and I will address them personally. They will obey my orders," Ramesses replied with a confident poking out of his chest.

The next day, the five Indians were sitting in a circle, telling stories as Francesco walked up to them, ready to deliver the message.

Sito looked up and saw Francesco in Egyptian attire. "What are *you* doing here?"

"I have orders from Pharaoh about you five, and there will be a few changes around here. First, you will dress like Egyptians. Second, you will not be permitted to leave these premises. And third, you will not have access to any type of weapons, and he doesn't like you ripping branches from the trees in his garden."

"Is that all?" Panthero retorted flatly.

"Yeah—you know—I love the skirt. It makes you look like the girl you really are!" Neiko punned.

Francesco looked at Neiko sourly with his hands on his hips. "I wouldn't be so smug about that if I were you because you won't be wearing that fancy Indian outfit anymore. Oh yes, there is a dinner tonight, and he expects you all to be there since he has very important news."

All of them laughed at him. "Yeah, right! You're just saying that because you want to try to pull a fast one on us. Go away," snapped Tito.

Francesco sneered. "Very well. I will just tell him you mocked him behind his back, and I'll let him deal with the lot of you."

"You do that, and we'll get you back," cautioned Mactalon, holding up his finger and waving it.

"I double-dog dare you to do it, and that'll give me a reason to beat you up," Neiko said.

Francesco threw up his hands innocently. "All right, have it your way," he said and then marched off to tell on them. He returned a few minutes later with Ramesses on his heels.

"Uh, oh. I think we're in trouble," said Neiko.

"You dare mock me behind my back? I suppose you prefer for me to address you personally—so be it. I want my commands followed to the letter, and you will change clothes now. Get up," Ramesses barked ruthlessly.

"Where do we get dressed?" asked Neiko.

"Come, I and a few of my maids will help you because your new attire is quite remarkable and very elegant," said Nefertari, taking her by the hand.

"Very nice of you to assist her, but don't tell her of our surprise," Ramesses said.

"Of course not. I'm very glad it's finished so she can try it on," Nefertari said, folding her hands and grinning.

"Try what on—what new clothes? What's this all about?" asked Neiko, scratching her head.

"Don't worry, you'll find out tonight," Nefertari said leading her off.

A few hours passed, and the four men waited to see Neiko.

"What is taking so long? How long does it take to change into a skirt, a head cloth, and no shirt? But in her case, she would be wearing a shirt," said Tito, rubbing his tawny, muscular chest, which was exposed. They were dressed in simple linen clothing.

A woman came into the room behind Nefertari, but no one could recognize her. "Hi, guys," she said, and it was Neiko.

Mactalon's mouth flew open. "Is that you, Neiko?

"Nefertari, what did you do to her?" asked Sito in shock.

"These are her new clothes. They were made specifically for her. What do you think?" Neferari asked.

Neiko was wearing a fine linen dress that shone like the rainbow and was covered in jewels complete with a jeweled collar. She had rings on her fingers including the turquoise one that Monchiska had given her. She wore gold bracelets and armlets that were encrusted with gemstones. She wore a large golden crown that was a vulture, and its wings wrapped around her face; it covered most of her head. Her hair was done in the traditional way and full of jewels, gold, and beads that clinked when she walked, and she wore traditional sandals of spun gold. She was dressed like an Egyptian queen, complete with outlined eyes. "Neiko, you're beautiful," said Tito in a whisper as he took in her breathtaking beauty.

Neiko tugged at her dress and her hair. "Guys, I feel like such a geek—
I look like Cleopatra. This is so uncomfortable—it feels like
Bloodhawk is standing on my head. And you think you feel stupid. This
is so awkward! I can't go to dinner looking like this!"

"Oh, you'll get used to it," said Nefertari.

Neiko looked at Nefertari like she was joking. "Huh? You mean
I have to wear this from now on? How am I supposed to fight in this?
No wonder women were such wusses in this time," Neiko grumbled.

"You are ready for dinner, and it will be in an hour. You will find out tonight."

"Goodie," said Neiko, scratching her collar. "All of these jewels are annoying."

They all went to the dinner hall to prepare for the dinner.

- CHAPTER 21 -

THE INDIANS SAT THERE at the dinner table for a while, and then Sito had an idea. "I know of something to spike up the evening. Be right back," he said. He returned with a whoopie cushion he had made. "We will find out where Francesco is sitting and embarrass the daylights out of him before the Pharaoh. Ramesses will think Francesco farted at the table which is not acceptable behavior here."

Everyone sniggered.

"Where is Francesco supposed to sit?" asked Mactalon to a servant.

"He will be sitting at the first seat next to the head on your side," replied the servant.

Sito inflated the cushion and put it in Francesco's seat. "Try not to laugh till he sits down," he said, and they started laughing.

Francesco entered the room, and they had to choke back

laughter. They were still sniggering and wiping their eyes from their tears of hilarity as Francesco approached the table.

"What are you laughing about? I find nothing amusing about this formal dinner. So stop laughing and stand up till Pharaoh arrives," Francesco snapped.

They stood up, while biting their lips, trying not to sabotage the prank. Ramesses came into the room with Nefertari, and the two of them sat down first. Then everyone else sat down including Francesco.

Pfft! said the cushion, and he had a look of shock on his face along with Ramesses. All of the Indians burst out laughing. They laughed so hard they were crying. Mactalon toppled over backward in his chair, and then they started laughing at him.

Ramesses was not amused. In fact, he was furious and aggravated. He folded his arms over his chest and looked at them sternly.

"Francesco, I think you really blew it this time," punned Mactalon as he wiped the tears from his eyes. "Brings back memories, don't it? How do you like that old practical joke from back home—a real blast from the past!"

Francesco pulled out the cushion and threw it at Mactalon since he was the prankster of the group as he glared at all of them. "All right, who did it?" he asked vehemently; they all pointed at each other.

"Enough, all of you! This is supposed to be a civilized dinner, not a zoo! Start acting like you are adults and not children because I have some very important news to share with you later," replied Ramesses crossly.

Everyone stopped, sat down, and tried to hold his or her animosity until the dinner was over; the Indians and the Crackedskull gave each other daggers as they ate.

"I want to run through that little—grrr," Mactalon muttered to Sito as he ripped a leg off of his roasted pheasant.

Thirty minutes passed, and Ramesses set down his goblet of wine, wiped his hands, and cleared his throat since he and everyone had finished their dinner. "Now, I wish to tell you why you are all here and why this occasion is so very important. You have heard that I have chosen another to sit beside me, and I have called you here to tell you who she is."

Everyone looked at each other in surprise, and then returned their looks to Pharaoh.

"Well, who is it? Why do you have to tell us anyway?" asked Neiko, fanning her hands in frustration. "It's not like it's any of our business."

Ramesses smiled at her, chuckling. "It is you."

Neiko's mouth fell open along with the other four Indians'. Cold fear gripped her stomach and churned it; this was not good, and it was everyone's worst fear. "I…I can't! I have a war to win, and I am no good to you. I'm not who you think I am. Will you please do me a favor and let me go? I promise I won't cause you anymore problems. I'll take everyone else with me, and we'll be gone. Please? I'm thankful of you taking care of us, but will you show me the door?" she rambled in her own shock.

"You are not going anywhere, my warrior," Ramesses said, standing up.

"You don't understand! I don't belong here! I'm not supposed to be with you—I'm not even supposed to know you outside of history class! I don't have time for this! I have important things to do at home! I need to go back to where I came from…" Neiko said.

Ramesses held up his hand and extended his first two fingers which meant to be silent.

"No! I will not be silent!" Neiko said, regaining her speech, standing up, and slamming her fists on the table in strong resistance. "You don't get it…"

Before Neiko could finish, Francesco chimed in. "He's not *asking* you whether or not you want to marry him—he's just stating the facts. Your opinion doesn't count! You will be joined to him in two weeks as you heard. There is nothing you can do or say to stop it. So be ready."

Neiko gave Francesco daggers covered in ice as she slumped back into her chair. Neiko slammed her head on the table and groaned. "I can't do this, and I won't. Guys, get me out of this!" she moaned.

"Neiko, there is nothing we can do," said Sito, and when she looked up, he winked, letting her know he was duping the pharaoh and promising that they will find a way out of the situation.

Neiko started rubbing her turquoise ring. *You gave me this for luck, and I need it right now, Monchiska,* she yelled in her mind.

Ramesses broke into her thoughts by saying, "Tomorrow we will start spending quality time together to get to know each other better—finally alone, and I want you to be ready at midday. Everyone is dismissed!"

All the Indians got up, muttering, but Neiko stormed out of the dining hall and headed for the garden. A door slammed and echoed in the hallways as she made her exit.

Sito looked after her as she disappeared in the hall.

"Oh man, she's really upset," said Tito shaking his head.

"Should we go after her?" asked Mactalon.

"No, I'll go and talk to her and see if I can cheer her up, but I must go alone. You go on to bed," replied Sito. "Besides, I have that secret she'd love to hear that the four of us have known for eleven years. It may be the thing to cheer her up."

"Okay, do it," said Panthero giving him thumbs-up.

The three went on to bed while Sito went to talk to Neiko.

Neiko was sitting on the steps, with her face buried in her hands, sobbing when she heard the footsteps behind her. "Pharaoh, if that's you, go away," she said curtly between sobs.

"Neiko, it's me, and I've come to talk to you," said Sito as he sat down beside her. "Why are you crying? It's not your style."

"Oh good. I was hoping you would come," Neiko said wiping her eyes. The kohl was smeared on her eyes and hands, and it looked as she had been beaten. "I'm just thinking about not seeing my family and friends again and Ramesses not caring," she said.

Sito bit his lip. "It's not that he doesn't care—it's just that he doesn't know, and it compromises his plans if he did know which he won't allow. His heart won't let him release you. I've been wondering, who's the guy you are in love with back home? It's been a secret ever since we were kids."

Neiko snorted. "What heart?" The she paused and gathered her thoughts to answer Sito's question. "It's Monchiska, but he doesn't love me back. He's still dating that snotty blonde, Rebecca Cunningham," Neiko said and then sniffled.

Sito chuckled. "Oh, he's got one—you'll see. Monchiska is still with that snotty blonde, huh? But he doesn't love her like you think. He is in love with someone else, but he thinks she doesn't love him back. He told me who she was before we came here."

"But that was eleven years ago! She's been pressuring him into getting the ring to get hitched, but he hasn't." argued Neiko.

"You see? He didn't just run and get it, did he? He has been making excuses to keep from marrying her, hasn't he?" Sito asked.

"Well—yeah, but—" Neiko stammered.

"Neiko, no buts. The girl of his dreams is you and has been for many years!" Sito declared.

Neiko smiled. "That makes me feel a lot better. When I get back home, I'll tell him exactly how I feel. But, what would Pharaoh do if he found out, and what are we gonna do to get out of here? We have two weeks to get that crystal, and if we don't make it, then I have to—" she thought, shivering. "I don't want to marry him—I don't love him. As a matter of fact, I can't stand him!"

"We will make sure Pharaoh never finds out. He would try to make you forget Monchiska. You better be glad he isn't here because Pharaoh would slay him so he could have you. People wouldn't care what happens to a slave—the Egyptians would think of it as taking out the trash and not the murder of a human being. They do this all the time all the way up to Pharaoh himself. I wouldn't be surprised if he would try to be rid of us shortly after your ceremony so he wouldn't have to worry about us ever again. We are in a race against Pharaoh's clock, and it is very short. He hates us more than he does the Hebrews."

Neiko shuddered. "If he ditches you guys, then I'll be here by myself with him and Francesco, and we all know my life will be Hades. I almost forgot—I got a date with him tomorrow at midday, and I have to go. Ugh! Will y'all try to get that crystal while I keep him busy?"

"Okay, I'll do my best, but don't count on the first attempt," warned Sito.

"I know, but the sooner I can dump Ramesses the better. I really don't want to be his wife or a queen of Egypt—or even his Great Wife if it comes to that. I just want to go home—I miss the action. Palace and Egyptian life are so boring compared to Hawote. I feel like I'm in prison, and Pharaoh is my jailer," Neiko grumbled.

"I know what you mean, and it'll get worse. It won't get boring if we have to fight Pharaoh to free you. I bet we will if everything goes wrong, and in the turn I'll tell him what I think of him and what a heartless scum he really is—at my own risk that is. Then I'd have to fear for my life because he already hates me," remarked Sito.

Neiko chuckled. "I'd like to see that. I feel much better—I was so upset at first because it was such a shock. I know, the more I reject him the worse he'll get because I know his type. I'm ready for that, but I was wondering is there is any way by law or anything I can do to thwart the marriage?"

"No. Pharaoh is above the law, and everyone must obey his commands whether they agree with them or not. Every word he speaks is law, so you are his wife right now—this very minute. All that ceremony is to honor your union with him and to show to all of Egypt that he has acquired you," Sito replied.

Neiko covered her face with her hands and moaned. "I thought a queen of the Crackedskulls was bad, but the Queen of Egypt? Sito, I can't do this!"

"You can moan and groan about it all you want, but it won't change a thing," Sito said firmly as he held up his finger.

"The only way out of this is for him to change his mind, and I know *exactly* how to do it!" Neiko said triumphantly.

"Neiko, don't count on it. He won't be changing his mind anytime soon, no matter how much you try to make him angry or make yourself repulsive. If there is one thing I know about Pharaoh, it's when he has made up his mind, there is no changing it, even if the sky is falling or if hell comes to earth. He is adamant and strong-willed when he has his heart set on something. Even if giants were smashing Egypt to pieces, he wouldn't give it up. You have no hope from the law anyway because you are a slave; a peasant Egyptian would be superior to a foreigner. Second, you are a female, and all females are inferior to men, especially the pharaoh. Your parents aren't here to object, and they have no say against a god-king. It's basically written in stone," Sito said.

Neiko thought hard, but then an idea popped into her head. "He can't make me if I'm not here then can he?"

Sito cocked a questioning eyebrow. "What are you getting at?"

"Like if I ran away, he can't make me go to that ceremony or do anything. That's what I'll do—run away—that is, if you can't get the crystal," Neiko said with a cunning smile.

Sito shook his head. "Are you out of your mind? You would be lucky if you made it to the outskirts of Thebes! You may be Neiko Kidd and a great warrior, but you can't run away from or fight against the Egyptian army with Ramesses the Great at the head—he bears that title in our day and age for a reason. You would be captured in no time, and that would make things worse. He would be more determined to force you to love him, and he'll put more restrictions of your freedoms. We could pay the penalty. You would be more of a prisoner here because that act of defiance would make him tighten his grip on you that much more. Neiko, you are so desperate that you aren't thinking clearly! I'm saying this for your own good."

"Well, that means I can't go on foot, so I'll just have to swipe a ride," Neiko shrugged indifferently.

Sito put his hands up. "Neiko, stop this—it won't work. This place is crawling with sentries and soldiers at night, and it doesn't take long for him to mobilize the army for pursuit. I don't think he'd be happy to be awakened in the middle of the night with news of your disobedience to his commands. Get this crazy idea out of your mind—and don't worry—we'll get the crystal. Come on, Neiko, let's go to bed."

Neiko followed him inside, but she tried to think of a way to run away if things didn't work out.

- CHAPTER 22 -

THE FOLLOWING DAY THE Indians tried to find a chance to corner Francesco to be able to retrieve the crystal before midday, but he wasn't there at the palace. He could be anywhere, but none of them could leave the palace.

"This is just great," Neiko grumbled. "I have exactly two more hours before I have to meet you-know-who. You'll have to try to get it without me."

Sito sighed. "He won't be back till late tonight because he had something he had to do, but I can go and search his room and see if it's there."

"Well, okay. I have to start getting ready now because I'm not sure how long it'll take, and I can tell he'd be mad if I was late—he'd probably think I did it on purpose. So I'll talk to you later?" asked Neiko with a timid shrug.

"Okay. We'll tell you of our progress, and you give us the juicy details," Tito said.

Neiko laughed sarcastically and then gave him a disgusted frown. "I will, but I know I won't be having fun."

Neiko ran to her room to get herself ready. She placed the crown on her head and put on her makeup. "I hate these clothes. I'll never get used to this," she muttered, seeing her dress was light material, and it was fairly short. "My mom would have a fit if she saw me in this," she said, tugging at her skirt. She went downstairs and met Nefertari in the foyer.

"You are already dressed? How did you do it?" asked Nefertari curiously.

"Oh, easy. I did it by myself," said Neiko with a carefree shrug. She guessed Nefertari was used to having just about everything done for her.

"Well, okay. He is waiting in the dining hall," Nefertari said, leading her down the hall by the hand.

Neiko fidgeted. "Uh, will you come with me?"

"Yes, I will accompany you to the dining hall, but he wants to be with you alone. I can't come in with you today. Do you know where Sito is?" asked Nefertari.

Neiko fidgeted. "Uh, he has a few things he has to do, so I'm not very sure," Neiko replied, shrugging, as they started to walk to the appointed place.

"Here we are, and I hope you have a good time. I'm so happy you are going to be a part of the family," said Nefertari, hugging her and then walking off.

"Why did you have to leave me here by myself with *him?*" Neiko grumbled.

Someone put his arm around her, and she jumped.

"Come on in and be seated," said Ramesses, ushering her in. He seated her at the table and sat down beside her.

Neiko twiddled her thumbs and tried to find something to talk about. The Egyptian words seemed to not fire in her brain or match with her fleeting thoughts. "Um…uh…well, I uh—nice day, isn't it?"

she managed to fight out. "The sun is…uh—really bright, and the trees are green. The obelisks are nice and tall. I learned that word yesterday—obelisk. It is very dry in the desert—it's not dry where I come from."

Ramesses smiled, watching her. "Really? Yes, it is a marvelous day, but the sun or nature is not what makes this day special," he said, looking at her and smiling.

"Really? Uh, is hunting fun here? I've always loved hunting, and I was hoping to go sometime soon. I also like to go fishing," mused Neiko as she fidgeted and twiddled her thumbs. She was extremely nervous.

"Really? How nice. I occasionally go, but not often. I would rather race than hunt or fish. I used to go with my father when I was younger." Ramesses said. "Father and I were close."

"Oh—well…Pharaoh, how are your treasure cities coming along? Good, I hope," Neiko said, trying to smile.

"Oh, they're coming along well. They should be finished within a few years. Call me Ramesses from now on," Ramesses said good-naturedly.

"Okay—Ramesses—when's the food coming? I'm starved!" Neiko said, trying to get her mind off of her situation.

"All in good time. It will be ready in a short while," Ramesses said as he looked at her deeply and licked his teeth nonchalantly.

Neiko tried not to look at him. "What are we having anyway? Tell them to hurry up—I'm wasting away over here!" she said as she looked at the ceiling.

Ramesses laughed at her until his eyes were watering. "You have a sense of humor. Do not worry; it will not be that long. I do not know what they are preparing."

"Well, okay, but don't worry if it sounds gross because I've eaten some pretty weird things in my life but they were good," said Neiko, trying to play the gross card to nauseate him and maybe call off the date.

"Oh, what did you eat?" Ramesses asked, as he reached and took her hand.

Neiko pulled it away and put it under the table and said, "Oh, stuff like slug casserole, beetle potpie, and some other stuff you don't have words for or never heard of. I've cooked slug casserole for a dinner in Hawote, and everybody loved it. If I told them what it was, then they would get sick. You wouldn't die if you ate it," she said, folding her hands and looking at him shrewdly.

Ramesses grimaced hearing this. "I am glad we are not eating now because hearing such things is making me feel sick."

Neiko's emerald eyes twinkled. "Aww, c'mon. You have never tried it! I knew what it was when I was putting it in my face."

"Please, no more," Ramesses said with his hands raised in surrender.

Servants then brought in the food and drink. "All right! Time to eat!" Neiko said as they sat it down in front of her.

They brought out chicken, bread, peas, figs, and other things. The scrumptious loaf of honey bread was Ramesses' favorite dessert.

Neiko prayed over her food and started to eat. "Wow, silver plates and gold cups—neat—I guess this is your idea of fine dinnerware," she said, after she swallowed a mouthful of peas. She grabbed her cup and took a large gulp. It was full of wine, and she spat it out. "Yuck! Ugh!" she said and got up. "I'll get me some water. Be right back," she said, elated, since she found an excuse to leave.

Ramesses seized her and forced her to sit back down. "Sit down. My servants will take care of this. I gather you wish to drink water in the future."

"Yeah. I can get it myself—it's no problem—really. I'm used to getting all my stuff myself. I've cooked my own dinner before, you know," Neiko said sarcastically.

"Well, you will not do that here—that is why we have servants. And you will stay seated until I say; you can't get up or leave until it is my wish," Ramesses said sharply.

Neiko rolled her eyes. "Okay," she grumbled as she folded her arms over her chest and curled her bottom lip in contempt. "Will you get me some water, please?" she asked politely to a girl. The girl nodded and looked at her, and she looked at Ramesses in terror and uncertainty since he hadn't given the order. He nodded, and she left running and came back in thirty seconds with her water. "Thank you," Neiko said, looking her in the eyes, but she turned away and walked off.

"There is no need to be overly polite," Ramesses said and then took a drink.

"I don't have to be *rude* either," Neiko said curtly. "Nobody gives me any eye contact when I talk to them, and it's annoying."

"They are not supposed to look at me or anybody who is royalty in the eye," Ramesses said. "You should remember that from the party escapade."

Neiko looked at him sternly. "You know, that's really silly. Whoever made that up needs a good kick in the pants because he must have been a real jerk. I mean, this is so ridiculous! It's kinda hard to get used to this when all people are equal in the place I came from, and everybody looks at you when they talk to you."

Ramesses shook his head and folded his hands. "Enough. I do not wish to argue with you about something so trifle. I don't know who created it—it's a tradition thousands of years old."

"Oh, okay. I hate all these laws and all this other stuff. It gets me all confused. Hawote had only ten laws and maybe a handful of rules."

"You had much freedom there, didn't you? Well, you will get used to your life here, and you will have much freedom—that is—you must earn it along with my trust. It will not be as hard as you make it out to be," Ramesses said gently.

"Oh," Neiko said as she ate her last bit of peas. "Well, I need more water," she said beginning to stand up and shaking her golden chalice.

"Sit down," Ramesses said harshly.

"Oh, I forgot," Neiko said sheepishly, but really she was annoyed.

"You, get the queen more water, and be quick about it," Ramesses ordered, snapping his fingers.

Neiko winced. "You know, you don't have to be so mean! They'd gladly do it if you were a little nicer." Her water arrived in less than a minute. "Whoa! Fast service!" *I wish I could give these guys a tip,* she thought.

"You may leave," Ramesses said to the servants and they left quickly. She watched them go and wished she could do the same since she knew where this was probably going next. "Alone at last. Now tell me what you think about me."

Neiko choked, and laughed nervously. "Uh—well you seem like a nice guy and a tough guy at the same time. You are kinda cute," she said, shrugging. She did think he was handsome, but she wasn't interested in a relationship with him, and she didn't care for his dominant personality and his condescending attitude toward her friends.

"Go on," Ramesses said, moving closer and reaching to embrace her, but she pushed him away and got up swiftly. He grabbed her wrist trying to stop her, but she pulled free.

"Sorry, that's all I could think of at the moment," Neiko said backing away. She backed against the wall, and he had her cornered.

"Maybe I'll give you a little inspiration and change your views about me," Ramesses said, oozing with passion and moving forward. He began to caress her face as he moved closer to kiss her on the lips. She turned away and shut her eyes in anguish when he was only a millimeter away from kissing her. He pulled away and looked at her smiling. Without thinking and solely on reflex, she pushed him away from her and started to make a hasty retreat; he caught her by the hand and held it tightly. She tried to pull free from his grasp, but he pulled her to him and held her close to him with an iron-clad embrace. "Leaving so soon?" he asked sweetly.

"Yeah! I'm outa here because you can't keep your hands off of me! This is only the first date for cryin' out loud! I'm sorry, but back off! I have rules for personal space on the first date!" Neiko shouted irately as she tried to fight free and resist his advances.

"You seem to have forgotten that you are my wife now and that I love you very much," Ramesses said, squeezing her hand.

"Just so you know, I don't believe in love at first sight," Neiko said crossly.

Ramesses chuckled lightheartedly since he had a secret he was carrying. "I have something very special to tell you in due time—at the right time. Very well, you are free to leave. I want to meet again with you in three days. Before you leave, I want to give you something."

Neiko held out her free hand as if he was going to hand her something. "Well, give it to me."

He laughed and kissed her on the cheek, and Neiko grimaced. He released her, and she ran down the hall wiping her cheek in disgust. He leaned against the door and propped his head on his arm as he smiled and watched her disappear down the hall. He rubbed the large amulet as passionate thoughts paraded through his head.

- CHAPTER 23 -

NEIKO RAN OUT into the garden to meet with her friends; they were outside waiting. "What's up?" asked Mactalon.

"Did y'all have any luck?" Neiko asked as she crossed her fingers.

"None. It seems he keeps it with him or hidden somewhere, so we have to corner him on a later date. Speaking of which, how was it?" asked Mactalon.

Neiko slapped her forehead and moaned in despair. "Dreadful. On the next date, I should take a dagger or something."

Sito chuckled. "Why is that?"

"He wouldn't keep his hands off of me! He tried to kiss me on the mouth—eww!" Neiko said, shuddering. "We've just met for cryin' out loud! He said he wants to meet again in three days. I hope he got the message that I ain't interested!"

Sito shook his head. "Don't count on it. I believe you have met your match. He will not give up until he has won you. I can say this—his persistence and stubbornness is equal to yours, but he has an edge—his commanding and demanding spirit and his high self-esteem will crush that iron will of yours, if he can weaken you. He thinks he'll conquer you and win you completely."

"Oh yeah? I'll show him! I won't let him get his way because I'll fight him with everything I have. He'll wish he never met me!" Neiko trumpeted, poking out her chest like she was a Siamese fighting fish. "You know, I'm not a country—I'm not a thing! I'm not something that is owned or conquered! You own a car or a camel—I am a *person!*"

Sito shurgged. "Neiko, that's exactly what he wants you to do—the conquering works the same way. He already has you where he wants you. You think this date was bad? You just wait because he is just getting warmed up. He went easy on you," warned Sito.

"What? You call that going easy on me?" she asked with her features. "Sito, I know what I'm doing. I know how to deal with conceited men. I've fared just fine against narcissistic Georgian guys—they're all the same. He'll give up in a month!" Neiko said with absolute certainty.

"Neiko, he isn't like them! You are totally unprepared, and you have no idea what you're up against—by the way, he's not narcissistic—he may be borderline at the most. He has very potent charms that he can use on you that can weaken you. It's just he doesn't get to use them that often—he usually doesn't have to because his money, power, and good-looks are usually enough for most women. You, in contrast, are a different story altogether. Others tell me his charms also have a keen edge you can't see. Prepare to face your ultimate challenge in strategic combat in the arena of love," Sito warned.

"Oh, Sito, come on! I can't stand Ramesses! His charms won't work on me! He'll have better luck charming a cobra!" Neiko snorted sarcastically. "I hope he tries to kiss it, and I hope it bites him!"

"That doesn't matter. He has a challenge for himself, and he loves a challenge. He views just about everything as a contest or a battle. Not only that, he sees the reward ahead of him and desires that prize very much—you have no idea how much—and nothing will stop him. He may have a long way to go, but don't count on him giving up. To Ramesses nothing is impossible, and he will not accept defeat when he finds something he really wants. 'No' is not acceptable and won't end at that," Sito replied. "What's more is that he's really going to enjoy the pursuit. Conquest will only be that much sweeter when he wins the war and that'll make the relationship that much more enjoyable. Guys like him like women who resist them at first the most."

Neiko rolled her eyes and tossed her head. Her long black locks whipped around her head and her hair beads clinked together and on her crown. "Well, I have news for him; he better get used to hearing the word 'no' since that's all he's gonna hear from me!" Neiko declared. "There goes that country thing again…"

"Like I said before, he is just getting warmed up. You are in a game of chess or cat and mouse—however you view it. You may want to adopt the war metaphor if you even hope to win or have a chance to withstand what's coming. You have to put up your guard and shield your weaknesses, because he will find them, and he'll hit them hard like a battering ram," cautioned Sito as he slammed his fist into his palm. "Once you begin to crack he'll move in with his charm and romance, and that will seep through the cracks and weaken you much more. Contrary to what you think, he does have a deep, fiery, passionate, and charming side; he's not all stone, iron, and ice."

Neiko put her hand on her head to take in all she had heard. "Oh boy, Sito, get that crystal. I don't know how much I can stand. I may end up going mad or killing him if he keeps it up, or if it gets worse!"

"Neiko, please, don't think it is hopeless. All I intended to do was warn you so that you would be prepared. If you tried to hurt him, you couldn't. He is also a fighter—he already knows what you are capable of and will take precautions since he has seen you in action. If you tried to kill him, all he would do is take the weapon away from you and probably pin you down and steal a victory kiss."

Neiko shuddered. "It seems easier fighting Bloodhawk hand-to-hand. Enough about him. Let's get that crystal tonight! Is ol' sourpuss coming back tonight?"

"Yes, and I suppose you want to jump him tonight?" asked Mactalon.

"You bet, and if all goes well, we'll be home tonight, and this nightmare will be over!" Neiko said in excitement.

The Indians waited late that night in the garden because Francesco would make his way out there to do his work. Night fell, and they remained in the bushes for a stake out and ambush. He came outside and walked into range.

"Get him!" shouted Neiko, and all five pounced on him and started beating him.

"Where is that crystal, you little weasel? Give it to me, or I'll break your neck!" growled Mactalon.

"You cannot use it, Indian, because you don't know how!" Francesco sneered.

"I do! So give it here!" Neiko retorted. "Hold him!" she said, and Mactalon and Tito held him.

"Let go, you stupid Indians!" shouted Francesco in hatred.

Neiko punched him in the stomach, winding him, and then dealt a hard blow in his nose. While he was gasping to catch his breath, Neiko reached into his pockets, searching him, and finally found the crystal. With the crystal in hand, Neiko started the chant, and it started to glow. Francesco kicked her hand and sent it flying in the air, and it landed on the ground.

"You scum!" Neiko growled, ready to punch him again, but someone seized her. The other Indians were surrounded by the palace guards.

The captain of the guard looked at them suspiciously. "What is going on here? I'll be delighted to enlighten Pharaoh on this outrage. So what is this quarrel about?"

"They started it!" Francesco said in his defense.

"Save your excuses for Pharaoh," said the captain.

"Here is what they were fighting over," said a guard as he brought the crystal to the captain.

"A rock? Is this all? Well, let's go. Bring them—Pharaoh awaits," he said, and they led them to the platform.

"What is this? I demand to know!" asked Ramesses moodily as he marched to meet them. He had heard the commotion and sent his guards to investigate.

"These six were fighting in the garden. They were quarreling over this, my king," the captain said handing the crystal to Ramesses.

"A stone? It has some importance, I gather. I'll keep it to ensure there is no more violence in my house," Ramesses said, holding out his hand, and the captain handed it to him. All five Indians gritted their teeth in dismay as he studied it and turned it over in his hand. "Who is responsible for beginning the fight?"

"They all are!" Francesco piped up, pointing at all five of the Indians. "Neiko punched me in the stomach and in the nose! They all tackled me and hit me!" he wailed as his nose continued to bleed.

"Is this true, Sito?" Ramesses asked. His eyes fell on Neiko, and she swallowed hard.

"Yes. He stole that crystal from our tribe!" Sito fibbed, trying to find some way to save the situation.

"Liar! I made it; you just want to save your little Indian hide. And oh—you want to take away Pharaoh's new bride-to-be and give her to another man!" Francesco thundered.

Upon hearing this, Ramesses grew angry, and his eyes filled with rage and jealousy.

Sito closed his eyes in deep despair. That remark was going to become a bane for the Indians. He was carrying a secret that none of his friends or his brother knew about, and he was forbidden to tell.

"Shut up, Oscar Mayer wiener! You better eat those words before I ram them down your throat!" Neiko shot back.

"You cannot outwit a genius such as me!" Francesco preached.

"What are you talking about? Are you the genius of the Dunce School for Dummies?" asked Mactalon. "You are a brainless moron. The only questions you can get right are the no-brainers!"

"You are so stupid, Frank!" Neiko added.

"My name is Francesco! At least I have a brain, Dodo Talon!" Francesco retorted.

"Oh yeah?" challenged Mactalon.

"Yes!" Francesco said.

"Enough!" Ramesses thundered, and his voiced seemed to echo in the palace. "I am tired of this endless bickering and fighting. I had better not see or hear about another quarrel, or I will turn you out. Is that understood? Leave my presence, all of you Indians, and go to your quarters! Francesco, you stay."

After everyone left, Francesco waited until the coast was clear. "I was hoping you would allow me to talk with you because I have so much more to tell you."

"Is that true what you said earlier about them taking Neiko away from me and giving her to another?" asked Ramesses. "Sito and I have fought our own battles over the course of eleven years," Ramesses sighed.

Francesco's eyes glittered maliciously; he instantly guessed what it was about. "It is. There are many young men in Hawote who are just *dying* to marry her—including Prince Bloodhawk I might add. Can you blame them? Oh yes, I will tell you the real reason why I'm here and why this crystal is so important. I just hope you can handle the truth."

Ramesses pressed his fingers together in a rhythm as he smoldered at hearing this. "Go on."

Francesco took a deep breath in anxiety, not knowing how Ramesses would take this since he was very hard to convince about anything he could not see or touch, let alone space and time travel. He was going to try to twist in lies to devastate the Indians' reputations. "That crystal is the gateway back to Hawote. We're from Hawote that is more than three thousand years into the future. You are dead in our world, and your mummy was discovered by people of the future. Many people learn and study your life. I studied and personally worship you. While the rest of Hawote mocks you and drags your name through the mud, I revere you," explained Francesco. "Neiko and her friends are not pilgrims by choice, as I sent them here with that crystal you hold in your hand because of foul deeds they did against me. I sent Neiko here to suffer. She turned the tables on me continuously and exposed me in my espionage when I was trying to help her people. I intended for her to be in servitude and anguish—to feel the pain she caused me. I came to see her anguish, and to learn firsthand how a pharaoh rules. I want to become the Pharaoh of Hawote and crush my enemies. I know if Neiko dies here in Egypt, then the land of Hawote will not know her because it would be like she never was born, and her great and not-so-great deeds will not be done. However, if she returns to Hawote, you will never remember her, no matter how much you love her. We are rewriting history as we speak, and that is the truth."

"That is a very entertaining story, but it is nonsense—all of it," Ramesses said curtly. He didn't believe anything Francesco said about Neiko. This report did not match what he had heard and witnessed. He would never have fallen in love with such a vile person.

"I know you are a man who requires cold, hard proof, and I'll give it to you. You aren't supposed to know any different, so you will be the first person to travel into the future from this time. Hand me the crystal and I'll show you. First, we'll go to Rome during the reign of Julius Caesar, and then I will send you to Texas in 1815," Francesco said, and Ramesses handed him the crystal.

"You wish to give me a demonstration?" asked Ramesses.

"Yes. It will not take long," Francesco said.

Francesco did the chant, and they appeared in Rome. Roman soldiers marched around. Then he summoned them back to where they were and sent Ramesses to Texas. Ramesses looked at the strange place. Before him, he could see Comanche Indians attacking a group of cowboys who were trespassing on their tribal burial grounds. Bows and guns were being fired, and people were falling off horses. Then he was summoned back.

"I believe you. So, everything you say is true about the future? Well, I accept some of it. Everything said about Neiko, however, is fabricated and untrue—that I know. She will remain with me till the day she dies. Do you object?" asked Ramesses challengingly.

"No, by all means you can have her. I will remain here until you two are happy together. Oh—by the way, I think you might want to keep Neiko from going back to the future since you will lose her forever, and you won't remember her or know her just like it should be. It would really be a shame," said Francesco with cunning.

Ramesses folded his arms and narrowed his eyes. "We'll see about that, won't we?" Then he nodded and sighed at Francesco's request. "Very well. I will say I will be losing quite a servant. I wish you well when you do leave, and you have my permission."

"Thank you. I greatly appreciate it," Francesco said and then went to go to bed.

- CHAPTER 24 -

THE NEXT DAY, ALL five Indians met in the garden, and Neiko told them everything she had heard while eavesdropping the previous night.

"Oh no. Now Pharaoh knows the whole truth, and this is going to add to his hatred of us because of those lies the little weasel told; he already views us as a threat, but this makes it worse. He's going to do everything in his power to stop you from going home. We won't be here much longer. He'll get rid of us probably after the ceremony for certain," Sito said in dread.

"He didn't believe everything though. That means I only have ten days left. Francesco is going to make sure I'm stuck here with him alone for the rest of my life. We can't make any sudden moves because Ramesses has the crystal, and we have to get it back somehow," said Neiko.

"If we aren't careful, he could destroy it if it becomes too much of a risk to his plans for Neiko," added Sito.

"Neiko and Sito are right. I just wonder how we'll get it back. How did Francesco make that thing?" asked Tito.

"With the Eye of Mohica—how exactly I'm unsure of," Neiko replied, and they looked at her like she was telling a science-fiction story.

She continued by saying, "I have more. I'm really not supposed to talk about this, but I need to tell someone if we don't make it out of here. You guys are my best friends. Y'all can't tell anyone if we get back. I know where the Eye of Mohica came from ... a land called Qari. It is in the First Universe and contains magic. Its real name is the Eye of Cygnus, and it was created by a Pharaoh name Rumi who began a line of the Pharaohs of Qari. Rumi created the black, simple magic of the pharaoh family. I found all of this out because I went to Qari, and I saw this spell of time travel before in a book of magic written by Rumi. Qarian pharaohs are just like Egyptian pharaohs, except mostly they possess magic."

Mactalon was perplexed. "How did you get there?"

"Before I say that, I'll tell you there is a very dangerous man from there called Ramses. He is after the Eye of Mohica and me. He is extremely dangerous and that's why I was sworn to secrecy. There is more, but I must stop there. You wouldn't believe me if I told you," said Neiko.

"How dangerous and mean is he? From what little you say, I don't think I would say anything either," said Sito.

"He is so mean, he puts Ramesses on a bad day to shame. Imagine Ramesses six foot eight and weighing six hundred pounds—including armor—with unlimited strength, potent magic, and a very short temper. He has a bigger inferiority complex, and he wants to kill anyone and everyone. The thing you can remember most are his eyes, because they are sightless and they glow with red fire. Say his name and all tremble," replied Neiko.

Everyone shuddered.

"Boy, that is the ultimate enemy—he could stomp Bloodhawk easily," said Panthero.

"That's because I know I'll be saved by my friends, the Attack Pack, but here, I have not much hope of escape. The Attack Pack has fought against him for a long time, but things are beginning to suck," said Neiko. "And I know if I marry Ramses, I'll be doomed to be his wife and live a life of solitude with him, and I'll never be freed from a curse. I may escape, but he will find me and get me back. At least I can say Ramesses is not evil—he may be a royal pain in the umph and a little mean—but he's not evil," Neiko replied.

"I guess so," said Panthero, biting his lip.

"Ramses somehow found out about Ramesses. He said that Ramesses the Great is a spoiled, arrogant palace brat who so weak and helpless can't even fasten his own sandals," said Neiko.

Everyone burst out laughing till their sides were hurting. "That fits Ramesses to a T. He is that helpless to someone like Ramses! Why don't we add on to what he started? Let's see, Seti never spanked him enough, so he thinks he can pitch a fit to get his way!" Sito punned.

"Ramesses is a royal pain in the butt!" Panthero said.

Tito couldn't wait for his turn. "He is such a snotty-nosed jerk that he has to keep a handkerchief on him to wipe his nose before he talks to someone!"

"He is so conceited he thinks he can kill a lion with his bare hands!" Mactalon said.

"He is so mean, and his stare is so deadly that he can kill one with his gaze," Sito pitched in.

"He's always so grouchy and moody, no wonder Neiko wants to give him the cold shoulder!" Mactalon said.

"Enough! How dare you insult me behind my back!" came an angry shout from behind them. Everyone turned around, and there stood Ramesses with his eyes gleaming in wrath and his chest heaving in fury. He understood them since he had decreed no foreign languages were to be spoken in the palace. "You dare make sport of me behind my back, and you think it's funny? You will not think it is very funny when I am finished! If you have something to say about me, then say it to my face!" he challenged as he stood tall with his brawny chest poked out and heaving in his wrath.

"Uh-oh, I think we just got ourselves in a sticky-wicket," Mactalon whispered.

"Look who just woke up in a tizzy and on the wrong side of the bed!" added Neiko.

"Shut up! No talking when I am talking, and you will not speak unless I say!" Ramesses ranted as he marched back and forth and shook his fists.

Wanting to speak, Panthero raised his hand.

"What?" Ramesses snapped.

"Er…um…we were talking about some other Ramesses—honest. You know that is a very popular name nowadays," Panthero said in hopes to alter the situation, but this just made Ramesses angrier.

"You lie! Do you think I am stupid? Come now—tell me how *stupid* I am now!" Ramesses snarled with his dark brown eyes nearly glowing and wild; the kohl just seemed to accent the fury.

The Indians shrank back.

"I will show you who is in command around here! I will make you work from sunrise to sunset in hard labor to teach you a lesson who is in charge here! Enjoy this day while it lasts. You will be gone *very* soon. You are only here it all in due respect for Neiko—don't try my patience and good will!" he warned.

All the Indians sighed with relief when Ramesses turned to leave.

"Well, at least I get to stay," Neiko said with a grin.

Ramesses spun around and came back a second later. "I forgot something. Let's go," he snapped as he grabbed her arm; he was holding it so tightly, it hurt. "You will be spending the rest of your time with me as it should be—you will have absolutely no contact with them for ten days."

"Oww, ouch. You're hurting me!" Neiko cried as he dragged her behind him, and they disappeared.

Sito shook his head. "We really did it this time, and someone is in a bad mood."

"Yeah, he's really cranky today—more than usual," Mactalon said.

"Well, we can't do what we were going to without Neiko, and she is forbidden to see us for ten days—maybe forever. That's the day of the ceremony, and I think it'll be permanently after that sometime—like he just said," said Sito glumly.

"Hi, guys. What's wrong?" asked Nefertari in a phrase she picked up from the Indians as she ran out. They told her what had happened. "Oh my. Why did you do that?"

"We were so mad at him, and we tried to get some of it out of our system. He wasn't supposed to overhear. I guess he was trying to eavesdrop on Neiko again. We can't see Neiko from today until ten days later—if ever again. We were going to play poker out here in the garden, and we can't now without Neiko," Sito replied.

"I'll take her place tonight. Can you teach me?" Nefertari asked.

"Yeah, but tonight is the last night we will feel like having fun, because we will be worked very hard."

- CHAPTER 25 -

THAT NIGHT THEY PLAYED poker and talked till they went to bed. Morning came, and the Indians began their hard labor.

Ramesses took Nefertari and Neiko to a chariot race he was contending in. He boasted of his chariot being the fastest in all of Egypt; he did this to impress Neiko. Neiko wasn't impressed by his arrogant display, but his racing chariot did catch her attention and gave her an idea. Neiko watched the race with her head propped on her hands. His chariot was fast; he won the race. She formulated a plan as they returned home.

When they got home, the other four Indians were lying on their backs, panting from their hard day's work. Neiko wanted to talk to her friends, but Ramesses forced her to go into the garden with him and made her spend the rest of the evening with him until bed.

Later that night, she sneaked into the garden, made herself a long staff, hid it in the bushes, and covered it with the discarded branches. Then she returned to bed.

Several days passed, and it was five days until the day of the marriage ceremony and feast. Neiko was ready for Ramesses' next chariot race.

It was an hour until they were supposed to leave, but the chariot was ready. She sprang into action. She ran out into the garden and retrieved her long staff. Then she sneaked past the guards to the awaiting racing chariot. Only one guard was watching it. She snuck up to him.

"Knock, knock," she said and punched him in the face. She jumped into the chariot, grabbed the reins, and set down her staff. "How hard can it be? It's a cross between riding a horse, driving a car, and riding a scooter. It's like a dogsled on wheels."

The guard she punched came at her ready to stop her, but she snapped the reins, and the horses started to run and almost ran him over. He started yelling to the others. More guards tried to stop her or cut her off, but she escaped by trying to run them over. They scattered like cockroaches when the kitchen light is turned on.

The guards' commotion got Ramesses' attention. He ran out the door, and all he could see was dust and her disappearing form.

"See ya, suckers!" Neiko called back.

"Don't just stand there! After her! Bring her back to me! I want her unharmed!" Ramesses commanded.

Soldiers and guards got on their horses and chariots and went after her. Messengers were sent to rustle up the army at the closest barracks.

Neiko was riding through the streets at a trot. People stopped to leer at the runaway future queen on her stolen ride while a platoon of soldiers tried to block the chariot's path. They were unaware that she was an escapee. Seeing her at the reins as she approached startled them.

"Stop her—Pharaoh commands!" called someone behind her to the soldiers in front of her.

Wasting no time, she snapped the reins and almost ran them over as they scattered. The horsemen and charioteers split up to trap her. She wove through the streets, trying to shake her pursuers.

She stayed well ahead of them, but then one horseman came in front of her to block her path.

Neiko bent down, got her long staff, and rested it in the front; it served as a lance. They charged toward each other, but before he could reach her, her staff caught him in the ribs. He flipped off his horse and landed onto the sand of the street.

Soon, she heard the rumble of many more chariots behind her; she looked back and saw hundreds. She gulped and kept on going, but suddenly a two-man chariot came out of the street and rode to her to intercept her.

"You wanna play chicken?" Neiko challenged and made the horses go faster. As she sped toward them, the driver jerked the reins to avoid a collision when she came dangerously close. The chariot turned over and sent the driver and his partner on a spill.

Neiko sped past them, laughing. She saw two chariots blocking her further ahead, and she made a hard left turn. But then there were two more blocking that street. She made another turn; the result was the same. She made another turn into a wide street, but there sat more chariots and horsemen completely closing off the street. All the chariots closed in and had her blocked in on all sides.

Neiko grabbed her staff, jumped off, and looked around, but she was trapped. "Oh crap!" she said in bitter defeat. She knew it was pointless to fight because there were ten armed men approaching her and many more to take their place if she took them out. She threw her staff down in disgust.

Two men seized her and tied her hands together in front of her, and the commanding officer walked up to her with a victorious swagger.

"Pharaoh is very displeased with this little stunt of yours, and he will punish you severely, I'm sure. Let's go—he's waiting," said the commander haughtily.

Neiko was brought back to the palace, and Ramesses was waiting outside in the front of the palace impatiently with his arms crossed as he paced. Two men escorted her to him behind the officer in charge, and the officer told him everything that was reported to him about her escapade. When he had finished, Ramesses glowered at her, and she gulped, knowing she was in deep trouble. They cut the rope binding her hands and shoved her to her wrathful husband.

He grabbed her and pulled her inside. When they were inside, he pinned her against the wall. "I hope you realize that you cannot run away from me. I am pleased you were not hurt, but this will not go unpunished."

"Aww, you're just mad because I swiped your chariot and got it dusty!" Neiko retorted.

Ramesses responded by tightening his grip till it hurt, and she gritted her teeth. "You are so wrong about so many things. You have much to learn about me."

"She did this to prevent marriage and the ceremony," Francesco said, coming up from behind.

"Is that so? Well, in that case I will change the day from five days away to two! I would like it to be final sooner myself. Francesco, go to Imenhotep and tell him I wish to see him tonight! Hurry," said Ramesses, waving his hand authoritatively.

"Yes, my king," Francesco said and left.

"Now, my warrior, you and I have unresolved issues to discuss, and they will not wait any longer. Let's go somewhere private," Ramesses said, dragging her off.

– CHAPTER 26 –

IMENHOTEP ARRIVED LATE THAT night, and they talked of the new arrangements. Neiko was supposed to be in bed, but she took the distraction of wedding plans as an opportunity to see her friends. They all met in the twins' room. "I can't believe you did this, Neiko. Now things are worse. I tried to warn you!" Sito said sadly.

"I know, but I had to try. It was going to happen anyway, and either way I lose. I'm not losing anything more. It seemed a good idea at the time," Neiko said, bowing her head in shame.

"Yes, I see your point. But he moved the date up from five days remaining to two. I gather that's why Imenhotep is here," Tito mused.

"Yeah, and Imenhotep is also one of Pharaoh's best friends. Yet, even Pharaoh gave me the same long lecture," said Neiko as she twisted her mouth.

Sito cocked an eyebrow. "About what?"

"Oh, something about putting myself in danger and stuff. I also made a remark about him just being mad because I got his chariot dirty. He got really ticked off about that. He said he'll prove his love one way or another," Neiko said, looking at the floor. "He called me that pet name again. He's been doing that a lot lately."

"Oh, you mean 'my warrior'?" asked Sito.

"Yeah," Neiko answered, nodding.

Everyone shook their heads.

Mactalon groaned. "That is what we were afraid of. Is that all he said?"

"Basically. But he says he will keep me on a leash and watch me like a hawk—even though he does that enough already," Neiko grumbled.

"Oh, you need to go on to bed, and hurry before he catches you in here with us, or you'll get in more trouble," cautioned Panthero urgently.

"Yeah. If we can find out how to escape, it won't matter," Tito proposed. "If not, she'll be forced to do the ceremony. If we try to stop it, he'll either kill us or throw us out."

"I don't know," said Sito warily. "I've heard gossip that there could be more going on than just the ceremony and feast."

"Like what?" asked Neiko.

"I don't know," Sito replied. "I can't get close enough to find out."

"You better get going," said Tito, reminding Neiko.

Mactalon looked out the door; no one was there. "Go now. The coast is clear," he whispered.

Neiko slipped into her room, cuddled on her mattress, and fell asleep.

The two days passed quickly; the big day had come. Neiko was dressed in a fine Egyptian dress, while her friends wore their native clothes—an exception granted by the Pharaoh. When everyone was dressed, they began their march to the temple with an armed escort. People were on both sides of the street, as they watched the progression. When they arrived, the six from Hawote as well as Ramesses and Nefertari walked in while the guards remained outside. Neiko was brought forward, and she stood before Imenhotep. The traditional marriage ceremony was performed, but that's not all that was performed.

After the ceremony, Imenhotep began to call upon the names of the gods and gave an eerie oration, casting some sort of a spell. Priests with the heads of the gods chanted and danced around her as they threw scented water on her, and she looked around in worry.

The ceremony lasted for hours, and Neiko became weary because of anxiety. Imenhotep took Neiko's hand and placed it into Ramesses'hand. Many other cryptic sayings were said and so where prayers and chants. The representations of the gods danced around and touched their united hands and cast a spell upon them. The strange second ritual was finally over, and they all returned. As they did, the people cheered. Neiko looked at them and laughed nervously. They finally made it home.

They had a feast at the palace that night. Soon after that Neiko went to her room early, shut the door, and cried herself to sleep.

- CHAPTER 27 -

THE NEXT MORNING, NEIKO stayed in her room most of the day. Then she made her way into the garden, climbed a fig tree, looked at the scenery beyond the wall, and thought of Monchiska. Francesco came outside to do his work.

Ramesses came out looking for her. "Where is Neiko?" he asked.

"I haven't seen her all day," Francesco replied.

"I can't find her. She is neither in her room nor in the palace. So where could she be?" asked Ramesses with his hands on his hips with his eyes scanning the garden.

"I wouldn't know. She is so unpredictable that she could be anywhere. I wouldn't be surprised if she is hiding from you," Francesco said and then walked under the tree she was in to begin writing. Suddenly a green fig hit him in the top of the head.

"Oww! What the—" Francesco growled and looked up as he rubbed his head and saw her near the top.

"Get outa here, Crackedskull. I don't want you near me," Neiko snapped irritably.

"Aha! So that's where you are. There is someone who wants to see you," Francesco said in a crafty manner.

"Who cares?" Neiko asked, sullen, as she grabbed another fig, threw it, and hit him in the nose.

Ramesses walked beneath the tree and looked up at her. "Come down here this instant! I want you to start acting like a queen! Climbing trees is not acceptable behavior of a queen of Egypt!" Ramesses snapped, shaking his fists.

Neiko folded her arms in defiance. "So? I want to spend time alone! The only way you'll leave me in peace is for me to be up here! Will you go away? I may be a queen, but I am still a warrior. I am an Indian, not an Egyptian. I do what Indian warriors do, and we climb trees all the time. I don't care what Egyptians do and don't do. You're just jealous because you can't climb trees. It's not my fault you didn't learn how to climb trees—you're the only guy I've ever met that can't climb a tree."

"Come down right now, or I'll—" Ramesses shouted shaking and clenching his fists

"You'll what? What are you gonna do—climb up here and get me? C'mon up here, big boy—I dare ya!" Neiko retorted, beckoning him with her fingers in challenge. "I'm not coming down; you're not coming up, so go away and leave me in peace," she said as she turned around and looked out at the sky.

"You can't stay up there forever! You must come down sometime! When you do, I'll be waiting!" Ramesses shouted.

Neiko ignored him and said nothing.

Ramesses stamped back inside exasperated.

Several weeks passed and the power struggle between Neiko and Ramesses was in full gridlock. She constantly dodged him whenever

possible. She tried to think of ways to make him hate her or become angry enough to get rid of her, in spite of the cautions that Sito and others had given her. She stayed in the tree whenever she could or kept herself busy by entertaining guests who came in and left him out on purpose. She would flirt with other young men while she ignored him. She also took in a few animals and spent time with them and her friends—whenever they weren't working. Other times, she bathed herself three to five times a day to avoid her husband.

The only time she was anywhere near him was when Nefertari was present or one of her friends. Whenever he tried to show affection, she pushed him away, rebuffed him, and ran away. She would not allow him to touch her, but it was not to say he didn't try. The entire time they lived together they never kissed. He tried, but she would always refuse him. She would lock herself in her room if she didn't want to deal with him, or if he was intolerable.

Locks were not supposed to exist in this time, but that was one of the few things Ramesses had Sito implement to his palace for better security. Nowhere else in the country had locks.

In Ramesses' anger and frustration, he retaliated by forbidding the men and guests to see her because of his intense jealousy and bitter rage; he was going to show her who was in charge. He also got rid of her animals. He was not fooled. He knew what she was doing; she was desperately trying to fight his charms. The entire thing was a contest of wills. He was going to get the upper hand, even if he had to do something nasty to put her in line. And, she was also aware of her vulnerability. Because her friends were involved, he may get rid of them sooner rather than later. They meant no more to him than the animals Neiko had tried to keep. Yet, he was feeling both stress and hurt by Neiko's defiance.

One day, Ramesses summoned Imenhotep and Francesco. "I have to find a way to stop this, so I can make her submit," he said, rubbing his forehead and trying to ease his frustration. "Where is she now?"

"She locked herself in her room again," Francesco replied.

"What has she been doing? And what have you tried?" asked Imenhotep.

"I try to get close to her, and she pushes me away. She ignores me and treats me with contempt. I want it to stop. I have to find a way to make her submit to me, but how? I am nearly through with being kind—I'll use brutal force if I must," Ramesses vowed.

"You must find a large weakness and exploit it with hard force—that's the only way. I don't know what it is, but I think you will find it," Francesco said. "She's not going to give you any choice."

"How much progress have you had since the first meeting?" asked Imenhotep.

"None. She will not allow me to lay a finger on her. I want to take her into my arms and kiss her, but she always runs away," Ramesses said sadly with intense longing.

"I have a solution to that. Just sneak up on her, grab her, and kiss her with all of your desire and affection. Make her head spin when you get done. Or, if she is no so approachable, then start trapping her in a room with you alone. You need to spend time with her," Francesco said in encouragement.

Ramesses smiled at Francesco's counsel. "Now, Imenhotep, I will show you what I have to work through. Come, let me handle this," he whispered, as they walked to her door. He pounded on the door with his fist. "Open this door!" he bellowed.

"Is that you, Ramesses? Did you say something? I can't hear you with all of this racket!" Neiko called back and banged on the furniture trying to create loud noise.

"You heard me—open this door now!" Ramesses thundered.

"I can't hear you, speak louder!" Neiko retorted.

"Open it!" Ramesses commanded.

"I'm not listening to you, so go away!" Neiko said defiantly.

"Open it, or I'll break it down!" Ramesses shouted, irate.

"I'm not listening to you--yadda, yadda--go away, Frightful One," Neiko sang as he continued to shout. She sang the impudent song louder and louder until he gave up, and they walked away.

"You see? That is the least of her bullheadedness," Ramesses said with a vicious frown and his chest heaving.

Imenhotep shook his head. "You have your work cut out for you, but I know you won't stop. Good luck. I will visit later," he said and then left.

Ramesses and Francesco had a private lunch, discussing what to do about the defiant, wayward queen.

— Chapter 28 —

NEIKO SAT IN HER room drawing pictures of Hawote battle plans, especially of possible maneuvers for both the Seven Tribes and the Crackedskulls as well as locations of Crackedskull reinforcements.

There was a knock on the door, and Neiko gritted her teeth. "Who is it? If it's you, Ramesses, go away!"

"It's me, Sito. May I come in?" Sito asked. "I only have a few minutes."

Neiko came, opened the door, and let him in. Then she shut and locked the door. "What's new?"

"Oh, nothing. I was just coming to see how you were doing. What are these maps?" asked Sito.

"Oh, I was going to bring these to dinner tonight to talk this over with you guys after Weenie Man and the ball-and-chain leave. Did you know it's the annual Seven Tribes' dance tonight? I was hoping we would join them—well—sort of. We have to make a fire. We can't have drums because we'll wake Ramesses, and then he'll cut it short. So we have to have the beat and music in our minds. Good enough?" asked Neiko wriggling in excitement. "We would have to chant quietly," she added and then grinned.

Sito smiled. "That's a great idea. I've missed that dance for eleven years, and now we can have our own small version of it. We will have to do it really late, though. Yet, we still have our Indian clothes, and we'll use your makeup as war paint. I'll see you tonight," Sito said giving her a brief hug and leaving in order to return to work.

Pharaoh had permitted the Indians to eat dinner together as a strategy. That night at the table—Neiko and Nefertari had begged him to let them come to dinner, and Ramesses had his own hidden agenda for allowing them to tag along. Neiko talked with her friends about the maps. Because of the festival back home, she couldn't wait. Yet, it was one more way to avoid engaging in conversation with Ramesses.

"Okay, I believe the Crackedskulls have something big going on here at Skull Mountain in the Etowah Territory on Scraah Land. So we need to send a few trackers or spies there to check it out. The main fortress, I believe, is here," she said pointing at the mark on the map.

"Raven set this fortress that is near my parents' house in the Central Territory to keep an eye on me when I lived there. Now, I've moved out, but they are still close by the way the crow flies. They may have to return to Skull Mountain because a Georgian is making a mobile home park close to it. This will help cut down on convenient attacks on me or anyone else that lives in the Central Territory—or— Raven may interfere with the construction with some kind of guerilla attack or equipment sabotage; he's done that before. We should spread our defenses because they may move troops at both fortresses at any time. We will have to worry about more outside/public attacks and larger numbers than ever before because Raven is ready for this war to finally end," Neiko said, pointing to the maps, indicating possible Crackedskull movements with her finger.

The Indians talked about the maps in front of Ramesses, but he didn't say anything; he only watched Neiko as she pointed to the places, talked, and illustrated. He said nothing to her most of the evening, but he watched her with cunning and a sly smile was on his face.

Nefertari noticed his odd behavior, and it worried her. He only had that expression when he was up to something. He was going to do something rash, perhaps resort to brutal force and craftiness. She knew he had been pushed to the limit of his patience by Neiko's defiance and her friends' intervention.

As soon dinner was over, Nefertari stopped Sito and Neiko both. "Did you both see that Ramesses was acting a bit odd this evening? He wasn't ranting about Neiko's behavior today, and he had a look on his face that unnerved me. I fear for you, Neiko, and possibly for your friends," She said as she turned to Sito.

"I didn't even notice. He isn't going to hurt Neiko, is he?" asked Sito with his eyebrows raised in worry.

Nefertari shook her head. "No, he loves her too much to harm her. He is going to do something brash, and it will be *very* soon. I know he is going to try to break her with force in a different way since browbeating isn't working. I just want to tell you to be careful, Neiko. He is tired of rejection; it is getting to a dangerous level now. I fear he may even threaten you to make you submit," Nefertari said, turning to Neiko.

"Thanks for telling me, Nefie. I hope to leave before then and head for home. Will you tell him the truth about us and how we must get home before the you-know-what?" asked Neiko referring to the secret dance.

Nefertari giggled. "Nefie? I like that. You may call me that—all five of you—but don't say it around Ramesses because he'll be jealous."

"Okay, I have some things to do, so I gotta go. See ya later?" Neiko said.

Neiko walked down the hall, humming while looking around, making sure Ramesses was nowhere in sight; he wasn't. Neiko was about to open the door. Ramesses came out of nowhere, grabbed her, spun her around. He held her tightly to him, pressed her against the wall, and held the back of her neck with one hand. He wasted no time and started kissing her. Overtaken with surprise, shock, and fear, she struggled to free herself. She squealed in fright because she had never been kissed before in her life. She was unable to move and her strength started to drain. Her head started spinning due to the intense passion that seemed to be seasoned a lot longer than a few months time—years or maybe even a decade. It also took her breath. He wouldn't let her come up for air. She almost couldn't stand up and started to teeter.

Finally, he stopped and released her. She panted in ragged breathing because of intense fear, exhaustion, and loss of breath. He walked away, smiling and without saying a word, but she got the message from his eyes that this wasn't finished—he'd be back.

Nefertari ran to her a moment later looking for him. "Have you seen Ramesses?" she asked, and Neiko pointed to where he had gone still panting with fear in her eyes. "Neiko, what's wrong?" she asked trying to steady her because she almost fell over.

Neiko told her what had happened. Nefertari escorted her into her room and tried to calm her; she talked to her about what Sito had told her.

Later that night, all five slipped out into the garden to perform the dance. They were painted and dressed in their Indian clothes. They had a pile of dead sticks ready for the fire they had gathered from pruning the garden weeks ago. Sito lit the fire, and they waited for it to grow. When it was burning steadily, they began the dance with the drumbeat in their head. They danced around the fire, chanting; their shadows were large and moving on the wall. More instruments of Hawote filled their heads, they saw images of their far home with other Indians dancing, and they felt they were back there in Hawote. Their chants intensified, and so did the images and sounds in their heads.

They were sent back to the reality of ancient Egypt by an angry shout. The Indians stopped in mid-dance.

"Oops!" gasped Mactalon as he saw Ramesses standing on the porch in his night robe with Nefertari by his side; his bald head glistening in the moonlight.

"I don't care, and I will not hear of it tonight! Go to your rooms right now! I will discuss this in the morning!" Ramesses snapped and stormed back to his room.

Nefertari stayed behind; she was interested in what they were doing.

"I felt I was back in Hawote with everyone else," Neiko said sullenly.

The others nodded.

"I know, but we're gonna get it tomorrow," Sito said.

"What are you doing here, Nefie?" asked Neiko.

"I came to see what is going on. You all live an interesting life. I want to be an Indian," Nefertari said, and everyone looked at each other.

Sito looked at her like he wanted to talk her out of it and shook his head. "It's late. We will talk more tomorrow. Let me take you to your room," he said, and then he took her to her bedchamber.

- CHAPTER 29 -

THE NEXT MORNING, THE five unlucky Indians had to stand before Ramesses for their little dance the night before.

"I am disappointed you are going behind my back and doing foreign rituals in my house without my permission or approval. Let me say this—I do not approve of anything that has to do with Hawote. I don't want to hear that name again or of any of its laws because they do not apply here. I'm tired of hearing about the history of things to come, and what is supposed to be and what is not. It doesn't concern me. Is that understood?" he said as he marched back and forth on the royal platform with crook and flail in hand, accenting his mannerisms. He had complete command of the situation and was laying down the law.

The Indians nodded without a word. Arguing the matter was a waste of time and dangerous. Not even Neiko could think of a sarcastic comment to add or a way to alter the situation.

Ramesses wasn't done yet. "Furthermore, I also want you to start acting like Egyptians—you are no longer Indians as long as you live here—I may be sending the other four of you on your way soon. I am just not certain as to when. If you will not abide by these rules, then leave now. I will not repeat myself. Francesco, take these clothes and burn them. The five of you may leave," Ramesses said, waving his hand.

They left shaking their heads. Neiko scowled.

"He's coming down on us really hard, and he's stripping us of our heritage and our identity—it's not fair," Panthero said, biting his lip.

"We have to do what he says to stay here. I think he is doing this for three reasons—one, he can't stand our kind or land, so he doesn't want to deal with it because we are against him having Neiko. Two, he is turning up the heat to try to make us leave sooner, and three, he is transforming Neiko into what he wants her to be and shaping her life for her. He's turning her into an Egyptian queen—soon a Great Queen," Sito said as he kept count with his fingers. "I've heard that a Great Wife ceremony is around the corner. I haven't been able to pinpoint a date yet."

"We aren't leaving. He has no idea how strong our friendship is. The only way he can get rid of us is if he exiles us, but we'd come back with a vengeance," Mactalon said with his eyes burning and slamming his fist into his palm.

"Well guys, I need to go to my room; I've got something I have to do," Neiko said taking out the key to her room from her pocket.

"I've been wondering where you got that key from to be able to lock yourself up," said Sito.

Neiko winked. "Nefie. It's the only key to my room, and she got it for me. See ya," she said, walking away.

Neiko walked to her room quickly looking for Ramesses, because she didn't see him in the throne room. Neiko was wary of another ambush. She quickly unlocked the door and walked inside. He came into sight just behind her, and she ran inside and slammed the door in his face. It missed his nose by a centimeter, and she quickly locked it. "Ha, ha! Nice try," she said like a rebellious teenager as she leaned on the door.

"We'll see about that," Ramesses laughed to himself as he took out a master key that he had in his hand.

No one, not even Nefertari, knew he had a master key. He unlocked the door and walked in, and Neiko turned around in surprise.

"How'd you—" Neiko stammered.

Ramesses held up the master key. "This has gone far enough. Come," he said as he pulled her out of the room and forced her to go eat with him.

Later that afternoon, the other four Indians were looking for Neiko, and Sito walked up to meet the three.

"I went to her room, but she wasn't there," Sito said.

Then Neiko appeared with Ramesses as he was holding her hand. She looked fed up, and she wouldn't grasp his hand back.

Before Sito could ask, Neiko muttered, "Don't ask. I'll tell you later."

"I am going for a ride on my private boat in the river, and you four and Nefertari are welcome to join us," he said kindly.

They looked at him shocked like their ears were playing tricks on them. Sito was wondering if there was some sort of ulterior motive for this gracious invite.

"Sure, we'll come. When do we leave?" asked Sito. He thought he could get to the bottom of things and maybe find out what kind of tricks Ramesses may be dealing.

"Now. Come," Ramesses said, waving his hand as he walked away leading Neiko by the hand with them close behind.

Nefertari met them in the foyer, and she walked beside her husband arm-in-arm. He kept a firm grip on Neiko's hand, and she struggled to free her hand from his grasp as the others followed behind the three on the way to the boat.

When they arrived to the boat, Francesco was there waiting, and everyone climbed on.

"You may spend this time with your friends, Neiko. You may also join them, Nefertari," said Ramesses kindly.

Neiko hesitated and then went with her friends. She and the rest sat in a circle in the front, while Ramesses sat under the canopy with Francesco watching them and smirking. The Indians were singing songs, poking fun at each other, and laughing as Nefertari observed.

"Francesco, how strong is the friendship of these five?" he asked, rubbing his chin as a plan began to form in his mind.

Francesco looked at him like "How is this important?" and shrugged. "Very strong. Why?"

"How strong?" asked Ramesses, pressing him harder.

"Well, they love to do everything together, and they are willing to do anything for each other even if it means giving up their life to save the other. Why is this so important?" asked Francesco, scratching his head.

"I believe I have found her weakness—her friends—am I so blind not to have seen it sooner? The answer has been right before my eyes all this time," Ramesses said, reprimanding himself for not paying attention to detail; his father would scold him for that, too. "I know they want to stay together to return to Hawote, and she will risk anything to make sure nothing happens to them—she will even please me. I will have to get her alone and threaten her with harsh comings to her friends if she displeases me or fails to obey me. She leaves me no choice, and neither do they. I must find a way to trap her," said Ramesses as he stroked his beard in thought. "They may have some use until I win this war, and *then* I will send them on their way..."

Francesco cocked an eyebrow. "That's it! Of course! She always puts herself in the line of fire to save another's life. For example, she ran into a burning house to save Eagle Claw and his family—they barely escaped alive. I could go on all day telling you stories of her heroic rescues and daring deeds. What do you mean by trapping her? How will you do it? You will have to put up with threats from her friends, and what would Nefertari think if she found out what you did to weaken and force Neiko into submitting?"

"I will make certain no one ever knows what I did, because I will make her sorry if she tells, and that's why I will trap her. I will not tell you how I'll do it. I will keep that a secret, so Neiko will never suspect," Ramesses said craftily.

"Good point. Well, you've got her now," Francesco said as he smiled with a wicked grin.

They boated for hours, and they were on their way home. Neiko saw someone in the water, drowning in the river; the man was several yards away.

"Neiko, what's wrong?" asked Mactalon.

"There's someone in the water! Oh no, they will be killed!" Nefertari squealed as she covered her mouth with her hands.

"If somebody doesn't hurry, he could he croc food!" Mactalon added.

Wasting no time, Neiko took off her crown, threw it on the deck, sprinted across the deck, and dove into the river. She didn't even think about crocodiles or snakes being in the water.

"Queen overboard!" shouted Panthero.

"Turn it around!" Ramesses thundered at the boatman. He ran to the bow of the boat and tugged at his crown in worry as she swam like a fish to the floating man.

Neiko made it to the man, grabbed him, and started pulling him to the boat by the collar of his simple tunic. Mactalon and Panthero pulled the man onto the boat, and Sito and Tito helped Neiko climb back on. They laid the man on his back, but he didn't move.

"Is he alive?" asked Nefertari.

Neiko put her ear to his chest. "Yep, but he's not breathing. He's got a heartbeat, though. I will have to give him air. Stand back." She rolled him on his stomach and chopped him between his shoulder blades, but he didn't respond. "C'mon!" she said, rolled on his back, again, pinched his nose, parted his mouth, and gave him artificial respiration.

Ramesses came to see what was going on, and hatred and jealousy rose within him. The man was a Hebrew slave, yet her lips were touching his even though she wasn't kissing him. Ramesses didn't understand what was happening. The slave finally heaved and cough up water. After a moment, he sat up and looked around in terror.

"It's okay, just relax," Neiko said, stroking his hair in reassurance.

But, he shrank back from her in terror because he saw she was a queen, and her angry husband was glaring at him.

Neiko stood up and spun around, put her hands on her hips, and stared at Ramesses harshly.

"Stop looking at him like that! You are doing nothing but harm so go back over there and let me take care of this man!" Neiko snapped as she crossed her arms.

Ramesses folded his arms. "You risk your life for a slave? You could have been killed. Your days of saving others are over—I will not hear of you saving anymore rodents from the river. And you dare kiss him in my presence?"

"I know what I'm doing! I know how to swim in rivers! Ugh! I just saved another human being! No one's better than anyone else in our culture, and a Hebrew is just as important as an Egyptian—a pharaoh is no better than a slave because we all are people! And, for your information, I was *not* kissing him! Go away—you're ticking me off!" Neiko shouted.

"You are wet, and you will not be anywhere near this lowlife. Come with me," Ramesses said, grabbing her arm and trying to pull her away. "My culture is now your culture. This Indian nonsense about everyone being your equal is no longer your way of life. Come with me!"

"Stop it, would you?! Let go of me! I'm staying right here! Let me go!" Neiko said, wrenching free, pushing Ramesses away, and running to the aid of the stranger.

Ramesses let her do her work as he watched in fury. "I will tame your wild spirit, Neiko—you wait and see," said Ramesses under his breath to Neiko in a harsh warning.

Yet, Neiko overheard his heated retort and snapped back sarcastically, "Whatever."

"I thank you for saving me, my queen. But what kind of an Egyptian are you? Please take no offense—I mean no disrespect," said the man with caution.

"My name is Neiko, and I've been recently taken in by Pharaoh. I'm from Hawote, and these are my friends. What's your name?" asked Neiko, trying to make friends.

"Benjamin," he replied.

"Well, Benjamin, how did you end up in the river?" Neiko asked as she started to pull off his wet shirt. She saw the whiplash marks on his torso, and remembered when her friends were beaten by Kenes. "They beat you like an animal. Who was your master?" she asked angrily.

"I was rowing a holiday barge with the rest of the men for Kenes, our master; I tired, so the taskmaster threw me in the river— unfortunately I never learned how to swim," he said as Mactalon draped a blanket over him.

All of the Indians furrowed their brows and frowned. They knew of Kenes' cruelty all too well. Was he going to drop back into Thebes unannounced?

Nefertari saw his ribs poking out of his skin because he was being starved. "He is starving—how dreadful. Kenes just left him to die, Neiko," she said pitifully. "What will we do?"

Neiko shrugged. "We can't take him back to the palace with us because Ramesses will not let us take him in, judging by the way he just acted. Let's just say if we did we talk him into it, he might treat him even worse than Kenes did because he's a little sore at me right now—he may even send him to Goshen if we're not careful. We have to find him a good place to stay."

Mactalon lit up as idea came to him. "I know! We can take him to Senu—he will take very good care of him. Don't worry, we were in his care at one time before Pharaoh came for Neiko," said Mactalon to Benjamin.

Benjamin looked at the five closely. "Are you the strange people that Kenes used to own, but escaped after the death of that Philistine? I remember only four of you. So you are the girl of the strange people who Kenes wanted, and you are now Pharaoh's wife?"

"That's right. This other one here is my twin brother, Sito. My name is Tito, and these are my friends, Mactalon, Panthero, and Neiko—or should I say Queen Neiko. And this is Queen Nefertari," said Tito. "Once we return, Sito and I will take you to Senu. Do you have any family?"

Benjamin shook his head. "No, my parents are dead, and I have no wife. But I thank you for all you are doing. Maybe someday I can repay you for your kindness," he said.

Once they returned, Sito and Tito took Benjamin to Senu, and everyone else went to bed.

Sito stopped Neiko on her way to her bedroom. "Neiko, I need to talk to you, and it's important," he said, and they went into her room.

– CHAPTER 30 –

NEIKO WENT INTO THE room first; Sito closed the door behind him and locked it.

"What is it?" asked Neiko in surprise at the urgency of the conversation and Sito's actions.

"I found out something more about that second ceremony, and it is quite disturbing," Sito replied. "I was also wondering how you ended up with Ramesses today."

"I slammed the door in his face and locked it just like always, but this time he had a key. You can figure out the rest. And what's the big deal about that stupid ceremony?" asked Neiko, folding her arms.

Sito sighed and ran his fingers through his hair. "It has never been performed in all of history. Ramesses was never supposed to have it performed on anybody including Nefertari. I have studied Egypt and lived here for more than eleven years, but never heard of this ceremony until now. There are many heathen women taken in by pharaohs, but they never undergo this. I talked to a priest about it, who is a friend of mine—he told me that I can find it written on a very old tablet. This ceremony is only performed when a pharaoh takes a wife—and under his command—wishes it to be performed. The meaning is that this woman is bound to him for all of eternity, nothing can extinguish the love, and she is no longer of her people if she is not Egyptian. It also has a curse along with it: the pharaoh's ghost will haunt any man that takes this wife after the death of the pharaoh, and many evils will befall him. Also, if the pharaoh dies before the woman, she will die and be buried with him—side by side. Even in death you'll never be separated or bad things will happen. If she doesn't die, then she will be cursed. The pharaoh's ghost will follow her and haunt her. So if something happens to Ramesses that isn't supposed to, you will be killed or you will be buried alive in his tomb. If you are killed, you will still be buried in his tomb beside him and not in a separate one like Nefertari will. If you die first, the same thing applies; you will have this inscribed on your sarcophagus with your funerary spells about your eternal union with Ramesses. You two can never be separated, even in death, or his wrath will be unleashed. If you ever run away, or if you try to stifle his eternal flame, it will not quench. He will find you wherever you go; his love will find you. So, Neiko, this is a very serious ordeal, and I'm sorry we didn't do something to stop it."

Neiko shook her head. "Oh, Sito, it's nothing but a bunch of superstitious nonsense! We come from the twentieth century, so we don't believe in that stuff! Ramesses would have made me do it, even if he had needed to hog-tie and drag me kicking and screaming, so no apology needed. We know that Egyptian curses are a bunch of baloney. That love stuff is really touching, but I hate Ramesses. Ramesses' ghost haunting Monchiska and jinxing his hunting days sounds ridiculous," she said and then frowned.

"Maybe so, but the rest will hold true. If Ramesses dies, you die. We have to make sure nothing like that happens," Sito said firmly.

"What happens to Nefertari if he dies early?" asked Neiko.

"Nothing—she just becomes a grieving widow and returns to her home, or she is picked up by the next pharaoh for a wife. We know she dies before he is supposed to," Sito stated.

"That's really not fair!" Neiko grumbled, shaking her fists. "I like Nefertari and all, but she gets all the breaks. I get curses and death threats if Ramesses bites the dust, but she gets to live while I get killed or buried alive. He is so jealous of anybody that looks at me cross-eyed. This whole curse thing is just another act of jealousy in my opinion. He is so possessive and overprotective; I can't do anything without him keeping an eye on me while she can go walking anywhere or do anything she wants. I know it'll get worse because he's so jealous of everyone I talk to. I'll bet I won't be able to even go to bed by myself without him escorting me to my room! This is so unfair!" Neiko fussed as she pulled at her hair.

"Neiko, I will tell you why this is. Your situation is really—complicated—Nefertari's is not. She has done nothing to make him doubt her loyalty, but you have been bucking his authority—that's the main reason—and this is sort of a punishment for your actions. He knows you'll be out of here at the first chance you get. He won't let that happen. Nefertari's situation has drawbacks, though. If she should ever betray him for any reason, she would suffer greater consequences than you ever would. She would pay dearly by losing his respect in that he may divorce her. She may even pay with her life depending on how bad the offense is and how angry he is at her. Right now, all that will happen to you is that he will take away more of your freedom or lock you in your room, so I guess it isn't much better either way. Nefertari has more dire punishment, but unlike you, she loves him very much, and I doubt she would ever betray him for any reason. You and she have become good friends. Let her assist you because she can. Confide in her, and she can help you work through your problems with Ramesses. She wouldn't do this for any other woman, remember that," Sito said.

"Okay, I wasn't saying I like her any less, but I was saying that

Ramesses is being unfair. It's not her fault that he is being a butthole," Neiko said cynically.

Sito laughed. "He doesn't want anyone else to have you. You're right, things will get worse. I believe he will make it forbidden for you to be even near us—sooner rather than later—definitely after that Great Wife ceremony. After that, we will never again be able to look at you or even touch you—and no—I haven't found out any more information on that," he said, reading Neiko's features. "Don't mention anything to Nefertari what we discussed about the 'mystery ceremony' or the curse. Don't complain too much to her about Ramesses because he may find out by eavesdropping since he keeps eyes and ears on you at all times. That's the last thing you need right now; I know she wouldn't tell on you intentionally."

"I think Ramesses needs to relearn a lesson in manners; it's not polite to eavesdrop on people," said Neiko with a cocky look on her face.

"You don't know how many times his father chastised him for that when he was young, but it hasn't stopped him yet. He was spying on me about 98 percent of the time. If he wants to know something bad enough, he'll find out in any way he can."

"Why was he spying on you?" Neiko asked.

"Nothing important. I'm off to bed. Good night," said Sito, avoiding the question as he gave Neiko a reassuring hug and left.

Neiko crawled into bed. She didn't buy that Ramesses would spy on Sito for no reason, but she couldn't think of anything that would be that important. It wasn't like Sito was inventing the atomic bomb for Ramesses' father Seti, and Ramesses wanted to learn how to make one, too. Neiko's thoughts faded as she fell asleep.

The next day, Neiko was looking at a picture she had drawn of Monchiska when there was a knock on the door. She looked up and put the drawing behind her. "Who is it?" she asked.

"It's Nefertari. May I come in?" asked Nefertari through the door.

Neiko got up. "Yeah—coming," she said and then opened the door and invited her in. "What's new?"

"I just wanted to commend you for saving that man yesterday. I also want to be an Indian," Nefertari said as she sat on the bed. She noticed the picture of Monchiska. "What's this?"

"Oh, that's Monchiska," said Neiko as she turned away. "Why do you want to be like us? I mean, you know what Ramesses would say. He'd go through the roof if he found out. He'd be ticked to know he had to un-Indian both his wives!"

Nefertari chuckled. "He won't find out; this will be our little secret. Is Monchiska special?" asked Nefertari with her brown eyes twinkling with curiosity.

"Yes. He's the man I love in Hawote," said Neiko with her voice filled with sadness and homesickness.

"Are you married?" Nefertari asked.

"No, we never dated and were nothing more than friends. I recently found out he loves me back. But I can't tell him how I feel because there are three thousand years and an ocean between us-- and not to mention Ramesses. He's worse than anything and wouldn't allow me to do that."

"Oh, I'm so sorry," Nefertari said, putting her hand on Neiko strong shoulder. "I don't care what he says about Indians—I want to be like you. Will you make me of your tribe and teach me how to fight?" Nefertari asked.

"Well…um…to make you a Desert Storm Falcon--let's see…I'm not the chief, so I can't do it this way—I can make you my blood sister," said Neiko as she thought out loud.

"What's a blood sister?" asked Nefertari, filled with curiosity and excitement.

"Well, we become sisters by sealing a covenant in blood. We basically become like we were born sisters. We agree to look after and protect each other until death and seal the pact in blood, either by slitting our wrists or pricking our fingers. I recommend we will prick our fingers so Ramesses won't find out. I don't want to try explaining *that* to him," said Neiko with a sideways grin.

Nefertari smiled and giggled. "Let's do this."

"Okay, I happen to have a needle right here," said Neiko taking out a needle from her gown. "Hold out your finger—this will hurt a little," Neiko said.

Nefertari put out her finger, and Neiko pricked it and squeezed it until a small crimson bead appeared on her fingertip.

"Ouch!" Nefertari cried and winced.

Then Neiko pricked her own finger, squeezed it, then took Nefertari's bloody finger, and pressed it against hers.

"We are now blood sisters; you are now Desert Storm Falcon. We promise to look after and protect each other until death," she said, sealing the pact. "Now, for the fighting part of the deal—I can only teach you how to fist fight because I can't have any kind of weapons," Neiko said, standing up and taking Nefertari by the hands. "Okay, now for your fighting lesson. Ball up your fist like this, and hit my hand as hard as you can," Neiko said as she coached and demonstrated the maneuvers and stance.

Nefertari tried to duplicate the maneuver. She hit Neiko's hand in the palm, but it was a weak hit.

"You didn't put all you had into it. C'mon, hurt me. Pretend my hand is someone's face you absolutely hate," Neiko coached and beckoned with her other hand as she held up her palm for a target.

Nefertari hit again, but this time it hurt. "How was that?"

"Very good," Neiko said, shaking the sting from her hand. "Actual combat is a lot more complicated than that. You won't ever have worry about that; I hope. Okay, now for some more advanced tricks."

Neiko taught Nefertari some evasive maneuvers and basic strikes points for a kick, punch, knee, or elbow. Neiko demonstrated the attacks on Nefertari's body in slow motion. Then they practiced the moves together in slow motion and slowly picked up the pace. Neiko instructed her to hit her hands for target practice.

"Practice this until it becomes natural. In a real fight you have to pay more attention to what they're doing rather than how you'll make your move. That's why it's important to practice," said Neiko.

"Oh, that will come in handy. Too bad I can't learn use a weapon," Nefertari said with a deflated frown. "You are a wonderful teacher."

Neiko shrugged her face and said "It's nothing". "Well, maybe another time. You can thank Ramesses for that one," Neiko added. "When I wasn't in battle, I was teaching the next generation," she added.

"Neiko, I have something I want you to know. You know that crystal you want so badly? I saw Ramesses put it on his clothes shelf in his room, but he doesn't know that I know," Nefertari said urgently like a double-agent meeting her contact.

Neiko looked at her elated and cheered. "Thanks, I'll have to find a way to take it when he leaves for a day."

"Good luck," Nefertari said clasping her hands. She hugged her and left.

Later that night everyone was at dinner, and Neiko did not skip even though had contemplated doing so earlier that day. She told them what Nefertari had told her about the crystal before Pharaoh had arrived. Moments later Ramesses and his scribe (and lackey, as Neiko liked to call him among other things) arrived at dinner. Ramesses cleared his throat to get everyone's attention because he had an announcement to make. "I will be at a meeting tomorrow with the master builder for most of the day about the plans for a new monument, but no one can leave," said Ramesses as he watched every move the Indians made.

Neiko and her friends had a history of making up codes in the past before their long exile from Hawote. Neiko immediately used a secret code to alert the others, thinking that Ramesses would not notice. She waved her hands in the secret code telling them that she would sneak into his room and take the crystal. She didn't notice that he was watching her. He was smirking, however, because she had taken the bait, and he wasn't fooled by the code at all. She was either going to fall into the trap or her friends were. Either way was a win-win for him. If he caught her friends in the act, they would be thrown out post-haste.

Neiko and the others got up to plan their escape shortly after dinner was over.

"We will go home as soon as I swipe that crystal. Good night, y'all," Neiko said.

They went to bed that night dreaming of being back home again.

- Chapter 31 -

THE NEXT DAY THE Indians were up and ready for their flight home. As soon as Ramesses went out the door, Neiko ran into his room. Nefertari and the rest went outside in the garden in hopes to cover their operation and to protect Nefertari from any ill fate. Neiko slipped into his room, partly closed the door, and then went to the shelf. She lifted up and looked underneath his crowns and pilfered through his headdresses, kilts, robes, and other royal regalia. She put on one of his crowns for show. She picked up a jeweled, polished bronze mirror from his cedar vanity and laughed at herself. She tried on many of his other clothes and jewels. She got onto herself for messing around and put the clothes back in their proper place, threw the heavy mirror on the bed, and looked through his jewels—nothing.

"She said it was right here. Let's see if he hid it somewhere else," Neiko mused as she stood there with a blank expression and her hans on her hips as her eyes scanned the lavish bedchamber. She twisted her mouth and clicked her tongue as her mind reeled of possible places the elusive crystal could be.

Neiko searched the bed and the room—nothing. "I coulda swore she said…" she thought as she tossed her hands in aggravation.

"Looking for this?" asked a voice.

Neiko spun around in surprise. There stood Ramesses with the crystal in his hand and a devious smile on his face. He tossed it as he leaned against one of the richly decorated gold tables that were by the door. He was enticing her and daring her to come get it.

Neiko's heart began pounding because she knew she was caught red-handed. She reached for the crystal, but he pulled it out of reach. "How…" she started to ask, but her throat closed up and cut off any words that may have tried to come out.

"Simple. I know how much you want this and how much you desire to be back home. I knew you would assume I would have it in my room, so I made up something to get you or your friends alone. Now, there is no escape," Ramesses said, approaching her.

"Wrong," Neiko said defiantly, running toward the door.

He was directly in her path, and he grabbed her, stopping her. She struggled, but it wasn't working. She finally kicked him in the shin, and he loosened his grip on her. That was what she needed. She pulled free, kicked him in between the legs, and socked him in the chin. He crumpled to the stone floor, groaning in pain, and looked at her in agony.

"Sorry, Ramesses, but the Indian foiled the Egyptian, and the admiral eluded the pharaoh," Neiko said triumphantly and ran to the door. It was closed. "I don't remember closing this," she said, and she tried to open it, but it was locked. "Oh crap! Sito, Mactalon, anybody, help! Nefertari, help!" she yelled, banging on the door and pulling it frantically. She looked back, and he was staggering to his feet and walking to her. It was obvious to her that he was a step ahead of her and well into the game.

"It seems the pharaoh outwitted the admiral, and the Egyptian just trapped the Indian. You cannot open it without this," Ramesses said with a smile holding up the key.

Neiko ran and tackled him, and she wrestled him for the key. She managed to get it and ran for the door, but he got up and seized her before she could put it in the lock, took it away, and threw it. She ran for it, but he tripped her by tackling her legs and retained his hold on her ankles. She lunged for it, but he kicked it out of reach while seated on the floor and still retaining his hold on her.

The key slid underneath the bed just beyond her reach. She tried to wriggle her feet free from his grip and commando-crawl to the key, but his grasp was like steel, and he was surprisingly strong. This eliminated her theory that he was a pampered, cowardly pantywaist who used protocol to get his way—Sito wasn't just overreacting. He pulled her to him and tried to pin her.

Ramesses stopped his advance and went on the defensive. "What do you plan on doing with that?" he asked with a grin and a flicker of excitement in his dark eyes. Nothing was more thrilling to him than battle— almost—*this* was just *too* perfect.

Feeling empowered, Neiko went on the attack. "This!" she yelled, swinging the mirror at him.

Ramesses ducked to dodge the first swing. He wove and leaned back to dodge other attacks. Not only was he big and strong, he had the reflexes of a mongoose. He also knew how

Neiko moved by secretly watching her practice and coach her friends and from seeing her in action. He had other reasons for watching other than learning her MO. All of them added up to one thing: he was well ahead of the game.

Neiko raised the mirror above the top of her head and tried to send the heavy object crashing down on top of his head, but Ramesses was ready for her. He stopped the attack by seizing her wrists and pinning her onto his cedar vanity. Objects clattered on the floor from the force of their combined weight and from Neiko

slamming down. Neiko struggled and writhed to get free. She tried to hoist her lower body and push him back again, but he pressed his body against her legs and immobilized her. He pried the mirror from her grasp and pitched it on the foot of the bed.

"You are so feisty. I like it when you play hard-to-get; I like rough play," he said as he bent down and nuzzled her neck. "Roughhousing with you is rather enjoyable."

Neiko yelled in disgust and discomfort. "Ugh! Eww! Stop it! Who said I was playin'? This ain't a game! Senet is a game—I really meant to hurt you…"

"On the contrary. I win this battle, so now for my reward," he said gripping her face and stealing a kiss. "Now, let's talk," Ramesses said as he picked her up and flung her over his shoulder. He carried her to the bed, threw her down on it, and pinned her back down.

Neiko was terrified. Was he about to do what she thought he was going to do? "You won't get away with this," Neiko growled.

Ramesses saw her terror, and she misunderstood his intentions. "Aww, I wouldn't do that to you—I am too much of a gentleman, and I now could charm you to love me that way and such an act is against the Code of Maat," he said.

Neiko gave him a silent retort about the gentleman part by giving him a look that said, "Yeah, right." "That Code doesn't stop some of you—like Kenes, for instance."

"You are comparing me to scum like Kenes?" Ramesses asked, appalled. "You don't even know me. I'm shocked. Where did such poisonous assumptions about my character come from? I am not at all heartless. Feel," he said pressing her hand on his muscular chest over his heart and underneath the large scarab amulet.

She could feel his strong, rapid heartbeat beneath her touch. "You're all the same to me! I guess facts and stories change a lot over 3,000 years. Apparently you got blamed for something you didn't exactly do, but you're still involved in it to some degree, so you're not totally sinless," Neiko shot back. "I'm not going to bother telling you that! It's not that important," she replied, answering his look that asked her "like what?" What implications would that have on the future? Would there even be a country called Israel in the 20th century if she did? When Moses was born and brought into the palace, if it was in his lifetime, Moses would probably cease to exist and complete genocide would follow. The future would then be really messed up. *I really screwed up. Maybe I shouldn't have said that. Hopefully he'll just forget about it,* she thought. "I don't want to know you; I don't want to love you. I just wanna go home!" Neiko yelled in protest.

"You *are* home. I tried to be merciful and do things the easy way, but you and your friends opted to do this the hard way, so we are now doing it the hard way. You will know my passionate side soon enough when you stop resisting me. I am so nigh to breaking through. I'm going to change your mind about me. You'll find that I am a cool drink of water and as sweet as honey; you will fall deeply in love with me."

Neiko gave him a "yeah right" look. "You just wait till I tell my friends…" Neiko said with a threatening growl.

"Tell them, and I will send them to Goshen," Ramesses interrupted savagely. "I have let you shun me long enough, and now it is time to show you I am in charge and that my forgiveness and patience are over. You will start obeying me in my every command to the letter if you want your friends to remain here. I may even exile them in the desert with no food or water if you try me further. I will not have any more attempts to take this crystal, or I will destroy it. And, if you utter a word of this to anyone including Nefertari, I will kill your friends. Is that clear?" he said harshly. "Also, if I call you, you will come running. And, you better be there, or else—"

Neiko knew he would live up to these threats because she knew how much he hated her friends and how much he would like to be rid of them. "Yeah," she said as hot tears of helplessness filled her eyes, and she began sobbing.

Ramesses smiled at his handiwork as she turned her back to him, but he wrapped his arms around her and kissed her cheek. She closed her eyes and cried harder. He was going to be getting rid of her friends soon anyway, but now keeping her friends around would be beneficial leverage for the time being.

Meanwhile the Indians and Nefertari were gathered in the throneroom waiting for Neiko. They were restless, and things were taking way too long. Stealing a crystal should take no more than ten minutes tops. Suddenly Neiko appeared about an hour later.

"Well?" asked Mactalon.

"It wasn't there. Sorry guys," Neiko said, bowing her head.

"Son of a gun!" Panthero said, stamping his foot in frustration.

Nefertari was confused and speechless, but she said nothing.

"I'm going to my room for a little while," Neiko said. "I just want to be alone," she said, answering their silent questions.

Neiko left abruptly and as she neared her quarters her face contorted in agony and the tears began to flow again. She flung herself on the bed and wept.

Several weeks had passed, and Sito became concerned about Neiko's strange behavior that seemed out of character for her. Neiko had been secretive and aloof. Why had she been responding to Pharaoh's every beck and call? Neiko was also avoiding her friends as well as Nefertari's concerns and questions. Neiko seemed ashamed and frightened in some ways, but she would not say why. When someone would ask her a question about it, she would avoid the question and run away. One evening, the four had the night off of work and decided to talk about it. Neiko had agreed to meet them for poker provided she could get a moment away from her demanding husband. She had not arrived yet.

"I wonder what's wrong with Neiko—she has been acting strangely. She seems to be afraid of something—we have to find out what," said Mactalon as he wrung his hands.

Agitated, Tito sighed. "I know. I don't buy that she is upset that she couldn't find the crystal. I'm wondering if Pharaoh threatened her or something. The thing is; she ain't afraid of him, so why would she submit to the point where she goes running to him every time he calls? He calls her every two minutes!" Mactalon said as he folded his arms.

Sito mused as he rubbed his chin. "Hmm, Mactalon, I believe you're on to something. I believe he *did* threaten her to make her feel helpless about something so he can crack her resistance, so he can start wearing her down with charm and romance. You know how much he wants her, and he will not stop—he will stoop low to get her and get his way with her. We all know it may have something to do with us. Things could get nasty for us whether or not she loses the war."

"Aye, he must be using her noble spirit against her," said Panthero, conjecturing a possible reason.

"The only person who can tell us for sure is Neiko, but she won't stay around and tell us. She won't even tell Nefertari, and that worries me. You know we can't ask Pharaoh," Tito said.

"We may have to tie her up and make her tell us. She knows she can trust us, so why is she avoiding us?" asked Mactalon.

"Guys, she's coming. Shh," said Tito, cutting off the conversation. He didn't want to talk about it until they decided to ask Neiko what was wrong—again. "Hi, Neiko. Ready for poker?"

"Yeah, come on," Neiko responded lightheartedly.

They went to their favorite spot and started to play.

"So…uh…Neiko, is everything all right?" asked Sito.

"Yeah, why?" Neiko said, looking over her hand of cards with fear.

"I was wondering if Pharaoh has threatened you or harmed you in some way," Sito said pressing her.

Neiko looked up from her hand again, folded it up, and laid it on the table. "Why?" she asked looking more scared and worried.

"I…I have no idea what you mean," she said standing up, and then ran away.

Her four friends shook their heads as they watched her disappear.

"I definitely believe he has intimidated her," said Panthero.

"I'll speak to Nefertari and see if she can talk to her. Nefertari had been concerned as well," added Sito.

Later that night, Sito told Nefertari of his and his friends' concerns. After that, she went to find Neiko and found her sitting on the feet of a statue of Ramesses looking at the ground and twiddling her thumbs. Neiko seem both exasperated and extremely upset.

"Neiko, I want to talk to you. I know you are tormented about something, and I want to help, but you must tell me what is going on. Has Ramesses upset you?" asked Nefertari.

Neiko looked up. "I…I can't. Please don't grill me about it. It is better if I say nothing."

Nefertari wasn't fooled; she knew Ramesses like the back of her hand. "Aha! He has threatened you. Please tell me—I can help you," Nefertari said, trying to comfort her and persuade her to open up.

"No—you can't. If I say a word to you, the consequences will be horrible. Not to you or me, but to others," Neiko said with a pained expression.

"Would this be your *friends* by any chance?" asked Nefertari perceptively as she put her hand on her hip. "Will your friends go to Goshen or die or be sent to the wilderness if you disobey? If I interfere, then will that be the cost of you telling me about this gambit?" asked Nefertari with a cross expression.

"How'd you know? Please don't tell anyone else—I'll get in trouble. Don't say a word to Ramesses—he will do in my friends and punish me in more isolation. I have to go to him when he calls so no one will be hurt," Neiko said, choking up. "I can't lose my friends again after it took so long to find them again."

"It will be all right," Nefertari said, hugging her. Nefertari measured up what to say to Sito. She also wanted to confront Ramesses while trying to protect her friend. Nefertari felt her brokenness, emptiness, and despair, and she knew something had to be done, and she was the only one who could do anything about it. Neiko was to the point of breaking. She wept with her as she stroked her hair.

"What is wrong, my warrior?" asked Ramesses to Neiko, and Nefertari gave him a dirty look.

"N-nothing…I—I was just telling N-Nefertari how much I miss home, that's all," Neiko fibbed, looking at the ground.

"Come with me—I will comfort you," Ramesses said, taking her hand, and Nefertari gave him an icy glare. He looked at Nefertari like she had gone bonkers.

"Let her be, Ramesses. She has spent most of the day with you. Now she wishes to be alone. Let me comfort her—you have done enough already," Nefertari said in a scolding manner.

"This is no affair of yours. If you are placing your nose where it does not belong, then you will pay," Ramesses said with a dark and poisonous glare.

Nefertari looked at him with an appalled and shocked look. "Are you threatening me?" she asked with a miffed tone. "I have something unsettled to talk with you about—alone. Now would be good."

"Later. Excuse me," Ramesses said, blowing her off and leading Neiko off and brushing past her.

Nefertari narrowed her eyes at him with a nasty frown. She watched them disappear and went to find Sito.

- CHAPTER 32 -

A FEW MINUTES LATER, Nefertari found Sito and told him everything she had found out.

"So, it is true—he has threatened her with our well-being. I should have known—Neiko always puts others' needs ahead of her own, and she would do anything for our safety," said Sito.

"Yes, I know. Ramesses also has been very cold to me lately, and he pushes me away—I don't know why. I mentioned something about talking with him about this situation, and he got very angry and threatened me. Sito, this is getting dangerous, and someone will get hurt. Something must be done and quickly. Neiko is very weak and vulnerable, and he is on the verge of breaking her," Nefertari said.

Sito knew the answer to why Ramesses was being cold to Nefertari, but it was forbidden information. "You're right—something must be done. Neiko is hurting, and breaking her spirit is part of the idea so he can move in with his charms—he'll eventually cut off her lifelines to Hawote by cutting her off from us."

"Yes. I tried to comfort her, but he took her away. If she heals, then he must start all over again—we seem to be refueling her resistance. He will not let anyone else around for long, not even me. I'm beginning to wonder when he had the time to do such a thing. I don't think that bruise on his chin was caused by hitting himself with the door like he says. I believe Neiko hit him. He has a bruise on his shin too which he says he got when he tripped over a stool. He is not normally that clumsy," Nefertari said, setting her jaw and narrowing her eyes in suspicion.

"Hmm, I believe you're right. So there was a fight, and it seems he won. How on earth did he find time to pull it off, and no one knows about it? We've been inside the palace every day since he won't let anyone other than you out," mused Sito.

"Except for the day she tried to find the crystal…" Nefertari said then gasped cupped her hands over her mouth when she realized she may have stumbled on a clue. "Oh no!"

"That's it! It was a trap! He had this well planned out. But, he doesn't seem to know you told us where he had hid the crystal. I guess he assumed that she would be thinking he would have it in there," Sito realized Ramesses' own cleverness and pure dumb luck were the only things that saved Nefertari's skin at this point. "You are still in the clear," Sito said, wiping off his brow.

"Oh dear, I really want to give him a piece of my mind!" Nefertari said as she clenched her fists and stamped her feet in peevish rage.

"Nefertari, be careful," Sito warned, extending his finger. "You may need to say something to him for personal reasons, but you must try to protect Neiko—and us. Neiko is in great peril—don't endanger her with your anger," Sito said. "Your involvement may actually put us all at risk."

"I won't endanger anyone; it's a personal matter between him and I, and I am the only one who can safely speak out about such a despicable act. I'll take the blame of how the act was uncovered to save her if I must. Now I must find him," Nefertari said, gritting her teeth and fuming. She stamped off to find Ramesses.

Nefertari searched the usual places he would be: the garden, the dining hall, his room, but he wasn't there. She asked several of the guards for tip-offs in order to track them down. She finally found them walking in the main hall, and she stormed up to them while their backs were turned. They turned around, and Nefertari was breathing hard and glaring at Ramesses.

"Nefertari, I..." Ramesses began.

"Don't you *Nefertari* me, Ramesses!" Nefertari interrupted. "Did you not think I would find out about this? You will stop this now!"

Ramesses put on an innocent face and laughed. "I have no idea what you are talking about. Stop what? Why are you so upset?"

"You know *exactly* why I am upset. Don't play dumb with me; I am not that naïve. I know you are up to something! If you wish me to remind you about what you have done, I will!" she said through clenched teeth and narrowed eyes.

Ramesses set his jaw and vessels popped out of his forehead and neck as he tried to contain his anger. "Remind me of what? There is no need to be angry. Oh, I see, you are jealous because I'm not spending time with you. Is that it?" Ramesses asked with a cocky shrug.

Nefertari snorted. "No. That's not it at all. It's what you have been doing to *Neiko*. First, you trap her to be alone with you, and then you threaten her and force her to be with you? I was wondering if you would actually consider doing something like this, but then you have the audacity to actually *do* it! Ohh, that is despicable! I *won't* let you get away with this. I don't care if you are my husband or if you are the pharaoh. They call you a god, but you are less than a man for doing something so vile. She will never love you because she loves another of her own kind."

Ramesses' face darkened with rage upon hearing the sting of her words. He turned to Neiko, and she shrank back not knowing what was going to happen to her friends. "Did you tell her? Answer me!" he snarled at her and tightened his grip on her arm; she began to plead and beg for her friends' safety.

"Enough, Ramesses," Nefertari interrupted, stopping the bullying. "She did not tell me. I figured it out by myself, and it was not that hard. Stop hounding her; just let her go. She will never be happy here with you. She wants to return home to Hawote. I am speaking on Neiko's behalf," Nefertari said.

"Never mention that land in my presence again! I will never let her go; she's now mine. And, Neiko has the ability to speak for herself. There are other things at work here that you couldn't possibly understand and that is *also* none of you business," Ramesses said with apathy written all over his face. "They *all* left me with no choice. Neiko wanted to do this the hard way, so we're doing it the hard way. I *won't* be ignored, and I *won't* be shunned! Be gone and cool you heels in you chamber before I lose my temper!" Ramesses said.

"You prideful scoundrel, you are lower than the scum of the Nile! How dare you! If you really love Neiko and value her happiness, you would grant her freedom! Above all, release her from this bondage you call a marriage. She is not your wife; she is your prisoner and a gilded slave!" Nefertari yelled. "Furthermore, there is nothing more that needs to be understood here—you are being selfish and pig-headed. That's quite enough for anyone to know!" Nefertari retorted.

Ramesses' feathers were getting even more ruffled. "You are out of line. And who asked you to be Pharaoh? It was not I—*she* is the one who is making this harder than it has to be. She will learn to be happy with me and accept her life here. What would a woman know about circumstances like this, and who are you to say you know Neiko's thoughts? She is not enslaved; she is extremely privileged."

Nefertari slapped him across the face. "You vile, self-centered, insolent dog! Neiko knows more about true love than you ever will! I hope the gods curse the day you were born for this outrage. I hope they make your days of being Pharaoh a nightmare. I hope your treasure cities fall to the ground while you are standing in them. I may even go to the temple of Maat to pray for justice to be done about this despicable act!"

Ramesses rubbed his throbbing cheek and boiled. "You brazen wench, how dare you strike me! You insult me with curses? If you were not one of my favorites, I would kill you for this. Try me no further because I will bathe my sword in your blood if you continue this insolence."

"Can I go now, please? This is none of my business—" Neiko said shyly, trying to break free from his grasp.

"You are not going anywhere, my warrior," Ramesses said, tightening his grip and forcing her to stay.

"Let her go, Ramesses! She doesn't have to watch us quarrel," argued Nefertari.

"Oh, you mean, something *you* started?" Ramesses snorted. "This argument is now over. Out of my way," Ramesses said, trying to walk past her, but she stopped him. She pulled Neiko's arm free from his clutches, and Neiko ran down the hall and disappeared.

"It is not over—I have just begun to tell you what I really think of you! There are words I wouldn't want small children to hear to tell you how much I despise you for what you have done to Neiko. I can say this, you are not the son of Seti, but the son of Set!" Nefertari snarled at him.

Ramesses pushed her violently against the wall with all of his strength and anger because she caused him to blow a gasket. Nefertari fell to the ground, motionless, since she hit her head on the wall. In his rage he cursed her and stormed down the hall.

Neiko ran down the hall out of her hiding place and saw her lying on the floor. "Nefertari!" she said, running to her fallen friend and scooping her up. "Are you okay? Say something!" she said, and she saw the horrible swelling on the side of her head.

Nefertari groaned, and partly opened her eyes. "Neiko? I overdid it, and he pushed me. He has shoved me a few times before when I refused to stop a quarrel, but never like this," she said weakly.

"Don't try to talk—I think you have what we call a concussion," Neiko said, explaining. She had to say "concussion" in English since there was no word for it in the Egyptian language, if there was, she didn't know it. "I have to go get help. Sito can help you. I'll help you to your feet and take you to your room," Neiko said, helping her up and letting Nefertari lean on her for support since she was dizzy.

Neiko helped her walk to her room and lay her down on her bed and covered her up.

After a few minutes, Neiko returned with her friends on her heels.

"How did this happen, Neiko?" asked Sito as he checked Nefertari's vitals and condition.

"Ramesses. They were arguing, and she let him have it and gave him a talking-to he won't forget, but she didn't stop and pushed him way beyond his breaking point, so he plowed her into the wall. Will she be all right?" asked Neiko. "I don't think she got anywhere though."

Sito furrowed his brow in worry; he hoped Nefertari didn't just make things worse. "Yeah, she will be fine. She only has a mild concussion. She did that, did she? No wonder. From what you tell me about what else she said, she's lucky he didn't really hurt her—he doesn't know his own strength when he gets mad—especially *that* mad. She has a lot of anger toward him about his treatment of you. She told me about you becoming blood sisters, and she did this to save you. She cares for our kind, and you are the one that is doomed," Sito said with more worry creasing in his brow. "I just pray this doesn't make it worse."

"Doomed, in what way?" asked Neiko, scratching her head.

"You're about to be cut off from the rest of us very soon. I believe you will be forbidden to be even near Nefertari for a little while till his anger blows over, and you will be forced to live in solitude in a palace full of people," Sito said glumly.

Neiko gasped. "No!" she exhaled in a whisper.

"I believe so," Sito nodded

Nefertari sat up. "I won't let that happen."

Sito pushed her back down. "Calm down, and try not to talk. You need to stay out of this unless we need your help—I don't think there is anything anyone can do at this point—even you. You can get killed if you keep pushing it too far. We are the only ones who can stop him and put an end to this. Besides, we need to protect your life. This is our fight."

Nefertari nodded. "Sito, there is something I want to confess, since all five of you are here. Ramesses and I have never gotten along like you think we have on certain matters, and I don't love him like you believe I do. I love an Indian too, but I can't say his name now because I definitely would pay, and so would he. I bet you are wondering is that why I care so much for your people, but that is only a part of it. The Indian people have mesmerized me, and I love hearing about their life."

Sito stroked her hair. "Shh, shh. That Indian would be lucky to have someone like you love him. Try to rest. Neiko and I will stay with you till you fall asleep."

Nefertari clutched Neiko's and Sito's hands. "I want the two of you to stay with me all night because you are my friends."

"All right," Sito said, as he made a pallet on the floor, and Neiko slept on the pallet beside him.

- CHAPTER **33** -

THE NEXT MORNING, NEIKO got up first and checked on Nefertari, who was sleeping peacefully. She slipped out the door, and someone grabbed her from behind. She jumped.

"Good morning. Sleep well? I was wondering where you were," said Ramesses, holding her close.

Neiko grimaced in disgust. "I slept fine," she snapped, trying to turn away.

"What are you doing in Nefertari's room?" Ramesses asked.

"That's none of your darn business," Neiko retorted.

"Everything you do is my business. And how has your morning been so far?" Ramesses asked with a grin.

"It was fine till you showed up," Neiko scowled, struggling to free herself.

Ramesses chuckled at her spunk. "Well, there will be some new rules now, and I will announce them to your four friends and to Nefertari in a short while. Come," he said, dragging her off.

A few hours later everyone was lined up in front of Ramesses before his throne awaiting the issue of his new rules. He swaggered back and forth looking at the six. "All right, these new laws will be concerning Neiko who is now my Great Wife. She will be crowned very soon. She is no longer of the Indians, and she is not your equal but your superior. You will no longer call her by her name; call her by the appropriate title: Great One. Never look her in the face if you ever talk to her. You will not be allowed to touch her in any way including friendly gestures. You will not look upon her at all, unless I give you permission, or if she is with me, and I say you can. She will not be in your company from this day forward, and that includes you, Nefertari, till I say so. Francesco, let these laws be written."

Everyone began to murmur in shock, and Neiko collapsed to her knees in shock and disbelief. Nefertari looked at Neiko, felt sorry for her, and bent down to touch her, but Imenhotep stopped her. Neiko grabbed the tail of Ramesses' kilt.

"No, please, Ramesses, don't do this to me, please. I'll do anything, just don't isolate me," Neiko wept, burying her face into his kilt and staining it with her tears. "I'll be your Great Wife—please don't cut me off from my friends—please," she sobbed.

"No, get used to it," Ramesses said mercilessly, enjoying his victory and seeing her begin to crumble at his feet. "I was going to do this a little later, but thanks to Nefertari and your friends, they forced my hand to do it sooner than I had planned."

Neiko then buried her face into the floor and wept sorely. "No!" she moaned into the floor and bawled. The fact that her home and her friends were pushed further away was almost too much to bear.

People in the court whispered and watched.

Her friends watched her, wanting to comfort her, but they couldn't and started to cry in silence.

Francesco smiled wickedly.

Ramesses picked her up off the floor and made her stand up. "Get up off the floor; you are making a mockery of yourself," he scolded.

Neiko was too sad to care, but she had to pull herself together nonetheless.

"Go, the rest of you. Neiko, remain beside me," Ramesses commanded.

Nefertari and the others walked into Sito's room to discuss the horrible outcome.

Nefertari felt very ashamed and bad that her anger could possibly be the cause of the sentence. "I didn't mean to do this, and all I wanted to do was help," Nefertari said, weeping and remembering how sad Neiko was.

"Don't worry about it—I knew he was going to do it very soon anyway," Sito replied. "He's merely tightening his grip on her and pulling her away from us to cut her lifeline from her past life and transitioning her to be his Great Wife. He's gonna fight us like we'll fight him—he'll fight dirty if he has to like we just witnessed. He's gonna do everything he can to hold on to her."

"Isn't he goin' a little overboard?" asked Panthero.

"No, not for making his Great Wife he isn't," said Sito, correcting Panthero.

"I'm gonna kill that lowlife scum for this!" Mactalon growled in hatred.

"No, Mactalon, Ramesses is not the enemy—Francesco is. We wouldn't be in this situation if it wasn't for him. He's the instigator and the reason the five of us ended up here in the first place! Besides, if you kill Ramesses, Neiko's death will follow along with our own—that wouldn't solve anything."

"Oh yeah, I forgot about the curse. But still, he is standing in the midst of our war, and he won't let us fight it. He's taking our friend away from us. I bet he will get rid of us or find a way to destroy us!

Sito, we have to find a way to get out of here. We really have stirred up the hornet's nest now. Haven't you realized that Ramesses has broken the arrow?"

"Why yes, Mactalon, I have, but we can't say a word about it to him. I don't know if that will help us very much," said Sito with a dismal frown. "It wouldn't change anything and he's already made it clear that our rules and ways of doing things don't apply to him."

"I think he hides behind all that Pharaoh protocol because he's a coward," said Mactalon with a hot-tempered scowl.

Sito and Nefertari winced.

"No, he isn't—I wished it was that easy. I don't think historians would have labeled a coward with the title: the Great, Mactalon," Sito said, reminding and correcting him. "The only other person in history that I'm aware of with that title is Alexander. He could easily pull this off without the crown. If he wasn't the king, we would have been butchered a lot sooner and would have no reasons for restraint. He's a lot tougher than you think he is. You, Panthero, and Neiko have all underestimated him at a dangerous level!" Sito said, shaking his head.

Macatalon and Panthero looked at him like "What could he do to us mano y mano outside of his palace and on a battlefield where it counts?"

"I don't think you want to find out," said Sito's counter-stare.

"What is breaking the arrow?" asked Nefertari, breaking into the stare-off.

"It is a very bad offense in Hawote. It is basically what Ramesses is doing to Neiko—taking her away from her people, forcing her to be his wife against her will, and holding her even though she wants to be free. But in this case, it is a more drastic offense because she is in love with Monchiska, and he is trying to drive him out of her heart. Breaking the arrow only applies to Indians," replied Sito.

"How does a person pay for this offense?" asked Nefertari.

"Usually with their lives, but if a foreign king is responsible for it, it starts a war. I have a feeling the four of us are going to have to fight a war to get her away from him," said Sito

Sito's twin brother, his two friends, and Nefertari looked at him like he just asked them to jump off a cliff.

"Uh, correct me if I'm wrong, but didn't you just say that Ramesses is basically unbeatable and never lost a war?!" interjected Mactalon. "He's undefeated against entire armies, so you are expecting four people to fight a war against someone who basically invincible that carries the title "the Great"? I don't know about you, but he won battles against petty things like money, land, and power. What do you think it's gonna be like when he fights a war over passion? That's a big deal, and it's a big driving force for a lot of things!"

Sito said nothing. How right his friend was; he just didn't know how big and how hot Ramesses' passion really was—he only had a vague inkling from the past and only what he saw in the present.

Nefertari snorted. "Are you out of your mind? Four Indians against the legions of Egypt with Ramesses at the head and leading the fight? That is impossible! You could never win, and he will slay you! I've heard the stories of how he charges hard into battle leading the army and killing all before him and in his wake! You have no chance! I've heard the rumors that his father's only complaint against Ramesses' leadership skills when he was young was that he was reckless," she added.

Sito had to find a way to salvage their morale. "Not with weapons, Nefertari, but with words, deeds, and strategy. If it comes to weapons, we will use some old Indian tricks and show him that Indians are not so humble that they can be trampled upon by tyranny," Sito said, poking out his chest in courage. "You're right, we can't have a full-fledged brouhaha on the battlefield. We'd be toast for sure," Sito said with a sigh. "If we did win, then that would be one for the record and that would be one battle he would lose, and that one would definitely count."

"You know, we're not named Hercules, Perseus, Theseus, or Odysseus," Panthero said, reminding him they were not demi-gods or god-chosen heroes; he loved reading the Greek myths in addition to

Indians' tales. He was doubtful even a demi-god could defeat Ramesses. He was on board with Mactalon on that one.

Nefertari's features asked "Who are they?", but then she said, "You know, Sito, I admire your courage, but he won't ever let her go no matter how much you cause him problems or how much you threaten him. He will just be all the more determined to destroy you. I know you are brilliant in many things, but you are now in Ramesses' domain—I am unsure if you can win at strategy alone. What will you do to him if you ever caught him in battle?" asked Nefertari.

"I would exchange him for Neiko, or I would like to give him a taste of his own medicine," Sito stated. "I'm sure Egypt would want him back post-haste."

"Well, say we did do that, but as soon as he got back he would hunt us down with a double-sized army the next time. As long as we have her, he won't leave us alone. It won't ever be over unless we either get back to our own time or move to Australia at this day and age if we can't get the crystal," said Mactalon.

"Could we even get to Australia from here?" asked Panthero. "How long would it take? Is there an easy way?"

Sito shrugged.

"Is that far enough away? Or, should we try Mars?" asked Mactalon with sarcasm. "Since I don't think we can invent a space ship, maybe he would stay out of Antarctica. I don't think Egyptians would like the cold. We would be living like the Inuit and Eskimos in the other direction of the world."

Nefertari chuckled at their conjectures; she had no idea where Mars or any of the other places were. "I will never understand the thinking of a warrior, but I do hope you can one day free her and return to your homeland. Egypt is no place for Indians," Nefertari said, shaking her head.

"You can say that again. I once said I always wanted to visit Egypt when I was a child and see the pyramids, but this isn't what I had in mind—or all of us for that matter," said Mactalon.

Nefertari chuckled. "If you ever return, I hope you never forget me."

"We won't," said Sito. From the crack in the door, he saw Imenhotep, Francesco, and Ramesses walking with Neiko in tow; she was still crying and gloomy. "And it begins," he said as he looked at Ramesses through the small opening.

— CHAPTER 34 —

AFTER NEIKO WAS *FINALLY* able to retire to her room, Imenhotep, Francesco, and Ramesses had a meeting.

"You know, Great Ramesses, I've been thinking it is time to rid yourself of those four savages," said Imenhotep. "I know you have been dying to get rid of Sito for some time. They propose a threat to your future plans. You also recall your past history with Sito and everything he has said is true about his other friends."

"I was thinking the same thing," Francesco said. "I can just imagine what could be at work here."

"I have been thinking the exact same thing, but I just do not know when yet—timing is key. I do not know what to do with them. I do not want them in my house making my life miserable. I don't know if they'll leave if I tell them to," Ramesses thought as he rubbed his beard.

"Yes, they are making tension between you and Nefertari, and they are the last roadblock in winning Neiko—they are her lifeline to what is left of her past life as you already know. They will continue to be a threat to you as long as they remain here," Francesco replied.

"I think they will make worthy additions to the labor gangs in constructing the treasure cities, and they would go well in the mud pits," mused Imenhotep.

"Hmm, that is a great idea. I will double the workload of those four than that of any other slave. Maybe I will be lucky and they'll die there," said Ramesses with a crafty smile. "If so, Neiko will never know. Such knowledge will remain unknown by both of us."

Later that day, Neiko walked in the garden alone. She thought of the day's events, and how her life was being shaped outside of her control. Next week was her coronation and ceremony. She found a concealed area and sat and played the flute that Sito had whittled for her. She would do this when she *could* get away from Ramesses—lately it seemed nearly impossible. After playing, she heard the cries of hawks, and she shut her eyes and began to meditate. Suddenly, her thoughts went into the depths of her soul—she heard the cries of a hawk and saw one flying; she and the hawk became one. She was flying over the countryside of Hawote, and she saw herself running in a field in happiness.

Suddenly, she saw an Egyptian god with the head of an ibis wiping away writings on a wall and writing new ones in their place. A sundial appeared, and the shadow began to move backward. She saw herself walking in Egypt, while the hawk was perched on the Great Pyramid which was her eyes. Neiko found Monchiska in Egypt, and they ran in the desert hand in hand laughing in joy. Suddenly, Egyptian gods surrounded them. Anubis took Monchiska, while Amon-Ra and Osiris took her. She was being dragged to Ramesses calling Monchiska's name, and they threw her in his arms. Monchiska fought

Anubis, defeated him, and came for her. He fought them and defeated all of them, and they returned to Hawote.

The sundial appeared and went forward as Neiko and Monchiska were living a happy life. There was a rumble on the ground and the four colossi of Ramesses and the sphinx were marching and destroying everything. The Abu-Simbal temple lay in ruins, stomped by the huge statues. The statues began to chase them. Then there was a great earthquake, and Ramesses came out of the ground and stabbed Monchiska in the heart. Anubis carried him off while Ramesses carried her off. Monchiska came back and defeated Ramesses freeing her. Neiko and Monchiska, with three unknown people, destroyed the marching statues.

The sundial showed again going forward. It showed Ramses and Ramesses—who looked very different and yet very similar—marching side by side after them, as they ran in terror. The two threw spells at Monchiska, while they tried to trap her together.

Suddenly, the images disappeared, and the hawk sat on a wall, looking at her. "Neiko, beware of Ramesses and the curse. He will one day try to win you back if you make it back to Hawote. He must never live again. Also, beware of Ramses. He too will try to win you, and beware of his curse. Ramesses must never become a Dark Pharaoh and never join Ramses. I will leave you a feather—keep it always for hope. However, Ramesses must never see it or all hope will be lost. Farewell, Neiko. I will be with you. Speak to Sito about what you saw and remember my words," it said and turned into a being of light, which was Great Spirit. Then the light being disappeared.

Neiko came out of her deep trance. A hawk sat on the wall, looking at her, cocking its head. Then it screeched and took off. A feather fell in front of her, and she picked it up and rubbed it against her face.

"The feather of hope," Neiko whispered, and hid it in her dress. Suddenly someone came up and put her hand on her shoulder. She jumped, but it was only Nefertari. "Oh, geez, you scared me! I thought you were..." she said, gasping.

"I know. I didn't mean to frighten you. I came to see how you were. I managed to smooth things over with Ramesses, and he will let me spend *some* time with you. I don't have to follow those laws now because he pardoned me. I will try not to anger him for your sake. You seem to have been deep in thought," said Nefertari.

"I have to talk to Sito. I had visions about Ramesses, and he and Monchiska were having battles over me. My guide told me to beware of Ramesses coming back to life. Nefie, I gotta get outa here and back to Hawote. I won't be safe anywhere else," said Neiko and then bit her lip.

"I see, but you will have to see him tonight when Ramesses sleeps. I will tell him you wish to speak with him, and you will meet in your room. Agreed?"

"Yeah. Thanks, Nefie," said Neiko, and Nefertari disappeared.

"You are out here alone? Come, let's talk," said Ramesses as he came from nowhere.

"Okay," Neiko said nervously, as she reached in her dress and stroked the feather.

- CHAPTER 35 -

NEIKO HAD TO SPEND the rest of that day with Ramesses, and she was in extreme thought. She was fidgeting and avoided to looking him in the eye.

"Is something troubling you?" Ramesses asked.

"Um, no. Why?" Neiko replied, biting her lip.

"You seem lost in thought and something weighs heavy in your mind. I was wondering if something was the matter," Ramesses said, concerned.

Neiko laughed. "Well, I…uh…um…well, it's kinda like this. It's just I'm stressed out, that's all—all these changes. I got a lot on my mind," she said, not alluding about the visions.

"I do not believe that is all. You seem to be hiding something from me. Why?" Ramesses asked, crossing his arms and looking at her with a grilling stare.

"I don't know what you mean. You wouldn't understand anyway," Neiko said with a flat expression and rolling her eyes.

"Try me," Ramesses said, tapping his foot and tapping his finger on his strong forearm.

"No! It's private—okay!" Neiko said, trying to be evasive.

"You shouldn't be keeping things from me. It makes me not trust you. We should be able to trust each other, shouldn't we?" Ramesses asked with his arms still folded and questioning her with his dark brown eyes.

Neiko rolled her eyes again. "Would you stop it already? I don't wanna talk about it!" she said.

"Very well—suit yourself," Ramesses said with a shrug. "Well, you are free to leave."

"Really? Great!" Neiko said and turned to leave.

Ramesses stopped her. "Not so fast," he said, and then he tried to kiss her, but she turned and ran away. In his annoyance he watched her disappear with a scowl on his face, and in his fury, he slammed his fist on the table.

From afar inside the palace Sito and the others saw this. "Oh boy, this is not good. He won't accept too much more of that!" Tito said.

"I agree. I bet he'll tie her down next time. Oh, I have a meeting with her tonight, and the rest of you can join us," said Sito.

"What is it?" asked Mactalon.

"Neiko has something to share with us, and it is important. We will meet in her room when old Attila is asleep," Sito replied.

Late that night, the five of them met in Neiko's room, and she told them about her visions.

Sito mused and twisted his long hair around his finger. "Hmm, a lot of it is very obvious, of course. Great Spirit gave me the answers to your questions. The god with the head of an ibis is Thoth, the

Egyptian god of history. When he erases the wall and puts new writing that is the changing of the past and history. The sundial is showing the passing of time. When it moves backward, it is where we are now, and when it moves forward that is the future. In the first part, Monchiska represents us, and Anubis represents death. When Amon-Ra and Osiris throw you to Ramesses that is showing your present state. We will defeat death and Ramesses and return to Hawote--maybe. The happiness and security scenes are when you are in safety. The rest is in the future, and I can't make that out. The future isn't set and could change on a dime. We aren't guaranteed anything."

"I can sort of make the other out," said Neiko. "It is showing what may happen if Ramesses comes back to life in the future—if that's even possible. But, I don't get a lot of it. How could he possibly be resurrected, and how could he possess magic? No one can do that—it's impossible. I don't think he could ever join forces with Ramses because I could see they would hate each other. I don't think Ramesses would be that desperate or that dumb! Ramesses may be a conceited jerk, but I can say for a fact that he's not evil. I don't think Ramesses would side with the greatest evil that ever lived," Neiko said, shaking her head doubtfully. "I dunno, all I need to focus on now is my present situation and getting outa here."

Sito nodded. "You're absolutely right. If we fail to return to Hawote, then the rest won't happen. Again, that vision is no guarantee we will make it back—I think it is mainly a warning of what could happen."

"Yeah, we need to leave because I can't keep hiding things from Ramesses forever. He already can sense my feelings. He will not accept me running away and giving him the cold shoulder or keeping secrets from him," said Neiko with a frown. "He already said his two cents about that."

"Aye, but we must have that crystal in order to get out. We can't try retrieving it now without the risk of him destroying it," Panthero said, fidgeting and massaging his forehead.

"I know. I'm tired, and that's all I had to say. Good night," said Neiko and then she left the room.

That night, Neiko was having dreams of her life with Monchiska. The next morning, she was still asleep, and Ramesses came in to see her. He came and sat down beside her and stroked her face and hair. She never awoke, but he smiled at her. He then bent down and kissed her, and when he had finished, Neiko said in English, "Oh, Monchiska, I'll be home soon. Kiss me some more," she said with a smile on her face.

Hearing this, he arose and looked at her frustrated because he couldn't understand what she had said; he went to find Francesco.

Francesco was writing on a scroll; he looked up and saw that Ramesses was exasperated. "What is wrong, my king?"

"Tell me, what is a Monchiska? I went to visit her this morning while she was sleeping, and after I kissed her, she said 'Monchiska' and much more gibberish I could not understand," said Ramesses.

"Monchiska is a person—a man to be exact. He is a member of the Scraah tribe, the same tribe that Mactalon is from. They have been good friends for a very long time. So it seems she has been dreaming about him, and she was happy about a kiss she thought she might have received from him. That can only mean one thing—that is the person she has loved for years," Francesco stated and then chuckled.

Ramesses' face darkened. "Oh, is that so? If I see a person that goes by that name, I will personally kill him. When she awakens, I will tell her to forget him!"

"No, say nothing. It is better to keep waiting and to rid her of anything she has with her to remind her of him. If you say anything about it now, it will make things worse and lead to another tirade and tussle between the two of you. It is good you found out," said Francesco.

"You're right. She will forget him once she learns she will never leave me and when she falls in love with me," Ramesses said with great confidence.

At breakfast, Neiko told her friends about the dreams she was having the night before. Neiko found it strange that Ramesses had allowed her friends to eat with them. She was completely unaware of both of his ulterior motives: to find out more about Monchiska and this could be her last breakfast with them. Neiko acted casual with her friends; she got onto them for calling her "Great One". She found it annoying. Every time she mentioned Monchiska's name, Ramesses became angrier—he looked as if he wanted to crush his goblet in his hand.

"I had a dream that we kissed, and it felt so real. I wanted him to kiss me again, but he left. Boy, I had no idea he was such a good kisser," Neiko said, remembering the vividness of the dream and sighing in delightful longing.

"Wow! I wish I could've had dreams like that about Phoenix," Sito said.

"Yeah, but y'all actually kissed," Neiko said, propping her cheek on left her hand that had the ring from Monchiska on it; this was the first time it had caught Ramesses' eye.

"Where did you get that?" Ramesses asked, taking her hand touching the turquoise.

"It was a gift from Monchiska," Neiko replied, not paying attention and not noticing the angry glint in his dark eyes.

Ramesses growled in rage and tried to rip the ring off her finger with his other hand.

"Hey, what's the big idea?" asked Neiko, trying to retract her hand and keep his other hand away from her prized possession.

"You will wear this no more!" Ramesses snapped. He finally got it off of her finger and out of her grasp and threw it in the garden.

It bounced, rolled, and blooped as it landed in the lotus pool. It began to sink in the murky water beneath the floating lotuses and lily pads.

"Hey, that's mine! You just threw my ring away! What's the matter with you?" Neiko protested with a look like he had lost his mind. "Have you gone nuts?" she asked, fanning her hands.

Ramesses looked at his hands took off one of his own rings from his left hand—from his left ring finger—and placed it on her left middle finger. "Now, this is my gift to you, and you will never take this off. I have given you my best and most special ring," he said with an emphatic and authoritative tone of voice.

"Sure, okay," Neiko said taken aback and confused. She held up her hand and looked at it. It was more magnificent than what she had. It was finely engraved gold with a large amethyst that was covered in gold designs. The amethyst sparkled beneath its shimmering gold accents. She rubbed the large amethyst. Everyone else's faces were written in shock, including her own.

"Ramesses, you are giving the ring your father had made for him when he was a boy by your grandfather? The same ring your father passed to you and you should pass on to your son?" Nefertari asked with a dumbfounded look.

"It is mine to give to whomever I choose!" Ramesses retorted. "You have no place to voice your opinion on such matters. I have no son, and I think she is more deserving—what if I have no son worthy of it? Hmm? It is my best gift and mine to give to whoever I see fit! Are you jealous that I didn't give it to you?" he asked with a caustic tone.

"No, that's not it at all!" Nefertari said in defense. "I just know that ring is very special to you since you and your father were so close. You have had that since you were a boy! Neiko doesn't return your love like you want, so I only thought..."

"But she will!" Ramesses interrupted.

Neiko felt awkward and a little squeamish when she heard how long it had been in the family and of its origin. "Ramesses, I can't accept this. That's kind of you and all, but…" she said trying to slip it off her finger and return it to him. She didn't feel like she deserved to take an heirloom as a gift and break the cycle of its passage from father to son.

Ramesses stopped her from removing it by clasping her hands. "Yes you can. I want you to take it—it is my best. I think you should have it. You may spend the day with your friends, Neiko. Now go before I change my mind," he said, and the Indians left in haste. "It may be the last time you ever see them," he muttered.

Neiko ran up to catch up with her friends. "What was he so mad about?" Neiko said looking at her new ring. "Why would he do something that rash and give me something so special to him?"

Sito knew the answers, but he couldn't say them.

"He really got mad when you said something about Monchiska, and I noticed that every time you mentioned Monchiska's name, he became angrier and angrier, but I have no idea why," shrugged Tito.

"Oh well, it's probably nothing. Let's have some fun, shall we?" said Neiko as she skipped around.

- CHAPTER 36 -

T HE NEXT DAY, EVERYONE went to Senu's house because he was hosting another party. When they arrived, Senu greeted them all. The only reason why Neiko's friends were there was because they were on work detail as attendants and servants. "Tito, it has been four months since I have seen all of you, and you are Sito, I presume," he said.

"I am. So nice to meet the man who helped my brother and friends," Sito replied.

"I am pleased to see you too, Mactalon and Panthero. Neiko, I am also pleased to make your acquaintance," he said, bowing to her and then acknowledging Ramesses. "Greetings, Great One. I hope you still do not bear me ill will."

"Of course not, I will let bygones be bygones," Ramesses replied, nodding his head.

"I am pleased you came as well, my queen," Senu said, bowing to Nefertari, and she grinned. "Go and make yourselves at home."

"I'm right behind you guys!" Neiko said, starting to run after them, but Ramesses stopped her.

"You will stay with me this evening where you belong and not gallivanting with your friends," Ramesses said, gripping her hand, and she bowed her head and looked at the floor.

Sut came up and saw her. "Well, well, look what just came in—the hussy that pretended to be an Egyptian. You know, I still want you."

"Look, Sut, I did that to keep from being in the situation I'm in now. I would leave if I were you," Neiko warned. "I don't know if you missed the memo, but I'm a Great Wife now," she said with a shrug and with "get lost" on her features.

Sut saw that Ramesses' back was turned, and he reached to touch her face.

Like lightning, Ramesses turned around, stopped him, and shot him icy daggers. He knew he was there. "How dare you. Touch my wife again, and you die," he said with a snarl.

Sut gulped and backed away. Many other young men looked at her, but Ramesses instantly stopped their gazes as he gave them cold stares. Several times, she tried to pull her hand from his grasp, but he responded by tightening his grip.

"I want to go with my friends," Neiko said, sulking.

"No, you are mine tonight and always," Ramesses argued. "You are not to associate yourself with peasants and commoners in public."

"My friends are not peasants or commoners!" Neiko shot back, trying to argue with him.

Ramesses gave Neiko a stern look that said "Don't tempt me" and held up his finger in her face, and then his features said "End of discussion".

Senu was talking with the Indians most of the evening, and he heard of their predicament. "He won't let her talk to no one else without him there. She's miserable. We are trying to find a way to get back home and get her away from him," said Tito.

Senu nodded. "Oh, I wish I could have stopped this from happening. I hope you can do something soon because you don't have much time. He is about to make another drastic move, but I'm not sure what it will be. I want to go see if I can speak with Neiko for a little while." He walked up to her. "Hello, Great One, I came to speak with you."

"Senu, I'm glad to see you. I've wanted to speak with you all evening, but as you can see, I'm restricted," said Neiko, pressing her lips in a line.

"Why, Senu, want to join us?" asked Ramesses politely.

"Actually, I wanted to speak with Neiko alone. I have something I want to tell her in confidence," said Senu.

"Senu, if you have something to say, you can tell both of us. There will be no secrets. You have my permission to stay if you like," invited Ramesses

"That is kind of you, but Sito has more to tell me. Pardon me," Senu said, and went to talk to the Indians. "You were right. I had a secret I had to tell her, and he wouldn't allow it. I suppose it will have to lie or you can try sending it to her for me," Senu sighed.

"We'll try, but we also have restricted time with her," Sito responded with an agitated sigh.

Everyone returned home from the party that night, but Neiko was still forced to remain with her husband. Neiko and Ramesses were sitting on the patio, talking, and then finally they went inside.

"Well, good night," Neiko said, pulling the door behind her, still holding the knob. Ramesses went for a kiss, but she pulled the knob down. Door knobs were another improvement Ramesses had Sito install in the palace. The door flew open, and Neiko stayed against it.

Ramesses lost his balance and tripped and toppled into the lotus pool with a loud splash. He stood up in the pool with a lotus hanging off of his head, and he spat the water out of his mouth with a look of disgust on his face. Neiko laughed and pointed.

"Oh, that's one for the record! You needed to cool off. Good night," Neiko said cheekily as she walked off.

The rest of the Indians saw what happened and were laughing at Ramesses and pointing at him.

Nothing was amusing to Ramesses about the occurrence. "They dare mock me? I will get even," he snarled indignantly as he wrung out his kilt, robe, and headdress. He picked foliage out of his collar, jewelry, and belt. He stamped inside the palace with water squishing out of his sandals and leaving wet footprints behind.

The next day, Neiko was poking around outside in the garden and playing the flute. She found a large bullfrog and caught it. "Oh, you sure are cute," she said stroking its smooth skin.

"What are you doing out here?" asked Ramesses from behind.

Neiko spun around and hid the frog behind her back. "Oh, it was such a nice morning; I decided to take a stroll in the garden."

"What are you hiding?" Ramesses asked.

"Nothing," Neiko said with a carefree shrug.

"I have something to ask of you, and you will do it, or I will be rid of your friends," Ramesses threatened.

"Well, ask away," Neiko said.

"I want you to kiss me," Ramesses pressed.

Neiko laughed nervously, but then a clever idea popped into her head. "Okay, but I want you to close your eyes because it'll make it more exciting."

Ramesses closed his eyes and waited.

Neiko put the frog in front of her face. "Mu-wah," she said.

Ramesses kissed the frog, but he instantly knew something wasn't right since Neiko's lips were not cold and slimy. It croaked and bulged its throat, and his eyes flew open. He was face-to-face and eye-to-eye with the frog—probably the biggest frog he had ever seen. A look of disbelief crossed his face as he spat, wiped off his lips in disgust, and looked at her while she was laughing. She knew he hated frogs and toads as much as some people hated roaches or spiders. One day he tore a room apart and went after a small toad with a khopesh sword to chase it down and kill it. The poor little toad didn't survive.

"Didn't know I could kiss so well, huh?" Neiko punned.

"Ugh! I hate frogs—disgusting, slimy creatures! I can tolerate asps better than those horrible things! Yuck!" Ramesses growled and threw a conniption. Then he said, "Now, I have a new dress I want you to wear, and you will put it on now! You will start bathing in scented water and oils. You will no longer smell like your kind."

Neiko went to her room with him behind her. The dress was lying on her bed, and she picked it up and looked at it; it was very skimpy. The top looked like a fancy bikini top with tassels of beads hanging from it. The bottom looked like a mini skirt accompanied with a fancy jeweled and beaded loincloth—almost like a very lavish, royal-looking belly-dancer outfit. She didn't have to be Einstein or Sherlock to figure out what his idea behind this was. "I am not wearing this. I mean, there isn't much to it. Madonna wore more clothes than this," she said, complaining. "I'm glad it's never cold here during the day."

"All right, fine. I'll just tell the master builder there will be some new additions to the mud pits," Ramesses said, beginning to walk away. For right now he was still using her friends as leverage to get his way.

"All right!" Neiko retorted and rolled her eyes and gave him a why-I-oughta look. "How do I get that other stuff you mentioned?"

"Better. I will send some servants to assist you. Come to me when you finish," Ramesses said and then walked away.

Neiko put on her dress, and it was uncomfortable. She looked in the mirror and groaned. "I can't do this. I hope I don't have to wear this often," she said. Then the servants washed her with scented water, covered her in oils, and put myrrh in her hair. She put on her eye kohl, lip stain, and rouge. She sniffed her arms, and coughed, wheezed, and then sneezed; the stuff was too strong for her sensitive nose and sense of smell. "Ugh! I can't fight like this—the enemy could smell me coming downwind! This stuff stinks. They literally bathe in perfume—so that's where the expression comes from."

Neiko walked down the stairs, and Sito saw her.

Sito's mouth fell open in a look of shock. "Oh my gosh! What in the…"

"Don't ask. Gotta go. Talk later?" Neiko said, hiding herself and trying to cover herself with her arms. Then she disappeared.

Neiko walked into the appointed place still trying to cover herself. "You look dashing. How do you like it?"

"I don't. My parents would have a fit if they saw me in this—I don't wear stuff like this back home. I hate all this perfume, because I smell awful. I feel like I took a bath in perfume!" Neiko shot back. "I can't even breathe," she said, continuing to complain.

"You would rather smell like a dog?" Ramesses asked.

"We don't stink! We don't smell like dogs, either," Neiko said. "Stuff like this stinks to Indians because we don't wear stuff that is so strong that it would take the stink off of a…uh—camel's hindquarters." She couldn't think of the word for skunk; there probably wasn't one. "I'd rather smell like a breeze in the woods, or like the woods after a rain, or like a nearby creek. If I went to war like this, the Crackedskulls could smell me coming downwind," Neiko said, fuming.

Ramesses chuckled. "You are no longer of your people. You will fight wars at my side now."

Neiko grabbed a curtain and wrapped it around herself. "Well, but I'm still an Indian—nothing can change that."

"Oh yes, you would rather spend the rest of your life in poverty than in a life of splendor? Do you enjoy being a savage, and do you intend to live a life with that Monchiska instead of me?"

Neiko looked at him, shocked. "Who said I live in poverty? You don't know anything about my life in Hawote, do you? And, for your information, we are not savages! How do you know about Monchiska?"

"I have my ways—as for your past life, it is of no concern to me or of our future or present together. You will never be a savage again, and you will stay with me. Tell me, how much does this Monchiska love you, and has he even paid attention to how much you love him? Has he ever kissed you?"

Neiko put her hands on her hips. "That's getting a little personal! Besides, my private life is none of your business," she snapped, turning away.

Ramesses came closer to her and ran his fingers through her black silky hair and ran his hands on her strong shoulders. "Oh, come now, surely you would be proud to tell me—that is—if there is something to tell. Tell me of one time he kissed you. Everything about your life is now my business," Ramesses said with a cocky grin. "You have no private life any longer to *my* eyes."

Neiko spun around and looked at him with a defiant stare, and then looked at the floor in defeat. "I…"

"I thought so. I found a perfect rose, and I was the one who was able to harvest it before anyone else. What a pity—Monchiska has what I want, and he will not accept what you have to offer. I will accept if you are willing to give," Ramesses said, shaking his head.

"Now, wait just a minute. I haven't told you the whole story. You see, he loves me too, but he don't think I love him, and I recently found out that he loves me. I can clear up this misunderstanding real fast," Neiko said, brushing off his hands and stepping back out of reach.

"Well, he will not ever know because I will not allow it," Ramesses said, stepping forward and catching her hands and clasping them tightly.

"Yeah right. If I get to Hawote, you can't stop me because you will never remember me. Put that in your pipe and smoke it," Neiko said defiantly, wrenching free.

Ramesses was miffed, but not deterred. He put his hands on his hips. "You may find a way to leave me behind, but you will not make me forget! You cannot hide from me. Love always finds a way, and I will find you somehow even in the far reaches of the future—death won't even keep us apart," Ramesses said in a cryptic way.

Neiko laughed at him in his face. "What kind of hocus-pocus is that? In the Hawote I live in, you're dead and nothing more than a dried up old prune that was dug up and put in a museum for tourists to look at. I don't know what you're mummy looked like, but I can say for a fact you wouldn't be very attractive coming back looking like that. Mummies are so gross! I definitely don't believe you can pull any of that cryptic stuff on me. I guess Francesco spilled the beans about us being from the future."

"Yes, maybe he did, but it was worth my while. You may be from three thousand years in the future, but I will find a way to get to you one way or another," Ramesses said, accenting each word by thrusting his finger at the ground.

"Whatever. Look, can I go now, please?" Neiko asked.

"You may," Ramesses said, waving his hand, and she stormed out of the room.

Neiko was walking back to her room to change into her regular queen's attire when she suddenly ran into Francesco.

"Well, well, well. Look at you now. You should dress like that more often," Francesco sneered as she tried to cover herself.

"Oh yeah? Why don't you try wearing this!" Neiko shot back and then cuffed him in the side of the head.

"Oww! I'll be glad when I leave you here, and you will resting in a tomb with your guts in jars, along with your brain, while you are forgotten! Huh, I guess I'll be seeing you in I guess—oh—in about three thousand years?" Francesco said with an evil grin. "I may even see you in the Cairo museum lying beside your husband as an old, decrepit, snowy-haired Great Squaw!" he said, taunting her more.

Neiko's emerald eyes narrowed to slits as she stamped her feet and shook her fists. "If you want my brain in a jar, then how 'bout I stick you in the gizzard with a sword!" Neiko retorted with her green eyes glowing with hostile battlefire. "I'll show you a Great Squaw, you pencil-neck geek!"

"I don't think you are dressed appropriately to be talking smack. Farewell for now, Great One," Francesco said with a cavalier sneer and swaggered off.

"Ooh, I'm gonna get you for this, Weenie Man!" Neiko snarled at him and shook her fists. "This is all your fault. I'll tell Raven and Bloodhawk about this even if I have to haunt them from the dead!" she yelled at him as he vanished.

Later that night, Francesco was walking in the hall, reading over a scroll he had finished. "Well, that's done. Now all I have to do is give it to Pharaoh in the morning," he said, stretching and yawning. But suddenly he felt a point in his back; he turned and Neiko was standing in front of him with Ramesses' broadsword, which was then pointed at his throat. He was lucky that she didn't grab one of his twin khopesh swords that he had inherited from his great-great grandfather; her attacks would have been even quicker. "What are you doing with the sword of Pharaoh, and do you know he would be angry to know you have it and that you tried to kill me?"

"Shut up. Prepare to die, Weenie Man," Neiko said ruthlessly as she turned to make a swing to cut off his head. He ducked as the blade whizzed by and dug itself in the wall with a loud clang. Sparks scattered, and small tufts of black hair floated to the floor from the top of his head. Noticing his close shave when he saw his hair fall to the floor, Francesco gasped. Wasting no time, he moved out of the way before she could make another attack. He desperately dodged her fast attacks with narrow escapes. He felt like a pigeon trying to elude a peregrine falcon.

Francesco breathed in ragged breaths, and started to run with her chasing him. "Ramesses, help! Ramesses! Guards!" he called in between ragged breaths and in desperation.

"You rat! You'll pay for what you have done to me and the others! Come and fight, you coward!" Neiko yelled, closing in on him.

"This isn't even a fair fight," Francesco pleaded and backed against the wall. Knowing he was trapped, he slid down and looked at his executioner with dread. Her outlined, fiery green eyes were fierce. Neiko's large, gold vulture crown just seemed to accent her battlefire-etched features.

"You don't even know what a fair fight is—you don't fight fair! You're dead, skank!" Neiko said as she raised the sword over her head for the kill.

Francesco closed his eyes waiting for the sting of death, but then he heard struggling. He opened his eyes, and Ramesses had apprehended Neiko and was trying to disarm her. She wrenched free and thrust the point at his chest. Then the guards drew their swords and put the points and curved blades to her back.

"If you kill me, then you die. Do you not know of the curse?" Ramesses asked.

"I do, and death is a release, not a punishment," Neiko said with defiance.

"Drop my sword—you have been caught. There will be no more fighting, and your war is over. Do you get that? This is my final warning," Ramesses said.

Neiko threw down the sword in disgust.

"Now, go to your room, and I will see you in the morning and discuss this then," Ramesses said, and Neiko stormed past him as he bent down to retrieve his sword.

Francesco struggled to his feet, panting and trembling. "Thank you, my king."

"I've had it. Go to the master builder at once and tell him to come and remove those four troublesome Indians. They are now more of a liability than leverage at this point. Leave now. I want them gone no later than tomorrow night!" Ramesses ordered.

"Yes, my liege," Francesco said with a bow and a sneer and ran out into the night.

- CHAPTER 37 -

THE NEXT DAY, THE INDIANS were in the garden most of the day except for Neiko. No one had to hire Sherlock Holmes to know where she was. Evening came, and they were still outside, but Neiko was forbidden to be near them. Suddenly, their poker game was cut short because several taskmasters made their way to them with chains in hand. "Holy cow! I know they aren't here to play poker!" Mactalon said in alarm.

"We gotta fight for our freedom!" Panthero said, motioning for them to get close together and putting his dukes up.

Several of the taskmasters tried to catch them, but the defending Indians punched them and proved to he fierce hand-to-hand fighters. The number of taskmasters greatly exceeded the four, so they were beaten down and shackled within minutes.

"Take them to the cages, and let's put them to work," said the leader.

255

The taskmasters began to drag them to the wagons.

Neiko heard the commotion and ran out to try to stop them. "No! You can't do this!" she yelled as she ran up to throw herself in the melee to interfere with the operation. Several of the palace guards stopped her, dragged her back, and threw her into the waiting arms of her husband. "No!" she yelled, and slumped down to the ground in total shock. Neiko was powerless to save her friends.

Ramesses held her to him tightly, and she buried her face into his chest and cried since she knew there was no hope now and her friends were history.

"We'll be back, Pharaoh! You can't get rid of us that easily!" Sito called from afar, but Ramesses acted as if he did not hear him.

The four Indians rode in the wagons to Goshen. When they reached the labor yards, the cages were opened, and they were shoved to the mud pits. Many of the slaves looked at the new arrivals.

"Get to work, savages," snapped a taskmaster as he cracked the whip at them.

They got into the pits and began to stomp in the straw.

"You are strangers here. Three of you are scarred by the whip, but one is not. Why?" asked one of the slaves.

"I served Seti, while my brother and my friends were in the service of Kenes; we have recently been reunited. There is one more of us, but she is in worse bondage than we are," Sito replied.

"How is that? So where is this other one?" asked another.

"Her chains are heavier than ours, and her burden is greater. She is forced to be the Great Wife of Pharaoh against her will, but we will get out of here, rescue her, and take her with us."

"You will challenge Pharaoh and take away his wife? You will die here in this mud hole with the rest of us," said an Assyrian.

"Faster!" snapped a taskmaster as he stung Sito with the whip.

"Wo!" Sito bellowed and rubbed his shoulder. "Man, I've been here ten minutes, and I hate it already."

"Got any bright ideas on how to fly this coop?" asked Mactalon.

"We have to steal some clothes, but I have no idea how we will get into the palace. He'll have the place well guarded to be sure," Sito said.

Several weeks passed, and the four were being worked more than anyone else. Sito knew Ramesses was going to have them worked to death and into an early grave and yet have no knowledge of it. They were also made to drag the huge bricks in addition to working in the mudpits. They had more scars than any other slave. One day, Sito collapsed from exhaustion while pulling a load of bricks with the others, and a taskmaster began to beat him. "Get up, you worthless piece of wasted flesh," he snarled and hit him again.

Seeing his brother being afflicted, Tito stormed up and jumped on the Egyptian; he began to beat him and wrapped his shackles around his neck. "If you mess with my brother again, then I'll kill you," Tito said with menace, but several more taskmasters came to the aid of the fallen. They beat Tito and freed the man from the death grip of the angry Indian.

The master builder came up to see what had happened. "Do you know it is death if you strike an Egyptian?" he asked.

"No, I didn't, and I couldn't care less," Tito retorted, and one of his captors hit him.

"You four are indeed troublesome just like it has been said. Scourge this one and send him to work; let his brother rot in the sun," the master builder said waving his rod.

The taskmasters took Tito to be beaten. A few Hebrew women lifted Sito up, and took him to their makeshift tent to take care of him. They gave him water to drink and let him rest.

A few days passed, and the four tried to make plans for an escape. They performed their normal duties for that day. Even though they were completely exhausted, the sweet scent of freedom triumphed. If they didn't get out of here soon, they were going to die.

While the taskmasters were asleep, Sito found tools to break the bands of their chains. Once free, they slipped into a one of the nearby tents. The Indians had not lost their touch with stealth. They pounced on the unlucky Egyptians. After a few moments of tussling, the Indians tied them up, took their clothes, and left them in their underwear.

Next they snuck into the next tent and knocked out some night owls playing late-night Senet. They raided this tent and stole food and water.

Sneaking about with the moon high in the sky, the Indians stole four horses, and rode them bareback into the night.

They arrived back in Thebes a several days later. They perfected their disguises and made their way into the palace to confront Ramesses. When they arrived, there were people presenting gifts to him. When it was their turn, they approached the royal platform.

"What do you four have for me?" Ramesses asked.

Sito took the stand. "We have no gifts, but we are here to confront you, Ramesses," he said in a disguised voice.

People in the court began to mutter, and Neiko and Nefertari looked at each other, confused.

"Confront me about what? How dare you call my name in contempt, commoner! Who are you?" Ramesses demanded as he stood up, erect, in a display of power.

Sito and the others took off their disguises. "We are here to confront you about a great evil you have done to our land. We demand you let Neiko go."

"You! You have come to insult me in my own court, have you?" Ramesses thundered and was blind with fury.

"We'll do more than that if you continue to harden your heart. We may even start a war against you!" Tito interjected.

"A war—against the four of you and what army? The one you conjure up in your own imagination? Do you take me for a fool? How will you fight against me and the armies of Egypt? I suppose you will hide in the crevices like the rats you are!" Ramesses jeered, and everyone laughed. "You may need to go pray to your Great Spirit for an army of warriors and hope that he hears you," he added with a scathing jeer.

"Now we will tell you what evil you have done. You forcibly took Neiko into your house and forced her to become your wife, and you sent us to slavery to be rid of us—that is called breaking the arrow—the payment for the offense is death—or in your case, a war if you refuse to release her. Let this sink into your hard heart and thick skull, Ramesses," Sito said insulting him. He now had zero respect for the Pharaoh now.

Francesco stood up. "The heart of Pharaoh is as priceless as that of the most costly diamond!"

"Yeah? And it's just as hard!" Mactalon shot back. "I second the thick skull part—he's got a skull thicker than a Pachycephalosaurus."

Sito nodded with a grin.

Ramesses was enraged at the insults and their display of insolence. "Enough! I do not care of your stupid laws, and they do not apply to me. Leave my presence! I will not let Neiko go—she's mine now. Get out of my sight! Get out of here before I kill you myself!"

"Then it begins," Sito trumpeted. "Don't say we didn't warn you."

"Have it your way, Ramesneeze!" Mactalon retorted.

Ramesses stormed up to him hit him in the head with his fist and Mactalon retreated behind Panthero with his hand on his aching head.

"I don't know what you've been sniffing, but you are making a big mistake," Panthero put in, and they left before things got really ugly.

- CHAPTER 38 -

THE FOUR OF THEM caused Ramesses many headaches, but they tried to avoid going toe to toe with him. They sent him scrolls with the notorious demand along with a broken arrow, which was a threat. Other threats, including: dead asps, dead scorpions, dead frogs, and crocodile teeth, were left at the palace. Other letters with more threats, including other Indian-type threats and the hieroglyphs that spelled *war* were left at his home. Spears were dug in the walls with seven feathers on them. Many fires and catastrophes happened. Flaming symbols of the present three tribes were lit in the fields. On the walls of the city was painted, PHARAOH, LET NEIKO GO.

Another letter was sent to him, and when Francesco had finished reading it, it was enclosed with the war hieroglyphs written with camel's blood.

Ramesses threw it down and stomped it. "Argh! I want those four destroyed! If it's a war they want, then it's a war they will get!"

he shouted as he shook his royal crook and flail violently in a tantrum.

Several groups of soldiers were sent out to kill them over the course of the standoff. Several days had passed and none of them had returned with any news—or better yet—their heads. The four had spared one of the officers from one of the patrols they had taken out, and Sito menaced him with the blade. "You go back and you tell Pharaoh we will continue our sworn duty, that is to free and protect Neiko, and we will use every means necessary and everything in our power to fight him."

"Bold words, but I would like to see Pharaoh make you eat them by ramming them down your throat," the general retorted.

Sito laughed, as he prodded him with the point.

"Get going," menaced Mactalon as he gave Panthero five.

Itet, the general, returned and told Ramesses what had happened and the message sent by Sito. Ramesses responded by throwing his royal crook on the ground. "They must be stopped! I will send out the entire army if I have to!"

"You can get this over with a lot sooner by letting me go and allowing me to take the crystal with me," Neiko said, toying with the crook by spinning like a baton and then making it fly like an imaginary airplane as she made the accompanying noises while she waited for his response. She picked it up off the floor during his tirade.

Ramesses sat down beside her. "You won't be going anywhere, my warrior, and neither will you be taking that crystal," he said, reaching and rubbing her thigh.

Neiko smacked his hand with the crook with a loud pop. He drew back, rubbed his injured hand, and looked at her with a frustrated glare.

"Paws off. You had that coming and deserved it for being such a jerk," Neiko said with sass.

Ramesses took the crook away from her and glowered at her, but said nothing.

Later that night, Panthero had an idea on how to free Neiko. "We could use some of the uniforms off of those soldiers we killed, and we can sneak into the palace and sneak her out. We have to take weapons, just in case."

Sito scratched his chin. "Hmm, that sounds like a good idea, and it may just work. We have to move carefully though."

They put on the uniforms, made their way to the palace, and made it inside. They posed as guards on duty when other soldiers and guards approached them.

"We have to wait until Ramesses goes to sleep in order to sneak her out. If he sees us, we're dead meat. Panthero and I will go search his room and see if you can find the crystal. Shh," said Sito as he placed his finger over his lips, and Ramesses and Nefertari walked past them, but there was no sign of Neiko.

"Where's Neiko?" asked Mactalon.

"She's probably in her room or in the garden. Be glad she isn't with the ball and chain," Tito replied.

"Okay, Panthero and I will go to his room just like I just said. Mactalon, go to Neiko's room and see if she's there. If she's not there, wait for her. When he goes to sleep, Panthero and I will come to meet you in Neiko's room. Tito, you keep watch and we'll meet you here and then we'll our escape. Go," Sito whispered.

Tito stayed behind, Sito and Panthero made their way to Ramesses' room, and Mactalon left toward Neiko's room.

Later that evening Neiko came from the garden and went into her room. Someone grabbed her from behind and covered her mouth, and she shrieked. Mactalon was lucky she didn't dish out a defense move.

"Shh, it's me, Mactalon. We've come to rescue you. Don't say anything," Mactalon whispered in her ear and released her

Neiko nodded.

About thirty minutes later, Sito and Panthero came in. Sito waved his arm for them to proceed and meet Tito. They tiptoed through the halls and slipped past several guards. Tito had knocked out several more, and he motioned for them to come on.

"What in the…" said a guard from across the throne room, and then he saw Neiko was up and about with guards. This wasn't right; he had just overheard Pharaoh take her to her room and get onto her for wandering about the palace in the wee hours of the night. Several more guards accompanied him on his patrol, and they brandished their weapons. The Indians drew their swords.

"Run!" shouted Panthero, and the five Indians tried to make a hasty retreat.

More guards appeared from the hallways from their patrols and went after them. Others heard the commotion and sounded the alarm. "You go and alert Pharaoh, and you stop their escape!" said Amenhotep the highest general and long time friend of Ramesses. He was talking to his brother Ahmose who was the captain of the guards.

Ahmose left to awaken Ramesses and to gather more guards.

The guards threw themselves at them, and the Indians fought bravely. Sito killed a guard who was trying to stab Mactalon, and he picked up his khopesh sword and tossed it to Neiko. All five fought with lightning speed in hopes to free themselves, and several Egyptians died, but more and more guards came in and surrounded them. Their escape route was then cut off, and the points of weapons surrounded the five of them. The soldiers parted as Ramesses walked to them behind Ahmose with a cross expression on his face. He was in his night robe and looked like he had been awoke from a peaceful slumber.

"Who dares come into my house to…" Ramesses began, but he recognized them instantly, and his cold, merciless eyes glowered at each of them. "I should have known you would try this, Sito, but you have failed, and I have won. You have a lot of nerve coming into my house in the middle of the night to steal what is rightfully mine and waking me up!"

"We won't give up. So what are you going to do, kill us?" Sito asked bravely.

"She may be yours, but not rightfully!" said Mactalon.

"All Indians are nothing more than unruly barbarians and savages who have no respect for anyone else's customs or beliefs or the personal feelings of others!"

"Yeah? And all Pharaohs are ugly!" retorted Mactalon.

"I am not ugly!" Ramesses scowled. "I happen to be the most handsome man in Egypt."

"Huh, coulda fooled me," Sito retaliated. "You don't have any respect for others' customs or beliefs, so you need to open mouth and insert foot on that one! We tried to mind our own business and stay out of you way, but you stuck you nose in our business and interfered. You also kidnapped our friend—"

"Kidnap—how dare you accuse me of a crime! That's it—you four have angered me for the last time. Tomorrow at dawn, the four of you will be exiled in the wilderness with no rations. Now you will feel the heat of my anger in the hot sun!" Ramesses said and then reached for Neiko, but Sito and Mactalon stepped in front of her in hopes to protect her.

"You will have to get by us first, Scarecrow!" Mactalon challenged, but the two of them were hit by a couple of guards. Ramesses grabbed Neiko and pulled her to him, and two guards stepped in front of them creating a barrier to block the Indians. Tito tried to break past them, but they prodded him with spears.

"Get a good look at them because that will be the last time you will ever see them and it is only for your sake that I don't have them slain for treason at dawn," Ramesses said and kissed her in front of them. Neiko screeched, and they were so angry they tried to fight their way to their tormentor. After he had finished, she spat and wiped her mouth in disgust.

"You will pay for this when we get back—I swear it!" Sito vowed, but Ramesses just sneered at him.

"You won't be back," Ramesses said, shaking his head. "No one survives the wilderness of the desert far from the river. Take them away and hold them till morning. We will take them to the wilderness at dawn. Let this be written, if they are ever seen in Egypt again after tomorrow then they are to be killed upon sight. I never want to see their face ever again," Ramesses said and disappeared with Neiko in tow.

The four Indians were taken to the dungeon and locked up.

The next morning at dawn, the four were blindfolded and taken to the barren desert. Neiko and Nefertari both wept as the Indians were turned out into the harsh environment and left there. Even though this was a dire situation, Neiko and Nefertari wanted to see them one last time even thought they were forbidden contact with them. A dust storm covered the tracks left by the chariots, and they took off their blindfolds and marched in an unknown direction since the sandstorms came and blocked out the sun. Days passed, and they marched on with no food or water in the sweltering heat and sandstorms. They continued on, but the lack of energy began to catch up with them. The four of them collapsed several times, but they couldn't stop or they would die. The hot sun beat on them, along with the stinging wind and sand. Finally, after a week and a half of traveling, the four of them collapsed, and this time they did not get up.

A few horses from a tribe of desert people rode and saw the four of them lying in the sand. It was anyone's guess how long they had been there They got off and inspected them. They were still alive. "Their clothes are Egyptian, but they do not look like Egyptians. I have never seen anything like this. Should we help them?" asked one man.

"I suppose we can, and I don't believe they will harm us. They seem to be lost," said another.

The horsemen then carried them to their fortress in the desert.

After a few days, the four were revived, and they told them the story of how they ended up in the desert.

"So, that's basically it. Now we have to return to Egypt to get our friend away from Pharaoh, but I know this time it will be much more difficult. We thank you for saving us," said Sito.

"It is rare we help strangers, but we saw that you were not really Egyptians so we wanted to know what type of people you were. Our people will be leaving this site in a few days, but you can stay if you wish. We will leave you some provisions and show you where to find water and food," said the leader.

"I greatly thank you. This place is just what we need to survive here," said Sito.

The few days passed, and the desert tribe left. The Indians had all they needed for survival, and they lived in the makeshift fortress. Sito also found time to make practical inventions to aid them in their survival.

Months passed and they made themselves clothes and weapons as well including some that did not exist in the present time such as: cannons, crossbows, longbows, and muskets. Of course, they had signature Indian weapons such as: clubs, tomahawks, spears, lances, shields, and knives. The cannons were rather dangerous to make since much could go wrong. Sito's strong science background allowed him to invent gunpowder in a place it wasn't supposed to exist. Iron was readily available since this was close to the time it was discovered and introduced in Egypt. Sito made the cannons out of cast iron. He knew the chemical make up of it and knew where to find the stuff to make it. His three friends had the muscle and practical knowledge to make everything happen; Sito pitched in where he could on that. The muskets they made were not perfect, but they were makeshift flint-locks that got the job done. Mactalon wanted to be cute and make a blunderbuss, but there was no time, and it was too dangerous with what they had to work with. They took safety precautions and test fired all of their firearms. They were lucky the cannons worked and didn't explode. They were going to need the advanced technology against Ramesses if they hoped to have any kind of an edge. A field battle almost seemed to be inevitable when it came to getting their friend back. Ramesses would be on the hunt once they took Neiko away from him. They were well aware of that.

- CHAPTER 39 -

SIX MONTHS LATER ...

The four talked to countless nations over the past months for help in their hopes to find allies in their fight against Ramesses, but no one volunteered. Ramesses had a well known reputation as a military leader and as a warrior. No one was going to fight a losing battle against him. They had already had punishing defeats with his father and Ramesses as a young man. Ramesses' reputation only increased into his manhood.

The last place they wished to consult was the Hyksos, the last conquerors of Egypt before the rise of the New Kingdom. They went in to see the king to ask him for their aid.

Sito began with the pleasantries and then said, "Great king, we have come to ask you for a favor. We have come…"

The king held up his hand. "I know who you are and why you are here. You wish for us to help you fight Pharaoh for your friend that he has taken as his Great Wife. Many peoples have told me of you four painted men and of his harsh treatment of you and how you ended up this far in the desert. We have fought against him and his father for years. We have lost another battle not long ago, and the blood of our people cries in the sand. We cannot help you since she now rightfully belongs to him, and this is not our war."

"You're right, he did take her for his wife—by force!" Mactalon protested.

"She isn't happy with him, and she wants to return to her homeland with us, but he will not allow her!" Tito added.

"Please, we would fight for other matters, but we will not fight Egypt for the wife of Pharaoh. Besides, a whole nation is not under his heel—just one person. And from what I saw in the last battle, I saw a female warrior fighting our kind by his side, and she slew us with the sword. If this is the person you wish us to fight for and save, we won't. Please be gone," the king said and left them in his court.

The four of them left the court shaking their heads. "I don't believe it—Neiko being happy with Ramesses and fighting in a war at his side? I don't get it," Sito grumbled.

"It has been more than six months since we were banished, Sito. She probably has given up on us," Tito replied.

"But Neiko isn't one who gives up no matter how bad the odds!" Sito protested.

"I know, but this is Ramesses we're talking about, and think about how long it's been. She probably cried herself to sleep and had many sleepless nights waiting for us to come and save her. She has no idea if we are alive or not. Imagine going through that and all he may be throwing at her. I wish we knew how bad the situation is and how she is doing," Tito mused, wiping away a tear with an angry brush of his hand.

"Yeah, and just thinking about him putting his hands on her just makes me want to start a war!" Mactalon scowled.

"We have to go back to Egypt and see for ourselves. There is one man that can help us," Sito said.

"Go back? Are you crazy?" Panthero asked in a shriek. "We will be dead meat for sure! If you need a refresher, he said we are to be killed on sight if we are seen again!"

"We can't just sit around and do nothing. Nobody will help us, and they don't have to. That king is right—this is our war. We are going to have to fight it on our own. We will have to use our brains to be able to fight against him—I know even that won't be easy. We will try to avoid a field battle if all possible—we wouldn't win that for certain. We have to try before we lose her forever. We will go into Egypt disguised as merchants, and we will make our way to Senu's house. We will find out from him how things are, and then we will construct a plan. We must try avoid any confrontation with Ramesses, or we will be done for," said Sito.

They returned to the fortress days later.

The next day, the four dressed up like Hittite merchants and prepared the wagon for their return to Egypt. Underneath many animal skins and wool, they put their weapons along with a canoe they had made. Using a compass Sito had made, they made it back to Thebes within five days traveling due south from the fortress' location. They arrived at Senu's house and knocked on the door.

A servant answered the door. "Yes? Can I help you?" she asked.

"We have things to sell to Senu. May we speak to him?" Panthero asked, and the servant allowed them to come in.

Senu looked at them and the skins they had brought in. "These are magnificent. How much?" he asked.

"For free if you want them," Sito said, and he took off his disguise along with the others.

Senu's eyes widened. "Gracious! You're alive! How…" he stammered, but fell silent. "Where are my manners? Come with me," he said, beckoning them to follow him.

He seated them in the dining hall and gave them food and drink. They told him everything that had happened and why they had returned as they ate.

"So how is Neiko?" asked Sito.

Senu shifted a little. "Well, I don't know all of the details, but life has been good to her since you were banished. Not too long after that she was crowned as Great Queen at the long lavish, ceremony that accompanied the recognition. Since then they have established trust with each other, and she has been granted more freedoms. He broke her three months after the day you left. When she showed good behavior, he would allow her to do the things she likes to do. He takes her hunting from time to time, and they ride chariots, boat rides, lavish trips to the beaches at the Red Sea and the Mediterranean when they go to Goshen and Luxor to see how construction is going, and they have had private trips to the waterfalls of the Nile. She now allows him to show affection."

Everyone whistled.

"Darn he's good!" commented Sito. He knew about Neiko's personal interests in the beaches and waterfalls in addition to hunting and fishing.

Mactalon winced at the notion about showing affection. "Yuck!" he said with a cringe. "But has he, uh…consummated the marriage?" Mactalon asked.

"No, not yet, but he has come close several times—it is now only a matter of time—I only know this since we are such close friends. However, he visited me today and said he would set the atmosphere this evening and try to seduce her again. But if she says no, he won't force her since he wants her to be willing and to be happy with him for all eternity," Senu replied.

Sito groaned and buried his face in his hands. "We gotta do something tonight! If she says yes, then she won't leave because they will be connected, and she won't break that level of a commitment! She'll think Monchiska won't want her any more!" Sito said. "Neiko is the type of person that marriage is forever if it ever goes that far…"

"That's what he wants anyway," said Tito, reminding him.

"We have to stop her from making the biggest mistake in her life," said Panthero.

"It's pretty amazing Neiko has survived this long against Ramesses' charms without giving in," remarked Sito.

"I would have thought he would have said screw it and let her go and went after someone else," Mactalon snorted.

"There is something else I have to tell you at a later time why this is not the case. We have to get out of here first," Sito said reading Mactalon's why-can't-you-tell-us-right-now look.

"Alright, but you better tell us!" Mactalon said poking Sito's chest. "Why the big secret?"

"Well…" Sito said, fidgeting and unable to answer the question.

Senu broke in by saying, "Maybe you should discuss this some other time. I must warn you that you can't just go in there like you used to. The palace is fortified and is crawling with soldiers. They check everyone who goes in, and you couldn't get to Neiko because of people trying to steal her from him," Senu said. "I might add that I think my long-time rival could be among them, but proving it is another matter. He would be a dead man if Pharaoh found out he was capable of such treachery."

"Do we have an alternative?" asked Mactalon. "It seems he took our threat seriously."

"He has also spoken of hearing a lot of rumors and hearsay about four strange men wanting to start a war against him and trying to rustle up other nations to aid them when he traveled to other lands for diplomacy matters. He took precautions just in case in addition to all the others who might have the gumption to trespass and try to steal his rare, trophy wife," Senu added.

"Yeah, that was us," said Panthero with an affirmative nod.

"Whoever would think to try and break in and snatch her in the middle of the night would have a serious death wish," said Mactalon.

Panthero snorted. "That's what we're doing," he said and face-palmed his friend on his forehead.

"Right," Mactalon said with his shoulders slumping in sheepishness. "I guess you can say we have a death wish."

An idea popped into Tito's head. "I got it! He values Nefertari as much as Neiko, and if we disguise ourselves as Hyksos bandits and take her, then he will come after us. We can then try to steal Neiko and let Nefertari go back, or we can use her as ransom for Neiko. Senu, you keep this canoe here if we ever need it."

Panthero and Mactalon look at each other and at the twins like "Are you serious?"

"Are you sure that would even work?" asked Panthero.

"No, but it's the best idea we've got. We don't even have a plan B. We don't have a lot of time," said Sito, trying to keep everyone on the same page about the operation and the very short timeframe.

"All right, good luck to you, and come back if you need any more help," Senu said, and he served them more food.

Benjamin was their server, and the Indians caught up with him; they talked about their adventures.

CHAPTER 40

THAT AFTERNOON, NEIKO and Nefertari were walking and talking in the garden. As they were chatting, they saw Francesco; he was holding and stroking the crystal, and it glistened in the sun. He marched up to them with a grin on his face. "Today I return to Hawote and leave you behind in your new life, Neiko, while your friends' carcasses bake in the desert. I have Pharaoh's permission to leave. Farewell," he said. "I'll be seeing you in about three thousand years."

"I think not," Neiko shouted, and she ran and tackled him. He dropped the crystal, and it rolled out of reach. They wrestled and tried to fight to get to it in a tangle of arms and legs. "Nefie, get it!" said Neiko as she pinned down the lanky man.

Nefertari ran, picked it up, and tried to run away with it, but Francesco tripped her. She landed facedown on the sand, and it rolled out of reach onto the stone walkway and at the feet of Ramesses.

"Time to end this once and for all," Ramesses said, and Neiko and Francesco stopped wrestling and Nefertari stood there helplessly. The trio watched in horror as he raised his royal staff and began to hit it with its butt. He hit it three times, and on the last hit, it shattered into small pieces. Then he ground the small pieces into dust with his foot. "I have changed my mind, Francesco. I want you to stay, and it is time to test your loyalty to me once and for all."

Francesco ran up to it and picked up the dust, but the wind carried it out of his hands. He turned and glared at Neiko while he pulled at his hair. "You stupid Indian! Look what you've done!" he yelled in terror.

"Well, at least I have comfort in knowing I won't die here alone, and at least I know you are now reaping what you've sown," Neiko said, standing like a victorious warrior. "You won't exist either, so now Hawote will be a better place without you. And, oh, you can kiss your promotion to "Pharaoh of Hawote" good-bye; I hope you like your demotion back down to Pharaoh's lacky," she said scathingly.

Francesco shot her icy daggers and then stormed off and cussed under his breath as he left.

Neiko and Nefertari talked about him and laughed.

"I need to borrow Nefertari for a moment, but as for you, I have something special planned for you tonight," said Ramesses with a cheery and broad smile.

Neiko shrugged. "Sure, no problem," she said and walked off.

That evening everyone in the palace watched a dance, but Neiko watched it halfheartedly and in boredom. When it was finished, everyone clapped. "That was good. Did you like it?" asked Nefertari.

"Not really. I'd rather watch an action movie," Neiko said with her chin resting on her hands and sighing. "I'm dying for some chocolate—too bad it doesn't exist here," she mumbled to herself. "Ice cream would be nice, too."

That evening, following the dance, Neiko was beginning her date, and the four of them moved in to make their attack. Francesco was walking around outside, and Nefertari was only a few yards away. Francesco saw them coming, but before he could scream, Mactalon knocked him out, tied him up, and gagged him. Then they sneaked up on Nefertari and threw a bag over her. She squealed, and they made a hasty retreat. Several guards pursued them, but they got away with their two captives.

"We must tell Pharaoh immediately that Queen Nefertari has been stolen by Hyksos bandits," said one guard to another pair. Their dress was unmistakable since they had occupied Egypt in the past.

The other two guards didn't argue and ran to find Ramesses.

"Where is Pharaoh?" asked one of the guards from outside to another pair that was patrolling the foyer.

"He is in his room with his wife and he wishes not to be disturbed," said one of the guards who were guarding the hall.

"This can't wait—Queen Nefertari has been abducted by Hyksos," the other said.

Hearing this, the guards ran into the hall with the others on his heels to alarm Ramesses about the news.

Meanwhile, the pair was sitting on the bed smooching. He began to undo her dress. Suddenly, there was pounding on the door, and the guards were calling his name, but he paid no attention to them. His focus was completely on her. The guards pounded harder and didn't stop.

Neiko pulled away. "It sounds like there's trouble," she said.

"We can't stop now—I've waited six months for this," Ramesses said kissing her neck, but it had actually been much longer then six months for his wait, and he was going to tell her the truth tomorrow at breakfast.

"But…" Neiko began, but he turned her head and silenced her by a fervent kiss.

However, the pounding and yelling didn't cease.

Finally, in frustration, he stopped. "I cannot do this with all this racket!" Ramesses grumbled, got up, and stormed to the door. He cracked open the door and said, "You had better have a *very* good reason for this intrusion! If it is not worthwhile, I will personally run you through!"

"Queen Nefertari has been taken by four Hyksos bandits along with Francesco. We weren't able to stop them," one of them said in a nervous whimper.

"Why didn't you say so instead of pounding on my door?" Ramesses said, and then released a long exhale to simmer down and to diffuse his frustration. His guards were loyal and did exactly as he instructed; it just was the worst inconvenience on the most special of nights. Finally, he said, "Never mind. Get me my armor, weapons, and war regalia. Make ready my war chariot. Those four knaves will die for this," he said in clenched teeth and contemplating taking his wrath on them rather than on his guards. "Do you know where they went?" asked Ramesses.

"No," one said while the others did as he commanded.

"Oh no! I'm coming too!" Neiko said, coming from behind. She had overheard everything.

"No, you will stay here because I do not want to lose you too. Remember those slimy dogs tried to take you in battle?" reminded Ramesses.

"Alright," she said sullenly, but he was right. She was nearly taken prisoner a month ago by these people because of a covetous Hyksos prince who met his end at her husband's very hand. "I hope she's all right, but they can do what they want to Francesco," Neiko said with no sympathy for Francesco. "But—you killed that prince, so there should be no fear there!"

"No, he has five more brothers, and one of them could follow in his footsteps," Ramesses argued, shaking his head. "My decision is final—you stay here."

"Your armor and chariot are ready," said one of the guards when he appeared. His appearance interrupted any further argument from Neiko.

Ramesses embraced Neiko tightly and kissed her. "For luck," he said gently, stroking her cheek and left, following after the guard.

The four renegades rode on the wagon back toward the fortress with Nefertari and Francesco in the back with Sito and Mactalon while Tito and Panthero were in the front.

"You won't get away with this, you filthy jackals because Neiko and Ramesses will fix you!" Nefertari snapped venomously as she wriggled her wrists trying to loosen the rope binding her.

"Geez, calm down, Nefie," Mactalon said.

"How would you pigs know that is the nickname given to me by my friends the Indians?" Nefertari demanded

Sito and Mactalon took off their disguises. "That is because we *are* the Indians," said Mactalon.

Nefertari shook with delight and in relief that they were alive. "Sito!" she cried, and she kissed him on the mouth; Mactalon's mouth flew open.

Tito and Panthero peeked over their shoulders.

"What's going on back there? Why are you feeling so fuzzy, brother?" Tito asked since his twin telepathy was picking up on something.

"You just missed it. Nefie just gave Sito one humdinger of a smooch," teased Mactalon.

Francesco sneered. "Just wait till I tell Ramesses about this, Nefertari. I've been meaning to get you back, too."

Nefertari's only response was her hitting him in the face with a baseball-like swing. Francesco's eyes rolled back into his head and he flopped down because she knocked him senseless.

"I learned from Neiko," she said, smiling.

"You won't need that," Mactalon said, cutting the rope from her hands with his knife.

"What are you planning?" Nefertari asked as she massaged her wrists.

"We were hoping to use you for ransom to get Neiko away from Ramesses. Everyone else will think we're Hyksos bandits, but you would know it was just us. Once we exchange you for Neiko, we will return to Hawote," said Sito.

"Very interesting, but it will not work. First of all, Ramesses will not exchange Neiko for me, and he will come after you and try to kill you for this and to rescue me. Also, if you make demands, then he may find out you are alive and will try to destroy you once and for all. Second, you can't return to Hawote because he destroyed the crystal," Nefertari said pressing her lips in a line that said "sorry".

Sito chuckled. "Oh, that old thing? That was a piece of green glass we ripped off some old peddler in Thebes. We got the real crystal right here," he said, holding up the real crystal. We've had it ever since we were banished. We pulled the old switcheroo."

On the way to the fortress, Sito shared with her all of their adventures in the desert, and when they arrived, she looked at their new home in amazement. When they got inside, they locked Francesco up, and the five of them had dinner.

"I was wondering more about the story with Neiko after we left," Sito said. "We'd like to hear your account," he said moving his cup of water.

"She was devastated when you were banished, and so was I. The first week or so she went through a dreadful melancholy, and she wouldn't have anything to do with anybody except me. But Ramesses still forced her to be with him, and finally she broke because she felt like you were dead, and he was putting a lot of pressure on her. She thought you would come for her otherwise. She would watch the horizon in hopes to see you riding to her rescue, but you never came. Even still she cries sometimes, mourning you, and because she feels that returning to Hawote is hopeless. What you saw and heard about was because she felt she had to accept her life with him and make the best of it. She knew she had to live in Egypt, and no one could change it. The saddest phrase she ever said was: 'I lost the four of them again, but this time it is for good, and now I'm lost as well'," Nefertari said.

Tito shook his head. "We couldn't have done it any sooner. We have to be prepared for anything, and fighting against Ramesses is and will be very difficult. We have to penetrate the defenses to get to her, and we would have to break out like lightning. We've perfected getting in, but getting out is the problem. Nefie, we need your help on this one."

"Well, I know just the thing. You could go in dressed like female servants, and I will accept you as my maidservants. Senu will bring you. I will return to the palace to settle things. I will stay with you at his house to make sure the plan is set, and I will pave the way for you. Take an extra disguise to sneak Neiko out," Nefertari added.

Mactalon nodded. "It may just work, and I doubt Ramesses would expect this."

"Yes. Sito, I have something I want to ask of you. Will you take me back to Hawote with you?" Nefertari asked with her brown eyes pleading him.

They all looked at her, startled.

- CHAPTER 41 -

SITO LOOKED AT HER, dumbfounded. "Why on earth do you want to come with us? Hawote is a very dangerous place, and it is no place for an Egyptian queen."

"I am not afraid of the Crackedskulls especially if they all are like Francesco. Besides, from what I hear, it is a beautiful and wonderful place to live. I want to live among the Indians. And I will tell you this—I'm in love with you, Sito," Nefertari said.

Everyone's mouths fell open.

"Nefie, listen to yourself. The rest of the Crackedskulls are *nothing* like Francesco; they are very dangerous people. We are at war with them even unto the day we live in. You wouldn't be safe there, and you play an important role here and in history itself. Besides, history would change if you came with us, and it would be impossible to get you and Neiko both away. You have to make certain we escape, besides, I can't give you the love and compassion you deserve because my heart belongs to someone else in Hawote," Sito said, holding her by the arms and looking her square in the eyes.

"No matter, I can find another Indian. I'm sure there are plenty of handsome men there," Nefertari shrugged.

Sito shook his head. "Nefertari, stop it! You are not going to Hawote. End. Of. Story. Period. You couldn't possibly live in the world we live in. You can't fight, and you would have to live a dual life—and in your case maybe a triple life. We know of mysteries you have no comprehension of, and Neiko has told of a new peril that threatens Hawote and her, and he is more terrible than anything. We have to stick to the plan, and it is only to free Neiko. Once we leave you, you must make certain Ramesses never remembers Neiko or us even in the afterlife. You are the only one capable of softening his heart or pushing his buttons. Will you do it please? If you really love me, you will do what is best for everyone."

Nefertari sighed. "Yes, I will. Will you promise not to forget me? Will you please give these to Neiko?" she said handing him Neiko's turquoise ring that was a gift from Monchiska, and one of her fine necklaces. "These are a gift from me to her. I will always remember how much she loved phoenixes, so I thought she should have it," she said smiling broadly.

"Sure. Is this that ring that Ramesses threw in the lotus pool? How did you get it?" asked Sito.

" I got it when it was her turn to be with him, and I could never give it back to her while Ramesses was around because he would never hear of it, so I kept it hidden with me. It brought me luck. But, now it is time to return it to her," said Nefertari. "I might add I had to make up quite a story of why I was so wet and why the guards found me in the lotus pool," she said with a chuckle.

Sito chortled and nodded. "You're amazing. She will greatly

appreciate it and the kindness you have shown her and to us. Every Indian will hear of how kind you are, and we would have never returned if it wasn't for you. What will happen if Ramesses ever found out about you loving me and you helping us?" asked Sito.

"He would kill me for sure, and I bet I would die with you, but that doesn't frighten me. I will fight with you till this is finally over. When do we leave for Thebes?" Nefertari asked.

"Tomorrow, and all of us are going. We will be in disguise and so will you. We will leave Francesco tied and locked up here, along with the crystal because we can't afford to lose it. Your gifts to Neiko will stay here too. That crystal is our ticket home, and we will die at the edge of the sword of Ramesses if we lose it. The costumes for the servant act are finished. So everyone, let's catch a few winks, and let us be on our way at dawn," said Sito as he sat the crystal and the trinkets on the table.

Ramesses searched for days to no avail. He was forced to return home to his station, but he kept his men on the search and were ordered to alert him when they found something tangible.

A few days passed and everyone left for Egypt, and they traveled the long journey back to Thebes. They changed their costumes and made a cover story for Nefertari's abrupt return.

They arrived in the evening of the fifth day of travel at Senu's house. The Indians and the "missing" queen told him the plan.

"My goodness, how ingenious, and I'm pleased to know that you are all right, my queen," said Senu, bowing to her.

"Senu, you will bring them in this evening. We will use them as dancing girls," said Nefertari.

"I will do it," Senu said with an agreeing nod.

"I want to help too! It would look suspicious if there are four instead of five," Benjamin replied.

"You're right! I did overlook that, but I do not have another costume for you," Nefertari said.

"I will take care of that and have one for him ready in time, Queen Nefertari," Senu replied. "Benjamin, why do you want to follow them into battle? You may be killed."

Benjamin poked out his narrow chest. "I am not afraid of Pharaoh. I'd rather die than be a slave. I want to fight for the freedom of the Indians who showed me kindness—I am indebted to them. You will never see me after this day, Senu. If I live, I will find a new life elsewhere, but I do thank you for the kindness you have bestowed me."

The Indians wanted to protest, but they knew it was a waste of time, and they may need his help after all.

"You are very welcome, but I will miss you—and all the rest of you as well. I wish you all the very best of luck, and tell Neiko likewise. I hope one day you will be free from the Crackedskulls as well," Senu said kindheartedly.

"Thank you, and we will miss you too, Senu. All of Hawote will know of you too," Sito replied, hugging him in friendship and shaking his hand.

The next morning Nefertari left for home to pave the way for the Indians and to settle down Pharaoh's dander as he still searched for the four mysterious Hyksos bandits. He had to send word to call off the search and bring the remaining troops and scouts home. She told Senu to bring the five "dancing slaves" to the palace in the evening.

Late that same evening, Senu brought in the five for the final battle. The direction of the tide was either way.

Many of the guards looked at them and whistled. They did make fine looking women.

Mactalon tugged at his costume; he wasn't very comfortable in a dress, and luckily for him it wasn't as skimpy as some dancers' attire. "Now I know how Neiko must've felt," he whispered.

Senu presented them to Ramesses and left, and they performed their dance.

"Now, Great Pharaoh, we would like to be taken in your house to serve you," said Sito in a disguised feminine voice.

"Very well, show them to their new quarters," Ramesses said.

They were shown to their new quarters by servants.

Nefertari met them in her room about an hour later. She gave them their Indian clothes for later that night. "So far so good," she said with a wink.

"Okay, you've got the horses ready so we can get to Senu's house, and we will get the canoe from there. We will then be back to the fortress," Tito said.

"Yes, there are fewer guards in the back, so you can get out that way. Use this rope to climb out her bedroom window, and ride out through the garden gate—I left it unlocked. Good luck," she said, beginning to cry as they slipped out to get to Neiko's room.

Neiko was lying on her back, staring at the ceiling, but then she was surrounded by the shadows. Before she could shriek, Sito covered her mouth. "It's us, we're here to get you out," whispered Sito.

"Sito? Is it really you?" Neiko asked. She hugged him, elated. She poked his arm to make sure he wasn't a ghost or a zombie.

"Yes, it's us and Benjamin. We don't have time to explain now—we will tell you on the way," Sito replied.

"Great!" Neiko said, jumping up. She was still wearing her clothes from that evening because she hadn't bothered to change. The six then tied the rope to a column in her room and climbed out of her window. The balcony of her room was too risky; it was normally watched by guards from down below. When everyone was down in the garden and hiding in the foliage, they looked toward the stable and the gate before proceeding, but there were guards in both places.

"Oh great! Now what do we do?" asked Panthero, frustrated.

"I've got a better idea," Neiko said, sneaking to the tree that they used to climb onto the wall in the training sessions. They sneaked to it and awaited further instructions. "We just climb up and jump off the other side—piece of cake. We have to make a run for Senu's house on foot. Who goes first?"

"You go first—ladies first, and we'll cover you," Mactalon replied.

Neiko began climbing, and the branches began to rattle in the quiet. She accidentally snapped a branch. The guards heard the noise and saw them standing at the tree and the branches moving as Neiko climbed. The guards raced to the refugees with their weapons drawn; it wouldn't be long until the garden would be full of guards and Pharaoh would be awakened. They had been down this road over six months ago, and exile wasn't their fate this time if they got captured.

Neiko made it and was on the other side of the wall.

"Move!" shouted Tito, and all the rest began to climb at lightning speed. They had to wait a few seconds for the other to move clear to proceed.

Everyone made it except Benjamin; he was fending the guards off.

"C'mon!" shouted Mactalon from the top of the wall.

"Go on!" Benjamin shouted, and he threw himself at five guards. He was able to slay two, but the remaining three threw him down and stabbed him. He died instantly.

The five Indians started running down the streets to Senu's house, remembering Benjamin's sacrifice. He died as bravely as any Indian warrior would have and would be remembered for his act of chivalry.

"We risked our lives to save his, and he is just repaying us," remarked Sito as she shook of the sadness.

The Indians ran, grabbed the canoe out of Senu's garden, and raced to the nearby river from his property to cover up Senu's involvement. When they had reached the river, they heard the thunder of hooves and chariots from behind. The Egyptians began to come into sight over the bank, and Ramesses was in the lead and still his pajamas; he didn't have time to worry about changing clothes.

"We got company!" Neiko shouted with her eyes wide in anxiety. "I guess it didn't take him too long to figure out I went AWOL!"

"Push it in! Hurry!" Sito shouted in urgency, and they pushed the canoe into the current and jumped in. Mactalon and Panthero grabbed the oars to begin rowing.

"Stop them! They are getting away!" shouted Ramesses as he waved his javelin with menace.

Neiko grabbed a bow, fired an arrow, and killed the driver of his chariot. Ramesses wasn't driving his own war chariot since it was not made ready in time so he hitched a ride with another man. Ramesses threw the body into the sand, took the reins and the whip, and continued to lead his army. Several nearby warships and boats tried to cut them off as they saw the pursuit of the army. Fishing boats threw nets at the Indians, trying to trap them. The fishing boats became blocked in by the bigger warships.

The Indians zigzagged expertly in between them, and several warships collided with each other and the rocks and ultra shallow sandbars. Several other warships put their oars into the water and pursued them.

"Paddle faster!" Neiko screamed.

"Hang on! We'll lose them in the rapids!" shouted Mactalon, and the canoe picked up speed as they approached the rapids. They

"Paddle faster!" Neiko screamed.

"Hang on! We'll lose them in the rapids!" shouted Mactalon,

went into the rapids and guided the canoe through the jagged rocks to safety, as several of the boats tried to chase but collided into the rocks. They left the boats and the pursuing Pharaoh and his army behind. The Indians held up their oars and bows in victory and let loose shrill war calls. Ramesses heard them, and he quivered in rage. He returned back to the palace to ready for war and mount up a huge army to pursue them. He also sent scouts to track them down before leaving for home.

– CHAPTER 42 –

T HE INDIANS TRAVELED downriver for three days to the
north and walked another two days in the desert to the east.
Neiko had forgotten that the Nile flowed backwards from
other rivers and the land of Egypt was backwards too with Upper
Egypt to the south. They finally reached the fortress in its desolate
desert wilderness in Sinai.

"Wow, cool place," said Neiko, remembering the stories they
shared on the boat. "So this is where you guys have been hangin' out
all this time."

"Well, Neiko, how are you going to explain this—I mean, to
your parents. I doubt they will believe you spent almost a year in
Egypt, and most of that time was with Ramesses," said Panthero. "I
don't even know if the chieftains will believe us either."

Neiko laughed. "I won't have to explain anything to my parents.
See, I can turn the clock to where I was gone for maybe thirty
minutes. I remember the month, day, and year, and I know the spell,

and it's different than the one Francesco uses. As for why I know, let's just say my time in Qari has a little pay off," she said with a wink. "As to the eleven years you guys spent, I can turn it back that far, but I don't know if that would be a good idea," Neiko added.

"Don't worry about us. We can use this as a battle wound we carry against the Crackedskulls, and we can put Francesco away for a long time for this," said Mactalon.

"Are you guys ready to rock?" asked Neiko.

"These are a gift from Nefie, and wait, where's the crystal? I put it right here!" Sito panicked as he gave the trinkets to Neiko and looked under the table and in the room.

Neiko looked at the necklace and put it on. "My ring! Oh, I'll miss her," she said as she took off the ring Ramesses gave her and put it in her pocket and put the turquoise ring in its rightful place. "I'll keep this other ring and these clothes as a dreadful reminder of the life I had with Ramesses," she said cringing. "Where did you have it last?"

"Right here! I remember exactly!" Sito said and then kicked a chair.

"The rats may have carried it off. We have a bad rat problem, you know—they're always totin' off shiny stuff," said Mactalon.

"Great," Neiko said with a sarcastic grunt.

Tito ran into the room with terror on his face. "Guys, we got problems," he said, putting on a face.

"Egyptians?" asked Panthero.

Tito nodded.

"How many?" asked Panthero, pressing him.

"All of 'em, I think—including angry Pharaoh," Tito replied.

"Great! We can't leave and fly the coop, because we can't find the crystal!" Neiko shrieked.

"You're kidding, right?" Tito asked, but everyone shook their heads. "Oh crap! We are going to die! Neiko is going back to Egypt with Ramesses the Grouch forever—permanently—for all eternity!

We better find that right now before the grinch gets in here and kills the rest of us!"

"There's no time! We have to pull off the search for it and brace for a full-scale attack!" Sito warned. He knew Ramesses well.

"Is there any way to buy some time?" asked Neiko. "How well will this place hold up against an entire army?"

"Not long enough with Ramesses the Great in command! He'll find the weaknesses really fast! We need to go out and survey the situation, come on!" Sito said and everyone herded behind him and followed him.

Everyone ran to the rampart to see the position of the Egyptians. They could see them coming over the desert like a plundering swarm of hungry army ants. Sito looked through the telescope to see that they came by the thousands with Ramesses in the lead—completely at the forefront. Chariots, horsemen, and foot soldiers followed behind him. Sito looked at him standing in his chariot, carrying his javelin and armed to the teeth. He was in full war regalia, complete with swords, daggers, bow, arrows, club, and an angry, vengeful, cold expression. Even though he was yards away his blue crown of war and armor glinted in the sun. He was truly an imposing sight on the battlefield.

Sito lowered the telescope with an open mouth. "He is really ticked off, and he is gonna to finish the job this time."

"Oh! We are in deep caca now!" Mactalon said, jumping up and down like he had to pee. "They're gonna be all over us like black on crows in a few minutes!"

"What are we gonna do?" asked Neiko as she scratched herself in a nervous tick like she was being eaten alive by chiggers. "We ain't never had to fight these kinds of odds in Hawote! If I get taken back this time it's gonna be permanently—I don't look forward to that and growing old and having children with him!"

"Neiko, don't panic! We have defenses, and there is only one thing we can do, fight," Sito replied.

"Are you crazy? We are gonna run outa weapons and ammo before he runs outa men!" Tito said.

"We have no choice, Tito. We can't run. It is time we show him what we're made of, and we won't go down without a fight; we'll take a few of them with us. Mactalon, Tito, go and get the cannons and catapults ready. Neiko, come with me and Panthero to get bows, crossbows, muskets, tomahawks, spears, and swords. And everyone, let's set the booby traps! Move!" Sito instructed. "We have to keep him out of the fortress as long as we can!"

"Yeah? Who's gonna brace the gate?" asked Mactalon sarcastically from a distance.

"Ha. Ha. Ha," Sito retorted in a fake laugh as he followed him inside.

Moving like lightning, the five prepared the defenses and went back to the lookout.

The Egyptians had surrounded the fortress, cutting off escape and putting it into siege with foot soldiers and chariots. Ramesses commanded his army from his mobile platform and dictated his movements with his javelin. He was even out of range for a longbow. The Egyptians cut down a large tree, one of the few that were nearby, to ram the gate. Archers were in position awaiting orders. All the Indians could do was watch as time painfully passed.

"I guess he wants us to stay," Mactalon punned.

"Mactalon, this is serious!" Sito scolded.

Sometime later Ramesses began calling to them, mostly to Neiko. Neiko came into view on the rampart.

"What is it, Ramesses?" she called down from her perch.

Ramesses looked up to her. "We can end this with no bloodshed and not a single arrow fired. Come to me now, and I will be merciful and spare your friends. Come back to me and come home," he said, calling to her with a very suave tone. He stood there and waited patiently for her response.

The Indians looked at each other.

"Do you buy it?" asked Mactalon.

"Yeah, he's serious. All he wants is her. He would graciously reward your obedience if you give in, but this is your last hope of returning to Hawote if we can find time to locate the crystal," Sito said. "It's up to you, Neiko."

Neiko nodded and then called out to her royal beau and asked, "What if I refuse?"

"Then I will break down the gate and come in there and drag you out myself. I will put your friends to death right here and burn this hovel to the ground. I'll make sure you never leave my side again!" Ramesses said in pure aggression.

"Oh," Neiko said to herself and cringed.

"Oooh," Panthero said. "We're so screwed right now it ain't funny."

"Well?" Ramesses demanded from below.

Neiko took a deep breath. She was about to unleash the beast and open a can of worms for sure. "I'm *going* home, you battle-axe! Go home, Ra," she said and gave him an offensive gesture.

Sito chuckled. "His name means "He Who Is Born of Ra" after all. How ironic."

"I guess that explains why he acts like he's king of the gods," added Mactalon.

Ramesses gritted his teeth and shook in rage. "Grrrr! So be it! I offer peace and you spurn me! I'm coming in after you, my warrior!" he shouted to Neiko and then he turned to his army. "In your positions. Break down the gate! Now!" he yelled and the army came alive with activity.

The Egyptians began to ram the gate with a battering ram, and more soldiers came from the distance. Mactalon and Panthero began to fire the cannons and catapults, killing many, and the reinforcements retreated out of range. Neiko, Tito, and Sito tried to pick off the rammers with bows, but others would fill their place.

"Fire in the hole!" shouted Mactalon as he fired into the siege, and many died from the cannonball. Several archers opened fire toward him, and he was forced to duck.

"Don't hit Ramesses!" said Sito.

"Man, are you nuts? That would end it really quick. Do you think he's gonna hold back from killing us? Screw history! If we don't take him out now, *we'll* be history!" Mactalon said defensively.

"If you kill him, we're all gonna die. If we have to die, and if we spare his life, at least Neiko will live..." Sito said, defending his position.

"He's got a point. I'll live, just not happily ever after," said Neiko.

"Fine," Mactalon said and fired another shot into the horsemen.

"What kind of sorcery is this?" asked Ramesses as he watched the cannons fire. "No sorcery of any kind will stop me from reclaiming what is rightfully mine and my vengeance! Archers, pin them down!"

The archers fired on the gunners, pinning them. They also fired at the three Indian archers, forcing them to take cover.

"Just warning shots! Don't hit Neiko!" Ramesses commanded.

"This ain't working!" Neiko said in distress as arrows hissed through the air and dug into the walls and wooden supports.

"Yeah—everyone back into the fortress! Now!" Sito shouted, and they stayed low and made it back into the fortress. "Our only chance is to find that crystal and brace for an inside attack!"

Ramesses gathered forty of his best men and summoned his generals. "Once they smash the gate, I and my forty men will go in. Keep the rest of the army in position, but they must stay ready. Give me two hours, and if I do not return, you have my order to crush the fortress. If you find my dead body, and if Neiko lives, kill her. If I come out, and I have my wife with me, then the rest of the army will crush this fortress. If you see Neiko, and she is not in my possession, I want her taken alive. I want Sito brought to me alive—you may do with the others as you please, but I want the pleasure of killing Sito myself along with my traitorous wife, Nefertari. They will die together. She thought she could hide her illicit affair from me and mock me by helping them."

The rammers finally broke through the gate, and the forty-one men charged in. A couple men stepped into traps, and the Indians shot them down from hidden locations. More chargers opened doors and were shot by hidden crossbows, catapults, and muskets. Others had fallen through concealed holes that led to a ten-foot tar pit, which was lit by Tito, and they were burned alive.

But the remaining force, which numbered thirty, pushed on to the stronghold. As soon as they broke into the door, the five shot and felled five more men. The Egyptians drew their weapons and charged after them. Each Indian killed a few more with their crossbows, but then they were useless, the Indians fought with swords. Neiko ran into another part of the fortress with Ramesses and four other men chasing her. She ran into the rooms, and the four men still chased her, but she lost sight of Ramesses. She went into a room that was a dead end, and the four men had her cornered. They charged after her and tried to capture her. One man tried to grab her from the left side, but she stabbed him in the chest and just barely had enough time to kick and slice another coming from the right. One man managed to seize her from behind, but he didn't have time to get a good grip. She jerked free and shot him with the last arrow in her double crossbow. She threw her crossbow and hit the other man in the face with it. While he was groaning, she threw a knife, and it went in between his eyes. Then Neiko went out of the room and went the back way to join the others.

Neiko wandered in the dark with a drawn sword, looking out for anyone who may try to attack her. She went into the room where the crystal had been lost. She was on a mission to find the crystal. She was aware Ramesses was definitely remaining, and could be anywhere. There was no telling how many of his men were left. After a brief search in the dark room, she started to exit the door, but then she heard a noise. Neiko spun around and breathed hard as she scanned the room with her sword ready, but a glint on the table caught her eye. There lay the crystal, and relief surged through her body, but then caution took over.

"There it is, but it wasn't there earlier…" she said trailing off in thought and searched the room carefully, but no one was there.

She quickly ran to the table and picked up the crystal. But before she could move, someone came out from his hiding place and seized her from behind—the perfect ambush. She dropped the sword and crystal. Neiko screamed in surprise and tried to struggle, but her captor had a secure grip on her and pulled her arms behind her back and tied her hands behind her back. She tried to look to see who caught her, but the shadow covered his face.

"Let go of me!" she snarled, but the attacker's identity was confirmed by a kiss on the cheek.

"Now, my warrior, this is the last time you will run away from me. Your friends will not live to see another day, and neither will Nefertari because she betrayed me. Let's go," said Ramesses in a harsh prophesy.

"No! Oh no! Poor Nefie! Help! Guys, help me!" Neiko cried, struggling as he dragged her down the stairs.

After they had killed the last soldier in sight, the four heard Neiko's cry for help. "Neiko!" they called, and they tracked the sound of her voice and ran after her. They found her sword and the crystal. Mactalon grabbed the crystal, and they sprinted down the stairs. When they made it down into the ground floor, they saw the pair. Ramesses was trying to make a hasty exit back out to his army with his captive in tow. Ramesses spun around and saw them, and they drew their swords and prepared to rush him. He pulled out his dagger and put the point to Neiko's throat; she grimaced.

"If you want to kill me, we die together," Ramesses said digging the point into her neck, and she whimpered. "I also have a little surprise—you have ten minutes before the rest of the army attacks. I suggest you let us go, and maybe I won't kill you."

Sito glared at him. "You're mad, Ramesses. You're a thief and a liar. I know you want nothing more than to destroy the rest of us so you can have Neiko."

"Sito, he's gonna kill Nefie too because he knows she helped us escape," Neiko said.

"I also know you were lovers, and both of you thought you could hide it from me! I was waiting for something like this to happen. I'll bet you had many nights alone when I was out, didn't you?" Ramesses snarled, glaring at Sito.

"No, we never did anything! You are blowing this way out of proportion, and I talked her out…" Sito stammered

"You lie!" Ramesses interrupted. "I bet you had a good time with her after you pulled that Hyksos bandit stunt! The purpose of that was to get her alone with you."

"It was not like that at all! I did that, so I could save Neiko from you! I was going to use Nefertari as a hostage…"

Ramesses grew angrier, and he narrowed his eyes and bared his teeth. "I believe you and she created this little game as well, didn't you? The games end now because you and Nefertari will die together for treason! I may even mummify the two of you alive together!"

"Ramesses, if you do that then I swear to God I will never love you! You'll never win my heart with such cruel actions!" Neiko vowed and threatened. If she was forced to go back to Egypt, she would do anything she could to save Nefertari's life in return for all she did for her and because of their close friendship and blood-sister vow. She didn't see any hope for Sito though.

"That's what you think!" Mactalon snapped as he held up the crystal.

"Give me that crystal, so I can send you to the underworld!" Ramesses growled as he seethed.

"How 'bout meeting some old friends?" Panthero said as he arrived from Francesco's room with Francesco in tow. He threw Francesco on the floor, and pointed the sword into the back of his head. "Now, Scarecrow, let her go, or the shrimp gets it!" Panthero tried to find something to stall Ramesses and buy time.

"Go ahead—do it. I don't care. I no longer have any use for him. So long," Ramesses said and then turned to leave with Neiko. He began to walk away with his captive, but Sito grabbed a nearby chair, threw it, and hit Ramesses in his strong, unarmored legs, sending him toppling over. He landed facedown on the ground with a loud crash of armor and weapons, and Neiko just barely cleared before he fell on her.

"Whoa, nice shot!" Mactalon said, congratulating Sito.

"You don't know how long I've wanted to do something like that at a safe distance from his twin pistons," Sito remarked, referring to Ramesses' fists. "Get him before he gets his bearings, or we'll be goners!"

Tito and Mactalon ran and grabbed him before he could make a move or before he recovered. Sito untied Neiko's hands and used the rope to bind Ramesses to the chair he had thrown at him.

"Unhand me, you filthy barbarians," Ramesses growled in venom as he struggled as they held him down and tied him up. "When I get loose, I'm going to kill you!"

"We're glad to see you too," said Panthero.

Outside, they could hear the army storming in.

"Time to go!" Mactalon said, tossing Neiko the crystal.

The Indians and the sole Crackedskull prepared to go back home. "Oh crystal of time, hear my voice. Send everyone in this room to the land of Hawote, except Ramesses II who is Pharaoh of this realm, to the year AD 2001, on October 15, at 9:30 p.m.," she chanted, and the crystal glowed brighter and brighter. The six were engulfed in the green light, and the images of Egypt began to spin and change to that of Hawote.

Ramesses squirmed as the light shone around them "No! I will get you back, and I will find you wherever you go—wherever you are, Neiko! Death and time won't keep us apart! You will be mine again! I will reach beyond the grave if I must—my ka will follow your footsteps wherever you go!" came the voice of Ramesses, and a bright light flashed and time spun around them. The light flashed and they were standing on her front porch.

"We're back," Neiko said with relief. Neiko looked at the night sky and estimated it to be 9:30 p.m., and everything looked like she remembered it almost a year ago when Francesco showed up on her porch. Neiko unlocked the door to her home and everyone went inside. She had managed to hold onto her house key for all this time as a reminder of her home.

A few minutes later Phoenix and Monchiska came into the house unannounced.

"Neiko! Oh, thank goodness you're okay. I thought Bloodhawk may have got you," Phoenix said in relief.

"What's the big deal?" asked Neiko, confused. *This is different than last time.*

"Phoenix and I both called your house for thirty minutes, and there was no answer," Monchiska said.

Neiko responded by running into his arms.

"I love you, Monchiska," Neiko said, sobbing.

Monchiska was a taken off guard by the sudden tender outburst. "I was hoping I would hear you say that," he said, hugging her back.

"Phoenix, my darling," said Sito as he walked to her.

Phoenix turned around and looked at him, and she saw the older version of the boy she loved standing before her. Shock and joy filled her, and she ran and embraced him. "I thought I had lost you," she said in a whisper and began to cry as he stroked her hair.

The seven Indians enjoyed their reunion, but then Phoenix noticed Francesco and Neiko's clothes. "What is he doing here? And,

Neiko, why on earth are you wearing those Egyptian clothes? And where did you get that tan? Who are you supposed to be the queen of Egypt? Halloween is two weeks away, and we were supposed to go shopping for costumes next week!"

"You two, the five of us have some explaining to do. And bring the loser," Neiko said, pointing at Francesco with her thumb.

"What is *he* doing here?" Phoenix asked again with her eyes darting in suspicion.

"I'm about to explain everything," said Neiko, ushering everyone to the living room.

Everyone went into the living room and told their part of the long story.

- CHAPTER 43 -

THE NEXT DAY, THE SEVEN TRIBES met together, and Neiko, Sito, Tito, Mactalon, and Panthero offered testimony on their Egyptian adventure as well as their complaints against Francesco.

"That's all, Xartna," Neiko replied after an hour and a half to wrap it all up in a nice little package.

Xartna pursed his lips and rubbed his chin as he tried to process the information. "Francesco is more devious and vengeful than anyone ever thought possible. As you can see, we have a strong case against Francesco, and now he has crimes against Raven and Bloodhawk as well. He nearly destroyed the lives of five of the best warriors in Hawote's history, and history itself because of spite. His hatred sent Neiko into the arms of Ramesses II, and nearly cost the lives of these other four and that of Queen Nefertari. We are thankful for her bravery that set them free and spared their lives. Now I present to you, Francesco, the cause of this outrage. Do you believe he should be sent to jail without trial for his crimes—past and present?"

"Yeah! Throw him in jail with his mom and dad, the rats, and throw away the key," Pike said.

All of the Indians decided to send him to jail, and it was done without much adieu. Neiko kept the crystal and a log of her adventures in Egypt along with her clothes, the necklace from Nefertari, and the ring from Ramesses as a reminder.

Everyone then went home and enjoyed the victory in one of the greatest battles over the Crackedskulls, and the defeat of the most dangerous Crackedskull ever known. The five home comers had a celebration held in their honor, and the four lost Indians enjoyed the life they had missed for eleven years and the freedom they had long waited for.

Weeks of peace followed.

The End

ABOUT THE AUTHOR

A.K. Taylor grew up in the backwoods of Georgia where she learned about nature. She enjoys hunting and fishing, beekeeping, gardening, archery, shooting, hiking, and has various collections.

She also has interest in music, Native American history and heritage, Egyptian history, and the natural sciences. A.K. Taylor has been writing and drawing since the age of 16. A.K. Taylor has graduated from the University of Georgia with a biology degree, and she shares an interest in herpetology with her husband.

FROM THE AUTHOR:

Thank you for reading! If you would be so kind, would you go to your favorite retailer, Goodreads, Booklikes, and leave an honest review? Thank you!

Would you like to get dibs on new releases and behind the scenes action? You also get a free book just for signing up. Join the newsletter today!

<u>ALSO BY AK TAYLOR:</u>

Neiko's Five Land Adventure
Book #1 of the Neiko Adventure Saga

The Newbie Author's Survival Guide

Bloody Klondike Gold
(A Randi Braveheart Mystery Short Story)

Many more things to come!

To read A.K.'s blog or
connect with her on social media please visit

www.BackwoodsAuthor.com